For Pete's Sake ⚉

For
Pete's
Sake

Linda Windsor

AVON
INSPIRE

An Imprint of HarperCollins*Publishers*

FOR PETE'S SAKE. Copyright © 2008 by Linda Windsor. All rights reserved. Printed in the United States of America. No part of this book may be used or reproduced in any manner whatsoever without written permission except in the case of brief quotations embodied in critical articles and reviews. For information address HarperCollins Publishers, 10 East 53rd Street, New York, NY 10022.

HarperCollins books may be purchased for educational, business, or sales promotional use. For information please write: Special Markets Department, HarperCollins Publishers, 10 East 53rd Street, New York, NY 10022.

FIRST EDITION

Designed by Elizabeth M. Glover

Library of Congress Cataloging-in-Publication Data
Windsor, Linda
  For Pete's sake / Linda Windsor. —1st ed.
    p. cm. —(The Piper Cove chronicles)
  ISBN 978-0-06-117138-3
1. Widowers—Fiction. 2. Fathers and sons—Fiction. 3. Neighbors—Fiction. I. Title.
  PS3573.I519F67 2008
  813' .54—dc22   2007038307

08 09 10 11 12   OV/RRD   10 9 8 7 6 5 4 3 2 1

PROLOGUE

My buddy Alex Butler, or rather Alex Turner, claims our *yutzi* senior class play brought our little group of friends together. It wasn't *Mame*, although there is a lot of truth about us in that *Bosom Buddies* song. Only real friends will love you, warts and all, and tell you the truth, even when it hurts. But I see us more as *The Four Musketeers* than *Mame*'s Depression-spawned ditzy rich woman, her floozy friend, and company. All for one and one for all.

We four happened on the infamous Night of the Flat Tire. My bud Jan Kudrow and I were on our way home from an away football game in Cambridge in the incredible, hand-me-down 1967 Chevy Camaro that Pop and I restored. When we turned onto Three Creek Road, we found a metallic red Corvette and Alex, the president of Decatur High's senior class, pinned by a spare tire like a turtle on its back, her arms and legs flailing.

It wasn't until Jan and I managed to stop laughing and get out of the car that we realized the problem—or one of them. Our president smelled like a brewery and had been wrestling for some time with that tire. Frankly, I was impressed that she managed to jack the car up and remove the flat without injury. As we helped Alex to her feet, Firestone-black streaking her white designer jeans and turquoise sweater, a miserable sound came from the other side of the car, where Sue Ann Quillen—now Wiltbank—retched into the ditch. Trust me, Miss Worcester County was no beauty queen that night. Oh, the dumb things we do when we're young.

Anyway, these wayward Cinderellas were in big trouble. Grounded by her parents, who were at a shindig in Ocean City, Alex had to be home before they returned at midnight. So, while Jan helped Sue Ann get herself together, I changed the tire. Piece of cake. And boy, was it sweet. These girls wouldn't have given Jan and me the time of day before that night. But they owed us now. I drove the Vette to the Butler place before the clock struck midnight with Jan following in my rig.

That night, Jan and I were surprised to find both Alex and Sue Ann were good folks and I think they were just as surprised about us. Face it—rich, poor, or in between, we were all in the same boat of life, and we've been bailing each other out of swamping storms and dangerous dips ever since.

Oh, and as for Alex owing me, she really didn't. My greatest dream had come true. To sit behind the wheel of a new Corvette and drive that little darling down the back roads to Piper Cove. What a ride. What a car!

CHAPTER ONE

W hat a car! A 2007 Atomic Orange Corvette swept past Ellen Brittingham's motorcycle as though in flight. It was the four-wheeled American eagle, in a class all its own. Her pulse, already thrumming as she rode in the saddle of her new Harley-Davidson, shot into an even higher gear. Ellen had been watching its approach in the rearview mirrors as she rode past green pastures that morphed into woods and then into a crossroads, occupied by a food and gas minimarket. It had been just a dot of orange, moving up through a herd of beach-bound cars and SUVs.

Revving up the speed of her Hog, she flipped on her blinker and swerved onto the passing lane to follow in the sport car's wake. Talk about the perfect end to a perfect week.

The Lower Shore Ladybugs, a women's biker group, had planned a rendezvous in St. Michaels on the Tred Avon River.

Just perfect to shake down her new bike—her *first* new bike. The gang, made up of women from all walks of life, had a blast taking day trips from St. Michaels to the farthest reaches of the Delmarva Peninsula. It never ceased to amaze Ellen how much the Eastern Shore's quaint bay and riverside towns, as well as their contrasting oceanfront resorts, had to offer and how much locals—including her—took them for granted.

And Sheba, the name Ellen dubbed the new bike because it made her feel like a queen, had done her proud. She'd roared like a lioness or purred like a cub all the way. Not once had Ellen had to break out the tool kit she kept in the left saddlebag. But then, for what she'd paid for the Harley, she hadn't expected to.

Watching the sleek Corvette swoop around an SUV as if it was standing still, Ellen accelerated to close the distance between them and get a better look. She'd read in one of her mechanics magazines that the GM 'Vette had a new color, and she liked it. With that metallic finish, it looked good to Ellen—from the front in her rearview mirror, the side as it passed her, and the back as she now followed it. She'd go at least as far as Route 90 with the kid and then head for Piper Cove and home.

That is, she assumed it was a kid who'd barreled by her. Probably a college grad in his new graduation present. Or even a high-school grad. Some families could swing that kind of gift. Not that she begrudged them or the fact that hers couldn't. No 'Vette in the world could give her the pleasure that she'd experienced helping her dad rebuild his classic 1967 Camaro. There were a lot of things in life that mattered more than money. Family. Faith.

Of course, money helped. And thankfully, her career as a landscape architect was lucrative enough to satisfy her meager needs and some of her wants.

With a grin as wide as her handlebar, she leaned into the wind and accelerated past the hot new car before her exit loomed too close. Sheba came to life beneath her, growling and clawing the road as if eager to show this four-wheeled eagle what its two-wheeled counterpart could do. But Ellen kept her engine semi-leashed. Safety first. She just wanted a look-see, not a blooming drag race.

As Sheba shot up beside the 'Vette, Ellen savored its sleek lines and made out a profile through the tinted windows. To her surprise, it was a mature, square-jawed one with a dimpled chin that turned toward her.

Shades of 007, he was checking her out, his designer sunglasses tipped ever-so-slightly in her direction! Sheba wobbled, betraying Ellen's shock. A teeth-grating smile locked on her lips by embarrassment, she did what she'd been taught to do since childhood. Blushing from her bones to the leather of her vest, she nodded a neighborly hello and gave Sheba the gas. It wasn't flirting, she told herself, but just in case the guy thought she was, the best thing to do was to exit. And if he'd been checking out Sheba . . . well, he could check out her dust.

"Go on, little Sheba," Adrian Sinclair chided, reading the custom tags on the back of the pearl-glow black-and-red Harley streaking ahead of him. "You might think you can run, but you can't outrun me."

He had no intention of actually catching the female biker. The preconceived image of badly colored and coiffed hair, tattoos, cigarette-breath, and a voice that could grate old cheese hardly appealed to him. Passing the chrome-bedecked Harley-Davidson served him just fine. It was a matter of power versus power, nothing else. And the five hundred and five horses under his hood were as anxious to break out as his own frustrated spirit.

At least *they* could.

"In one mile, turn right onto Route 90 East to Ocean Pines," his OnStar lady told him in a pleasant, yet indifferent voice.

One mile in which to show Sheba she'd bitten off more than she could chew. He gunned the engine and shifted gears. That was definitely doable. He might even make it to the closing for his new property a few minutes early.

In a matter of seconds, Adrian caught up with the bike. He couldn't help but admire the way the lady moved as one with the bike, dipping and swaying in those tight jeans as if she was glued to the seat. Sheba and her rider definitely showed a poetry in motion that a man behind a steering wheel couldn't.

Adrian wondered who the second helmet strapped on the back of the bike belonged to. A husband or boyfriend? Not likely, he decided. It matched *Sheba's* accessories. Would a rough-riding Harley man name his bike *Sheba?*

"In one half mile, turn right onto Route 90 East to Ocean Pines."

Adrian grimaced, shifted, accelerated, and shot past the

lady on the bike. She looked over, just as he expected. But instead of consternation on her mouth—he couldn't see her face behind her goggles—he saw a smile. Not flirtatious, but one that complemented her gracious, gloved salute of admiration.

Classy lady. A twinge of guilt pinged him for stereotyping her. He had little use for people who did that sort of thing. He subscribed that it was *who* they were, not *what* they were. But there it was.

"*Turn right onto Route 90 to Ocean Pines.*"

"Alright then," Adrian replied in annoyance.

Downshifting, he entered the curve of the exit. A glance in the rearview mirror showed the Harley lady right behind him. Not riding his bumper, but keeping a practical distance.

Although he had no interest beyond curiosity, Adrian couldn't help but wonder who and what Sheba was. Gracious, he knew. Adventurous. She had to be to ride a Harley. Slender, almost boyish in shape—keyword *almost*. The wind plastering her tank top and inflating her vest revealed modest curves in the right places.

Not at all like Selena. The tall, blonde, and curvaceous software marketing rep of Alphanet Security Corporation was more like the bike. Exotic, built to take a man's breath away, with an ambition that left other women in the dust. Maybe that was why she and Adrian had clicked. They were two of a kind. Neither would settle for anything less than winning.

The total opposite of his son's mother. Carol had complimented Adrian's ambitious nature with her artistic one and serene sense of who she was. And when Peter came along, she'd adapted to motherhood as if born to it, while Adrian had never quite been able to make his son the center of his priorities. Especially since Carol had sacrificed her life to give Peter his. The doctors had wanted to treat the cancer they'd diagnosed and terminate her pregnancy.

Maybe if they had, things would have been different today. Adrian had been emotionally and spiritually torn. There would be other babies, but no other Carol. But the decision had been hers. His wife would not hear of doing anything that would endanger the life growing within her. And on her deathbed three years later, she'd made Adrian promise to make Peter his first and foremost priority.

The promise was easier made than kept. Of course Adrian allocated time for the boy and saw that his eleven-year-old was well provided for and cared for by a nanny after Carol's death. Adrian's fingers tightened on the wheel. Had it been eight years? Despite having gone on with his life, thinking about Carol still stirred a raw place in his heart that perhaps would never heal.

"Turn left at the Piper Cove Road exit."

Adrian took the exit and stared ahead at a shoulderless county road that cut through farmland where corn, dried yellow in the late August sun, contrasted with the green of pasture where black and white cattle grazed lazily. A farmer driving a tractor waved as Adrian cautiously eased the 'Vette around him.

Selena had chosen well. This remote setting would be a refreshing change for all of them. After a long visit to his family home in Cape Cod, it was painfully obvious that Adrian hardly knew his son.

"Spending two evenings a week over dinner isn't exactly bonding," his mother had told Adrian. "You need to spend more leisure time with the lad." Thirty-eight years of marriage to one of Boston's oldest families hadn't eradicated his Scottish mum's accent. A bit of it lingered with Adrian, as well.

Adrian slowed again as he approached a large, rust-infested pickup loaded with debris from a construction site toddling at its own pace around a bend in the road. Glancing in the rearview mirror, he spotted Sheba. As he entered the curve, the 'Vette rumbled over something high enough to bang Adrian's teeth together. It scraped the bottom of the car and dragged for a few feet before the vehicle shook it off.

A post of some kind . . . or a piece of a post. Must have fallen off the truck—

Ahead the road sharply snaked in the other direction. He shifted again and hit the brake to slow down. To his horror, the pedal went straight to the floor.

The 'Vette shot off the road like a bullet, cornstalks passing Adrian in a blur and whipping the deluxe finish.

Adrian had no idea how far he'd gone before the mounded rows and soft soil brought the car to a stop. Dust and field debris littered the windshield and expansive hood. Behind him, clouds of it rolled in his flattened wake.

Glancing at his watch, Adrian groaned. Two forty-five. The closing was at three. Of all the fine fixes he'd found himself in—and some had been stellar—this one was his fault. His full attention should have been fixed on the road, especially an unfamiliar one that could have broken a snake's back.

"Continue on your current route," the feminine voice, totally unruffled, advised over the Bose sound system.

Adrian struck the wheel with both hands, then promptly shut her up before she had him running over cows, as well. Exhaling heavily, he slipped a cell phone from his waist, flipped it open, and punched in the realtor's speed dial number.

The roar of an engine behind him drew his attention to the side mirrors.

Sheba. Adrian closed the phone, watching as the young woman struggled for a moment to find a spot in the field firm enough to support the big bike, then hastily dismounted the Harley, and kicked down the stand. She strode toward the car with long booted strides and pulled off her helmet.

Dark hair, long and subdued in a braid. An oval face. All-business approach, knocking aside cornstalks like gnats. Tucking the helmet under her arm, she tapped on the window. The engine stalled as Adrian opened the car door.

"You okay in there?" she asked in an accent that took Adrian a moment to place. A surprising cross between Brooklyn and Southern.

"I've been in better spots." He climbed out of the cockpit, no easy task for his six-foot-plus frame. "A blasted time for my brakes to go out. Late for an appointment," he explained, straightening with a grunt.

Sheba lowered her sunglasses, taking him in from tip to toe and back with a curious gaze, not quite green, but not brown either. Hazel was the color. Warm, full of depth . . . and direct. "Wow, there's almost as much of you as there is car," she observed with a chuckle.

Actually it was a snort . . . a dainty one that embarrassed her because she hastily covered her mouth and nose. Color crept to her tanned face, darkening it even more.

"I could say there's more bike than there is woman, in your case."

Wrong thing to say. The friendly look sharpened. "I can handle *my* ride."

"I lost my brakes on the curve." She had him repeating himself.

"Yeah, I saw you hit and drag that chunk of four-by-four." She winced as though she'd felt the impact. When she looked at him again, the warmth was back, along with a hint of amusement. "I figured right then, the brake line was gone."

Made sense. Not that Adrian was mechanical. He paid someone to keep his vehicles in prime shape. "I'd better cancel that appointment and call OnStar to send help." He flipped open his cell phone.

"Where are you headed?"

"A real estate settlement at my new river property a few miles away. At the least, I'll be late."

"Where?" Sheba asked. "I live nearby."

Disconcerted, Adrian glanced at the Corvette. "The address is programmed into the navigation system. The land belonged to the Addisons."

"Hey, that's right up the creek from me. Ellen Brittingham, your friendly neighborhood landscape artist and next-door neighbor," she said, extending her hand.

Like everything about Sheba, her handshake was firm, self-assured. Landscape artist. That accounted for the crinkling tan lines around her expressive eyes. Brackets made by laughter in the sun.

"Adrian MacAlister Sinclair, security consultant at your service, Ellen Brittingham." He had no idea why he sounded so formal. But then, conversing with a Harley-riding, girl-next-door-pretty woman in a dusty cornfield was surreal in itself.

"Sheesh. You sound like a spy. Of course, you've got the car . . . an American model, that is."

She gave the Corvette a look of longing that would make a man jealous. At the least it would make his throat go dry. Suddenly those delightful eyes shifted back to him. One naturally sculpted eyebrow arched at him in challenge.

"You up for the ride of your life?"

Adrian dismissed his first thought before he made a fool of himself. There was no double entendre in her remark. She meant what she said, and she meant the shiny motorcycle awaiting her like a loyal steed.

"I'll deliver you to your appointment on time and while you're signing your future away to a mortgage company"—

she hesitated, shooting another glance at the car—"I'll call our local towing company for you."

"I shall be forever grateful," he said, falling in behind her as she turned and headed for the Harley as though his answer was a foregone conclusion.

"You bet you will." She took off the spare helmet and handed it over to him. "And I intend to collect."

Once again Adrian mentally staggered. "Oh?" He admired the lady for her style, but she was definitely not his type. Far from it. Yet there was a deep primitive part of him that had begun to growl from the moment the game of road tag started.

"I expect a neighborly ride in that 'Vette sometime." She climbed on the bike and looked over her shoulder. "And if you let me drive it, even if it's just for a few miles, I'll owe you forever."

Idiot. Adrian donned the helmet and got on the Harley behind Ellen's lean, lithe form. The woman wasn't hot for him. She was hot for his car.

Ellen fired up the engine and revved it. As she engineered a wide, unwieldy turn with one long, denim-clad leg extended inside as a precaution, Adrian looked for a place to hold on. A handle or something.

He was accustomed to driving some of the world's finest sports cars, but motorcycles had never caught his fancy.

"You better hold on," Ellen called over her shoulder.

Adrian complied, shoving aside disconcerted thought and reaction for the sake of safety. There wasn't a lot to the cycle nymph. He could nearly circle her waist twice with his arms. But seated in the low, leather saddle of the giant Harley, she was as much a part of the roaring beast as its chrome-adorned chassis. The brain to its brawn.

As the Harley shot forward, bouncing across and clawing into the horizontal mounds of dirt that had eventually stopped his Corvette, Adrian held on for dear life . . . *tightly.*

CHAPTER TWO

"Well done. I don't believe I've ever had such an . . . exhilarating ride," Adrian said over the rumble of the engine as Ellen pulled up behind a sleek silver limo parked in front of the Addison home.

"You're welcome, Mr. Sinclair." Ellen couldn't help but grin.

Ellen loved taking a guy out of his four-wheeled cage and putting him on two wheels with nothing between him and the abrasive paving. It separated the men from the boys. And Sinclair was definitely a man. He'd leaned with her on the curves in the road and kept her from wobbling all over creation like stiff, first time riders tended to do. And that rock-hard chest under his silk shirt and business suit was definitely that of a manly man.

Still, she'd never been held quite so . . . whole-heartedly. Not that he'd been feeling her up or anything—

"Call me Adrian," her new neighbor insisted.

The opening of the front door drew their attention as Hugh Thomas, owner of Atlantic Realty, stepped outside.

"Mr. Sinclair, I see you've met your neighbor."

"Hello, Hugh," Ellen called out as Adrian greeted the red-haired realtor with a handshake. A member of Ellen's congregation, Hugh lived his faith both in and out of church. His volunteering to work at the youth center—Ellen's pet project—made him special in her eyes.

"Indeed, I have, Mr. Thomas. She came to my rescue earlier when my car lost its brakes and shot off the road."

"Saints be blessed, are you alright, Adrian?" an older woman exclaimed from the front hall door. "I've never trusted them little cars." From the way the lady looked at Ellen's bike, she had even less regard for it.

"As you can see, Mrs. Duffy, I'm just fine, thanks to Ellen."

Ellen hadn't invited Sinclair to address her by her given name, but the flair with which he rolled it off his tongue sounded good to her. Almost royal.

"Come out and meet our neighbor, Ellen Brittingham."

"Is the car okay?" A young, serious-looking boy with a black shock of hair in need of cutting and wire-rimmed glasses emerged behind the bustling Mrs. Duffy. A bit like Harry Potter, Ellen mused. Since it looked as if Ellen were in for a short social, she cut the idling engine of her bike and dismounted. She wasn't in that much of a hurry to get home, anyway. Once the kickstand was down, she tugged off her helmet and tucked it under her arm.

"The car is sitting safely in the midst of a corn field," Sinclair replied. "Nothing a good detailing won't take care of." Adrian drew the boy under his arm. "Ellen, this is my son, Peter, and Mrs. Duffy, whose position with my family, I can't begin to explain. Suffice it to say, she has been the real boss on the home front since Peter's mother passed."

So Adrian Sinclair was a widower. *Please God, don't let Ma find out,* Ellen prayed. There would be no end to the matchmaking attempts. Besides, not even Ma could make a silk purse out of a sow's ear. And Ellen would have to upgrade to a silk purse to be in this guy's league.

Prompted by Mrs. Duffy clearing her throat, Peter extended his arm, his handshake weak and reluctant. "Pleased to meet you, Miss Brittingham. Impressive bike." Peter walked to the other side of the Harley, examining more than admiring.

"Thanks, Pete."

The boy's head shot up. "It's Peter, thank you." There was no reprimand in the boy's tone. It was simply matter of fact. Almost robotic.

Still, heat flushed Ellen's cheeks. "*Peter,*" she repeated. "Sorry about that."

"Peter is a stickler for formality, but we hope the move down here will help him enjoy himself more as the lad he is," Adrian explained.

Peter did not exchange the affectionate glance his father sent his way. His focus was on the bike, as if the assortment of people watching him didn't exist.

"My mother has the opposite problem with me." Ellen shrugged, nodding at the bike. "I'm too casual." *Heathen* was the word Bea used when Ellen had particularly frustrated her. Ma had wanted a girl in ruffles and bows but wound up with one in denim.

"Actually, Ellen is a great influence on the local kids. She started the community center, almost single-handedly, to keep the kids 'busy, not bored,'" Hugh told the group, quoting the center's motto. "All the kids love her."

"A Pied Piper on a Harley," Adrian observed with a wry twist of his lips. But it was the devilment in his gaze that curled Ellen's toes inside her boots. If she didn't know any better, she'd swear he was not the least surprised. Like maybe *he'd* been guilty of following *her*. Of course, that was nuts. That Prince Charming brogue of his was giving her Cinderella notions. And she was no Cinderella.

"Well, I should hope you're careful on that thing. It looks too big for the likes of you," Mrs. Duffy told her, giving Ellen a firm handshake. Her hand was wrinkled and soft, reminding Ellen of her late grandmother.

Ellen resisted a strange urge to hug her to see if she smelled like Gran's Camay soap, too.

"Nonetheless," the housekeeper went on, "I'm pleased to meet you, Miss Brittingham. By the by, is that your home popping up amidst that cluster of trees in the distance?"

"Actually, it's her parents' home," Hugh said. "They own the local nursery. Ellen here is a landscape artist. In fact, the very one I was going to recommend to do your grounds."

"I live down there." Ellen pointed to a small dock where her houseboat was tied up. "And I work in that building there," she added, indicating the nursery office and garage combination.

"Cool." Peter's remark was the only acknowledgement that he was even a part of the conversation. Maybe he was talking about the bike. Wherever he was, it was a world of his own.

"I knew that was a nursery!" Mrs. Duffy's gray eyes took on the glow of polished silver. "I couldn't help looking about our grounds upon arrival and discovered what must have been a garden in its day. I so love flowers."

"Ma's the flower expert," Ellen told her. "And there was a garden here, until the Addisons got too old to care for it. I tried to help out when I could, but everything is so overgrown."

"Adrian, *what* is the hold-up?"

Ellen shifted her attention along with the others to the front door where a tall, stylish woman with upswept blonde hair stood all but tapping her pointed stilettos in impatience. "Mr. Stanford has been ready since three."

"The attorney's here? I didn't see his car."

The woman leaned against the doorway and crossed her arms. "That, dearest, is because I sent the limo for him." She cast a dismissive look in Ellen's direction and then aimed a smile at Adrian. "So we are all waiting on you."

Dearest. Ellen groaned. Prince Charming just fell off his horse.

"Then he can wait a moment more . . . come meet our neighbor and landscaper. How soon can you start?" he asked Ellen.

Ellen shook herself. "I'll check in with Pop and let you know. I've been away from the office for a week."

No job was too small or too big. That's what Pop always said. But Ellen wasn't her father and lately, she'd had serious thoughts about doing something else. She'd prayed about it constantly. Gone away to think about it, but—

"Selena Lacy, this is Ellen Brittingham," Adrian said as the svelte blonde sidled next to him, something of a pout on her red lips.

Ellen never could figure out if these Vogue-types were peeved or trying to look sexy. The possessive arm Selena slipped behind Adrian's back reminded Ellen more of Marley, her family's chocolate Lab, claiming his rubber hotdog squeaky toy.

Like *she* should worry, Ellen thought, extending her hand. "Nice to meet you, Miss Lacy."

"Selena is my PR manager and personal right arm . . ."

Real personal, if Ellen got the woman's ice-cold drift.

"And fiancée," Adrian finished.

As Adrian told the story of his rescue via Harley-Davidson, Selena's dark-lined gaze widened in surprise. "You, on a motorcycle? I'd like to have seen that."

"Actually, he's got a natural feel for the ride. Surprised the dickens out of me." Ellen wanted to bite off her tongue and swallow it at Adrian's disconcerted expression. Even Peter was looking at her. "I meant for someone who dresses like that."

No, that wasn't what she meant either. She knew plenty of

suit-types who shed them every chance they got to ride their bikes. And she hated stereotyping.

"Adrian is always full of surprises. That's what keeps me around," Selena said, unwittingly bailing Ellen out. "And right now," Selena said directly to the man on her arm, "you need to sign some papers for *our* summer home."

Adrian straightened. "Thank you again, Ellen. I look forward to seeing what you can do with this place." He paused, a mischievous light settling in the bluest eyes Ellen had ever seen. "And maybe taking a few riding lessons, eh?"

"Any time," Ellen shot back. "You, too, Selena. I've got a couple of bikes." Not spanking-new Harleys, but those Ellen had rebuilt and used to work her way up to the big Hog. She suppressed a smile. Just the thought of Selena holding onto a bike for dear life filled Ellen with a wicked delight.

It wasn't like it was really going to happen, Ellen argued against her better self.

"Herself, on a motorbike. That'll be the day," Mrs. Duffy *harrumph*ed beneath her breath as Adrian and Selena followed Hugh Thomas up the steps. "Nothing less than the lap of luxury for that one."

It appeared that the housekeeper had a darker self to wrestle with, as well.

The Harley was the lap of luxury to Ellen, but she got Mrs. Duffy's meaning loud and clear. A power play was definitely afoot between the women in Adrian Sinclair's household.

"But it's none of my affair," Mrs. Duffy added. "Tell me now, what is the name of that tree or bush in the front yard?

It's perfectly lovely. I don't think I've seen one like it in New England." The lady pointed to a large bush-like tree covered in scarlet blossoms.

"That's a crape myrtle, *Lagerstroemia indica*," Ellen replied. "They usually don't do well north of the mid-Atlantic states. And *that* is definitely a keeper . . . unlike all that overgrown privet," she said, pointing to a hodge-podge remnant of what had been a hedge separating their properties. "So you all are from New England?"

"Massachusetts. Cape Cod," Mrs. Duffy told her. "That's where Adrian lives—*lived*. His family, that is. He kept the house so that Peter would remain close to his grandparents, while Adrian commuted back and forth as needed to Bethesda. Moving here was *herself's* idea." And Mrs. Duffy clearly did not approve.

"It *is* closer to Mr. Sinclair's work," Ellen pointed out. Although she didn't know why. Selena wasn't the most endearing person Ellen had ever met. *Snob* was the first word that came to her mind.

"Adrian does most of his work from home," the housekeeper said, adding with an almost motherly pride, "He's an internet security genius. It's why the government hired him."

"Actually, he subcontracts security for government defense contractors," Peter broke in. Hands shoved in his pockets, he strode toward them. "When Father was a teen, he hacked into NSA computers, and they've been interested in him ever since."

"National Security Agency?" Ellen was impressed. "Wow, I guess they *were* interested."

And so was Peter. "That's what he does . . . searches for possible holes in clients' networks and security software and seals them. I've worked on designing a game that does the same thing," he added. "The challenge is to get inside without being detected."

"Your dad must be really proud." While Peter looked like a potential computer nerd, Adrian Sinclair did not.

"Of course he is," Mrs. Duffy said.

Peter was noncommittal.

Definitely a strange kid, though. And for some reason, Ellen felt as though they had something in common. What, she couldn't imagine. Unless it was that they were both square pegs in a round-hole society.

"So . . ." Ellen stalled, catching Peter looking back at her bike. "I guess I'd better head home. Peter, would you like a ride first?"

"No, thank you."

"Peter doesn't like loud noise."

"Yeah?" Ellen walked over to the Harley and dug into one of her saddlebags. "That's what these are for," she said, tugging out a pair of earphones designed to cut down on road and engine noise. "Or you can do what I do and listen to music on my earphones."

Peter looked tempted. His blue eyes all but caressed the shiny Harley from handlebars to the companion pad, but he shook his head. "Not today, thank you."

Ellen shrugged. "Any time. If you take a notion, just pop on over for a visit. But I'm warning you, my mother lives to stuff kids with all manner of baked concoctions. Come to think of it, she stuffs anyone who comes around." Ellen snickered. At the inadvertent snort that escaped, Peter locked soulful eyes with her. It was as though she were being searched from the inside out. *Could you be a friend?* Ellen sensed the boy's unspoken question probing her heart, pulling at it. A hint of a tug at the corner of his mouth broke his quiet interrogation.

"So does Mrs. Duffy."

This young man didn't smile a lot.

"Well," Ellen said to the housekeeper, "you can be sure Ma'll be over to exchange recipes. And to bring flowers. She loves sharing her flowers with anyone who'll have them."

Mrs. Duffy clasped her hands together, her crinkled eyes twinkling. "I'd be delighted."

Ellen swung her leg over her bike and kicked back the stand. The Harley started with a roar and settled to a purr as she pulled on her helmet and fastened it. When she looked up to say goodbye, Peter was headed into the house like a scalded pup, his hands over his ears. Mrs. Duffy wasn't kidding about his sensitivity to noise.

"Glad to have you as new neighbor, Mrs. D. Do you mind if I call you that?"

"That would be fine, Ellen Brittingham."

"You can call me Brit if you want. Most of my friends do."

Mrs. Duffy shook her head. "With a pretty smile like that,

Brit doesn't do you justice. Ellen suits you more." She leaned in closer so that Ellen could hear her lowered voice. "And about Peter. I know it appears he doesn't care a lot about anything . . . you know, showing emotion and such, but he's a special boy with a heart big as all get out."

"His heart is in his eyes," Ellen observed. "They say it all, I think."

A mingle of surprise and satisfaction claimed Mrs. Duffy's softly wizened features. "I knew it!" Ellen braced herself, certain the animated housekeeper was about to give her a bear hug. Instead, Mrs. Duffy gave her a pat on the arm. "You two will get on just fine. Just don't be put off by his temper. It's all a part of his condition."

"Condition?"

"When we've more time, I'll explain, dear," Mrs. Duffy replied. Her dampened expression brightened again. "You nearly made him laugh, you know."

"Yeah, I make a lot of people laugh. It's the one thing I'm *really* good at." That and self-deprecation.

"Proverbs 17:22." Mrs. Duffy gave Ellen a sly wink. "'*A merry heart doeth good like a medicine.*' Lord knows, this family needs more of it. I'm so glad you'll be around for a while."

Mrs. Duffy's words haunted Ellen as she pulled out of the long cedar-lined driveway and headed for her own. She wondered what Peter's "condition" was. He didn't seem terribly abnormal. A little socially challenged, perhaps. His answers were canned, as if they were being read from the dialogue of a how-to-speak language book. A very intelligent face, almost older than his age, which Ellen guessed to be around eleven or twelve. And a bit sad.

Ellen wondered when he'd lost his mother. Or maybe his melancholy was because Ms. Stiletto was about to fill the vacancy. Alright, she was being bad again, but there was something about the blonde *femme fatale* that had rubbed Ellen the wrong way the moment their eyes met, making Ellen feel like a slug—repugnant and unloved.

Not that any of that was Ellen's business. Her job would be arm's length. If she took it. Which she would, even though she wanted to give up working at the nursery.

God, what is wrong with me? I love working in the earth, planting and growing. I love designing yards and grounds for people. It's what I went to school for. But my heart just isn't in it any more.

If God was answering, it wasn't over the noise of the Harley. Ellen pulled up to the office-garage near the waterfront and cut the engine. She was home, the place she loved, filled with people she loved. Yet the heaviness she'd abandoned for a weeklong ride settled once again like a brick in her chest.

Aw, God, take it back . . . please.

CHAPTER THREE

Marley raced toward Ellen as she dismounted her bike. Upon reaching her, the black lab sat obediently and waited for her to secure the kickstand before inching closer for his head rub.

"So, how ya been doing, boy? Holding down the fort?"

From the way his tail swished, he'd not only kept things together while she was away, but done so with great enthusiasm.

"Ma and Pop home?" she asked, straightening to head into the two-story farmhouse where she'd been raised.

T-shaped to catch the breeze from every direction and with a sun porch on the south side, the house was designed to afford the most comfort from the Shore's flighty weather. Ellen went in through the side sun porch door and stopped long enough to dig a handful of dry food out of a galvanized garbage can for Marley.

"Here ya go," she said, dropping it into his dish.

She'd thought a couple of times about getting a dog, but the limited space on her houseboat wasn't the best home for a puppy, especially one that would grow as big as Marley. Besides, the Lab did his best to visit daily. And on the rare occasion when her parents went away, Ellen made room for him aboard the *Sassy Sparrow*.

"Oh good, you're just in time for supper!" Bea Brittingham said, straightening from the oven. The scent of baked chicken tantalized Ellen's stomach, making it roll in anticipation.

"Dumplings?" she asked her mother hopefully. Ellen loved slippery dumplings, a thin mouth-watering pasta, Eastern Shore-style.

"Of course," Bea replied, as though it were a given. Ellen added another place setting to the colonial-style table in the eating area of the country kitchen. Paneled in knotty-pine with matching cabinets, it was always warm and inviting, both in scent and ambiance. The television built into the fireplace wall was tuned to a cooking show. A pie that rivaled anything the lady on the show could turn out sat on the counter. Ma was addicted to cooking. Take her out of the kitchen, and she might as well be shot.

"Pop watching the ballgame?"

"Yanks are playing Baltimore." Petite, with dark, age-salted hair, Bea carried the steaming roasting pan over to the sink counter and put it down. "How's about a hand with this, dear? Get me the platter."

Ellen fetched the meat platter that matched Ma's everyday

rooster dishes. She'd never seen a green and brown rooster, but she'd had many a scrumptious meal on those plates since she was kneehigh. With the practice of many years of cooking, Bea coaxed the roasted chicken off the rack and onto the platter.

"Perfect!" she declared in satisfaction. "So how was the ride?"

"Perfect!" Ellen mimicked. She leaned over and gave her mother a kiss on the cheek. A head taller, Ellen had inherited her father's long lanky frame. "I almost hate to go back to work."

More than her mother knew. She and Pop had put everything into this business. It was their source of income, as well as Ellen's. How could she tell them that she wanted to move on?

"You've worked hard this summer. You deserved a vacation."

"How'd Pop make out?"

"Fine. Why shouldn't he? It's not like he's a cripple." Ma rolled her eyes toward the ceiling, and Ellen grinned at her imitation of Pop. Or rather Pop with a Brooklyn accent. Thirty-eight years out of New York and Bea still had that accent, lightly touched with an Eastern Shore drawl. Talk about a weird combination. Add to that her Messianic Jewish roots and Bea Brittingham was a walking melting pot, both ethnic and spiritual.

"So did the crew finish the Tobias house in Piney Banks?"

"All but a couple of shrubs from the field that didn't look too good. Eddie ordered replacements." No one called Edward Brittingham by that name other than Ma. To others he was Brit and Ellen had inherited the same nickname from her own peers. She guessed that technically made her Brit Jr. "But between you and me," her mother went on, "he was worn out at the end of the day."

If only Ma knew how that made Ellen feel. Not that Bea intended to hurt her, but it did. No, it frustrated her, because she couldn't be in two places at one time. In the field over-seeing the grunt work and in the office doing the planning and ordering. And Ellen had tried to do both for the last two years, with Pop helping out as he could after a serious heart attack warning.

"We're getting older," Ma went on, "but who isn't? How's about *schlepping* to the living room and telling your father he has five minutes till dinner."

The game wasn't going well. Ellen could tell instantly be-cause Pop sat in the chair with his head tilted back, softly snoring.

"So the Birds lost, eh?" she said, rubbing the bristle on the top of his head. Unlike Ma's, Pop's hair was more salt than pepper and still cut in an Army buzz. "Yep." He twisted in the chair to look at her. "How'd she ride?"

Ellen's heart melted at the sparkle in his eye. There'd been a time when he'd have gone with her. "Like a kitten," she said. "Not a lick of trouble."

It was Pop who got the idea to switch from farming to establishing a nursery for wholesalers. Then Ellen took it further in landscaping and design. Which made it even harder for her complain to them that the business had grown to more than she could handle. More than she wanted to handle.

"Well, you bought the cream of the crop," he said.

"Speaking of cream of the crop, I met our new neighbor."

The crinkling about her father's eyes deepened. "Oh?"

"Not *him* per se," Ellen backtracked. Hot color crept up her neck. "I mean, him too, but I was talking about his car. He was driving a new Z07, Atomic Orange Metallic."

"A hotrod, eh?"

"Pop, *hotrod* doesn't do a 'Vette justice."

"Single?"

"What?" Ellen blinked, blank until her father's meaning caught up with her. "You've been around Ma too long."

"Is *who* single?" Bea said from the living room doorway. Her voice perked higher. "Have you met a *man*?" One might have thought from the way she said *man*, that Ellen had discovered an extinct species.

"Yep and she's in love with his car." Pop gave Ellen a wink and got up, addressing his wife. "Dinner ready? I'm starved, woman."

"Better you should tell me what you know first about our daughter and this man."

Ellen exhaled heavily. That was exactly why she hadn't burst into the house to tell Ma about Adrian Sinclair. Already a pair of itsy, bitsy wedding bells dangled where her pupils had just been.

"He's a widower—" Ellen began.

Bea caught her breath, her dark brows arched.

"—and engaged to a walking, talking Barbie doll."

"Oh." The brows lowered, flattened by disappointment. "Dinner is all but on the table," her mother informed her with an indignant sniff. "So you come pour the iced tea and tell me all about this man and his Barbie. You know, just because she's built like Barbie doesn't mean she's right for him."

Ellen groaned aloud. Before Ma was finished with Ellen, she'd know the color of Adrian's eyes, about Peter's special ways, Mrs. Duffy's favorite flower, and Selena Lacy's stilettos. The CIA would never know what it had missed, not having Bea Brittingham among their ranks.

It was going to be a long meal.

The next day, Ellen escaped her mother's well-intended, but ongoing interrogation and headed toward Piper Cove Golf and Country Club. Newlywed Alex Butler Turner had left a message on Ellen's answering machine not to forget that a *sundae* meeting had been planned for Monday lunch. Ellen and her three best friends from high school tried to get together at least once a month for sinful indulgence at the club's coffee shop, and more often when something special was afoot. This was a regular get-together, just to catch up, since their busy lives made it hard to keep in touch, despite living in the same small town.

Although Piper Cove wasn't so small any more. Ocean

City's popularity as a resort and retirement haven had spilled across Assawoman Bay, to what was once a small fishing village. The growth had started when the storm of 1933 cut the inlet and opened the bay to the Atlantic, but in the last ten years, the population had skyrocketed. Who'd have thought condos and canals would fill the marshland where Ellen and her dad used to hunt? Or that million dollar homes and multi-million dollar developments would line both sides of the St. Martin River?

At least the town planners kept Main Street intact, Ellen thought as she passed the brick and awning storefronts, and turned onto North Cove Road. Golf course green spread to the left of her pickup while the water to her right sparkled blue, set with diamonds of sunlight. Once lunch was over, she had to deliver the shrubs that came in that morning to the crew at Piney Cove. Something she could not do on her motorcycle.

"There's just somethin' 'bout a girl in a pickup truck," she paraphrased in song, pulling the red Ford F-150 into the club parking lot.

After slapping on her straw cowboy hat, Ellen climbed out of the vehicle, landing squarely on her booted feet. She'd donned a tank top, jeans, and boots in anticipation of having to pitch in at the work site. The guys could handle the job, but Ellen couldn't keep her hands out of the mix of peat and fresh-worked earth.

So why did she want to quit and run the community center? Was it God or her biological clock shoving her toward working with kids? She'd always loved them, no matter what age. Or was it both?

"Hey, Brit, wait up!"

Ellen stopped and turned to see Jan Kudrow heading toward her. With Ellen's tall, lanky frame and Jan's petite one, they were physical opposites.

"I just got off," Jan said, falling into double-step to Ellen's longer stride.

Jan clocked in at four in the morning at the Food Mart bakery, so by noon, she'd put in a full day. She always smelled good—cinnamon and 4X sugar with a hint of apple today.

"I hope you're headed to bed," Ellen told her, noting the dark circles under her friend's eyes. Today, they were a faded green, rather than their usual enigmatic shade.

"I am. Scott and I spent the weekend in Atlantic City."

Which meant, knowing Scott Phillips, owner of the Baysider Hotel and Condo at South Point, that Jan had had little or no sleep. Ellen could never understand the gambling bug, which Scott had big time, much less why her friend went along with his addiction. But then Ma always said that love makes people do strange things. Ellen could buy strange, but not stupid.

"Sue Ann and Alex are already here." Jan pointed to the back corner booth that they always came early to get. Catching sight of her baker hat–flattened pixie cut in the mirrored wall behind the counter, she fluffed the short, blonde strands with her fingers. "Aw, man, am I sight or what?"

"What," Ellen teased. She snickered as she sat down next to Alex.

"Well, I just can't believe it," Sue Ann Wiltbank exclaimed in her southern drawl, pinching Ellen's arm.

"Ow!" Ellen pulled it away. "What'd I do?"

"I just spent two weeks at a spa in the Bahamas and your ol' field tan still looks better than mine."

"Will it make you feel better if I tell you that when we're rocking away our golden years in Shady Pines, I'll look like a leathered old crone, and you'll be glowing like a peach?"

"You do use sunblock, don't you, Brit?" Alex asked. She'd dressed for business today in a power suit, basic black pin-stripe, white cuffed shirt.

Ellen nodded. "Of course, I do. I lather up in it daily."

"Ellen's got her mom's olive skin tone as a base," Jan observed with a hint of envy. "She'll always have a natural glow."

"Remember back in the days of our sun worship how Sue Ann and Jan always burned, while Ellen and I tanned so easily?" Alex reminded them.

"I shed more skin than a snake," Sue Ann complained as the waitress approached their table, "even with special lotions."

"Hi, ya'll. Can I get you ladies the usual?"

"I think so, Candy," Alex replied.

Ellen grinned. "You got it. How's Hattie Mae?"

"Grandma's in the kitchen, doing just fine. I'll bet she'll know you're here when I place your sundae order. Three hot fudge sundaes and," Candy looked at Ellen, "a banana split, right?"

"Gee, you'd think we'd been here before," Alex quipped as the girl left. It had taken them a while to get past Candy's teen disparagement for anyone older than twenty, but now the young girl seemed to hang around just to hear the banter when they got together.

Once Candy left the table, Sue Ann leaned over in a conspiratorial stage whisper. "A little birdie told me Ellen has a new handsome hunk of a neighbor. She's already taken him on that motor bike of hers."

Alex stiffened in mock indignation. "You aren't holding out on us, are you, Brit?"

Ellen groaned. "My mother has enough mouth for two sets of teeth . . ."

"And he's single, even," Sue Ann drawled in her best Brooklyn imitation, belying the wide innocence of her blue gaze.

" . . . more tongue than a high top shoe," Ellen continued, her expression doleful until Jan kicked her under the table. "Ow!"

"You took him riding on your Hog and you didn't tell *us,* your very best friends in the whole world?" she accused.

"I've been working and there's *nothing* to tell. At least nothing that couldn't wait until our sundae meeting. No big deal."

Sue Ann wriggled in anticipation beside her. "So tell us *everything.*"

Ellen did. From her love at first sight with his car to meeting his family. Every detail, except the fact that her heart had taken up gymnastics since Adrian smiled at her as she'd passed him for a better look at the 'Vette. What was the point?

"He is *so* taken," she concluded, envisioning Selena Lacy in her mind.

"Taken," Alex said, "isn't *taken* without the gold band." She wriggled her fingers in the sunlight, which danced off the gold set on her left hand. Love had softened Alex's *got to be in charge* nature, but she spoke her mind.

"Trust me, his fiancée is tall, blonde, sophisticated, and gorgeous . . . how *taken* can it get?"

"What's her name?" Jan asked.

"Selena Lacy," Ellen told her. "I mean, even her name is sexy."

"Sounds like a stripper to me," Sue Ann observed. "Not wholesome, like our girl Ellen. And if he has a kid, he wants wholesome in his house, not bombshell."

"Look, there's enough of a rift in that house over the fiancée without me adding to it. Not that I could compete, even if I wanted."

Sue Ann brushed aside Ellen's protest with a wave of her manicured hand. "Nonsense! Sweetie, we could do a make-over on you that—"

Ellen put on the brakes. "Oh no, I'm just fine. I like who I am."

"So do we, Brit," Alex said, "but there's room for improvement in all of us."

"I always thought the layered look would look lovely on you," Jan said, her gaze all but whacking away at Ellen's simple, ponytailed style. "More feminine."

"What is it about the word *engaged* that you three don't

understand?" She threw up her hands in exasperation. "I am not changing for anyone, especially not a man and more to the point, a practically married one."

"Here you go, ladies. Three hot fudge sundaes and one banana split," Candy announced. "Grandma put extra nuts and whipped cream on everything."

"Bless Hattie Mae's heart," Sue Ann moaned as Ellen helped Candy disburse the confections from the tray she balanced on one hand. "My diet is going to *you know where* in a handbasket."

"No ice cream there, Susie Q," Alex teased, "so enjoy."

"Yeah," Ellen chimed in. "And no more talk about Adrian Sinclair."

Jan sighed dreamily, a spoonful of chocolate-covered ice cream poised at her lips. "Even his name sounds hunky."

Ellen raised a warning finger to her. "Just eat before it melts."

But the subject was moot. Ma had unleashed her friends like hounds on scent and Ellen felt like a fox.

CHAPTER FOUR

The good thing about ice cream was that it didn't permit lengthy conversation before it was consumed. And by the time their spoons scraped the bottom of the sundae dishes, the conversation had shifted from Ellen. Alex's husband Josh was really getting into the development business, in addition to penning some Top Forty lyrics for his former band. Jan's beau had been pressuring her to quit her job at the Food Mart and work full time in the bakery for his restaurant.

"He wants to control you, Jan. Don't you dare give in," Ellen advised, along with the others. Scott Phillips was all about Scott Phillips, too in love with himself to love Jan the way she longed to be loved. But that was as much as any of them ventured to say. They loved Jan, despite some of her poorer choices in life.

"So when is Martin due in, Susie Q?" Ellen asked as they left the coffee shop.

Sue Ann's architect husband traveled extensively and was often gone for weeks at a time. Not that it seemed to bother her much. At least on the surface.

"He's flying into Salisbury at seven-thirty tonight from Florida." Her eyes flashed with mischief. "I'm having a special dinner prepared, his favorite wine, and I bought a new outfit just for the occasion. *Lace*," she added, glancing around the parking lot as if she'd just said something naughty and might be caught.

The roar of a finely tuned engine pulled Ellen's attention from her friend to where a familiar Corvette pulled into the club parking lot and zipped effortlessly into the space next to her pickup. Even though her buddies were not into cars and engines, their eyes were drawn to where Adrian Sinclair emerged from the vehicle and straightened, adjusting his tie as though it were second nature.

Sue Ann feigned a step backward. "My stars. Hunk alert."

"*Mega*," Jan agreed, steadying Susie Q's arm.

Always the cool head, Alex slipped on her designer sunglasses. "Heads up, he's looking at us, ladies. Make that, coming this way . . . and waving," she added in surprise.

Ellen pulled her straw cowboy hat down, shading her forehead, but there was no avoiding introductions. Piper Cove was too small. Sooner or later, she'd have to suffer through them with her matchmaking hounds at her heel.

"Miss Brittingham," Adrian said. "That *is* you under there, isn't it?"

If a cat had a smile like that, no mouse on earth would be safe. Ignoring Jan's sharp elbow to her ribs, Ellen tipped her hat. "In the flesh, " she said. And speaking of flesh, hers was burning with . . . well, she didn't know what.

"Well, for heaven's sake, Ellen. Where are your manners?" Sue Ann chided sweetly. "Aren't you going to introduce us?"

Or maybe it was from the sudden grilling of her friends' nudging gazes. Two sets. Sue Ann's had never left that of the handsome stranger. "Well, *aren't* you?" she cooed.

Some of Susie Q's devilment infected Ellen. "Adrian Sinclair, this is Jan Kudrow," Ellen told him, making Sue Ann squirm with impatience beside her. "Jan's the best pastry chef in Piper Cove . . ."

"Miss Kudrow." Adrian engulfed Jan's small hand between his own. "Pleased to meet you."

"And this is Alex Butler . . . er . . . Turner—she just got married—of *Designs by Alex*. If you need any decorating ideas, she's the one to call."

"I'll keep that in mind, Mrs. Turner," he replied with a nod.

"Delighted to meet you, Mr. Sinclair." Ever efficient, Alex produced a card. "You may contact me here if or when you're interested."

"And *this*," Ellen said with a grin, "is Mrs. Sue Ann Wiltbank . . ."

Sue Ann extended her French-manicured hand, forcing Ellen a step back, and drew "Charmed," into two, drawled syllables.

"Piper Cove's incorrigible flirt," Ellen finished. "She can't help herself. She was born winking at the doctor."

Sue Ann gave Ellen a playful smack on the arm. "Why, Ellen Brittingham, speaking of incorrigible." After giving Ellen that fleeting moment's attention, Sue Ann shifted her curious gaze back to the tall, suit-clad man. "We've been naughty today. Ice-cream sundaes for lunch."

Only Sue Ann could make eating ice-cream sound as though they were perdition-bound, three times over. And the way Ellen's heart catapulted to her throat as Adrian met her gaze, that's where she was headed, too. *The man's engaged,* she reminded herself.

"So . . . o," she began, her thoughts tumbling for something to say. "Was it the brake line that sent you into Willis's cornfield?"

"Ellen told us all about it," Sue Ann exclaimed with a rose red purse of her lips. "I'd have been rattled witless."

"It was more annoying than unsettling," Adrian told her, turning to Ellen. "But that is precisely what the mechanic said. A broken brake line. You have an impressive knowledge of mechanics."

Ellen's pulse couldn't have raced any faster if he'd said she was beautiful. Okay, maybe *that* was exaggerating. "Guess I was born with grease in my blood. Ow!" At the sharp pressure of Sue Ann's spiked heel, Ellen glared at her. "What?"

Innocence blossomed in Sue Ann's blue-eyed gaze. "Was that your foot, sweetie? I'm *so* sorry." Which meant, *hush-up* in her friend's body language. She extended her hand to

Adrian. "Mr. Sinclair, I can't tell you what a pleasure it was to make your acquaintance. I'm sure we'll be seeing each other again soon. That's just the way of small towns."

"Sue Ann's *husband* is flying home this evening," Ellen put in for some reason beyond her. After all, Susie Q was just being herself. If she ever caught the men she flirted with, she'd be as befuddled as the dog that caught a car. "He's an architect," Ellen explained, aware of Alex and Jan's bemused stares. "Travels a lot."

She was babbling. She never babbled.

Sue Ann glanced at the watch on her wrist. "And I have a hair appointment in twenty minutes! My goodness, where does the time fly?"

"It was a pleasure to meet you as well, Mrs. Wiltbank, but don't let me make you late," Adrian said. "I happened to see the landscaping truck and wanted to catch Ellen before she left."

Sue Ann stopped short. Ellen was mildly amused by Susie Q's insatiable curiosity. *Looks like the hairdresser can wait.*

"So what's up?" Ellen asked, more than a little self-conscious with her buddies watching for any innuendo that might smack of interest between her and Adrian.

"I'd hoped that you might speak with Mrs. Duffy and my fiancée about the landscaping soon. Selena fancies a spring wedding there."

Ellen ventured an *I told you so* glance at her friends.

"You *have* decided to take on the project, haven't you?"

Her attention snapped back to Adrian's bluer than blue appraisal. "You bet! I was planning on heading over this afternoon. I promise you," she said, giving Adrian a friendly punch on the bicep. Wow, there was muscle under that expensive jacket. "Um . . ." She mentally regrouped. "By spring, it will be a beautiful setting for a wedding."

"A spring wedding," Jan said dreamily. "That is so romantic. Is your fiancée a local girl?"

"Selena is from D.C. Like myself, she's a diplomatic corps brat. Perhaps when we're settled, we'll have an open house to show off Ellen's work."

"Ellen can work wonders with landscaping," Alex said, her enthusiasm falling just short of a *Rah Rah* from her cheerleader past.

"I look forward to it." Adrian glanced beyond them to the entrance where a sedan pulled into the lot with a magnetic *Atlantic Realty* sign on the door. "Ah, here is my appointment now." He practically clicked his highly polished heels as he bowed slightly. "Ladies, my pleasure. Have a grand afternoon."

With that, he walked over to the realtor's car.

"Well I *nevah*," Sue Ann marveled.

"Oh, yes, you have," Alex told her mischievously, "and you enjoyed every minute of it."

"I thought Martin was continental," Sue Ann continued, ignoring her, "but that one even comes with an accent."

"Scottish, British?" Jan ventured. "He's so proper."

"Yeah, he talks like a spy or something." Ellen's friends swung their attention her way. "Well, doesn't he?"

"Grease in your blood," Sue Ann quoted with a derisive grimace. She gave Ellen a little smack on the arm.

"Honestly, Ellen," Alex chimed in. "You are never going to get a man like that."

"Especially with that dribble of chocolate on your chest." Jan pointed to a wayward streak of syrup on Ellen's tank top.

Ellen cringed at the unsightly stain. "Aw, man," she complained, wiping at it with her fingers. "And I wasn't trying to get him. He's *gotten*," she reminded them.

"I think our Ellen has caught his eye." Jan sighed. "His eyes smiled every time he looked at you."

"That's because he's too polite to laugh outright and call me a klutz." Despite her disclaimer, Ellen's pulse burned rubber in her veins at the idea. "And you all haven't seen Selena Lacy. They could model a *Sexy* Barbie after her."

"I don't like her," Sue Ann sniffed.

"Me either," Jan chimed in.

Alex spoke with the voice of reason. "Now ladies, you haven't met her. Granted, it bites that she's got her hooks in one of the best catches I've seen in these waters, but I think Adrian Sinclair was just being friendly with Ellen. You know how guys always take to her."

"Yeah, I'm like a puppy." Ellen snorted, giving up on the stain. She drew up her paws and leaned into Jan with her best puppy imitation, eyelashes batting. "They can't resist."

Sue Ann pushed her away. "Say what you will, but I agree with Jan. For some bizarre reason, I think that debonair hunk of a man is able to see past the foot in Ellen's mouth and the chocolate dribbling down her bosom to the diamond we all know her to be."

"Aw, cut it out." The last thing Ellen's stepped-up pulse needed was fuel for encouragement. The only thing she had in common with Sinclair was his taste in cars. "The guy's just being friendly and grateful. End of story."

"If you say so." In Sue Ann speak, that meant *fiddle faddle*.

After his meeting with the realtor, Adrian maneuvered his newly repaired Corvette around the curve that had taken it out a few days earlier. This time, the vehicle clung to the road like gum to a shoe. No side trips through the corn. His mind flicked back to his first motorcycle ride, holding on for dear life as the Harley bit into the dirt, wobbly until the roaring engine propelled it forward with whiplash speed. The tall, wiry wildcat reminded him of Carol with her homegrown style and quirky sense of humor. Although to his knowledge, Carol had never been on a bike or worn leather, save the stylish two-tone leather coat he'd bought her their last Christmas together.

The memory constricted Adrian's chest until he recalled his late wife's wisecrack after a chilly January trip to an elite Boston cancer treatment center. They'd just gotten the news that everything that could be done had been done. It was just a matter of time. He'd hardly been able to see through his pain as he drove toward their Cape Cod home. Carol, a shadow of her former self from the chemo shivered in the confines of the coat, despite the full blast of the car's heater. With a humor that never abandoned her throughout her ordeal, she'd sworn the cow that had provided the skin for the wrap had died of pneumonia.

A half smile playing upon his lips, Adrian drove up the cedar-lined driveway toward his new home. He missed her comic relief and that look-at-the-bright-side attitude. It had been the color in his black-and-white world of software design. That his new neighbor, who looked nothing like his petite blonde-haired wife, had been able to trigger the same reaction in him had taken Adrian by surprise.

But then, Selena's picking an older home on the water, something Carol would have loved, had surprised Adrian, too. Somehow, he'd imagined his city-girl fiancée in one of the exclusive townhouses along the bayside. Yet, here she was. Of course, it was her attempt to find a home that suited raising an eleven-year-old boy. Adrian appreciated it more than she could know.

As he got out of the car the subject of his thoughts appeared in the doorway. Clad in a tailored, but decidedly feminine pantsuit, Selena had been at work in the make-shift office Adrian had set up for her in her temporary bedroom. The bold red silk blouse she wore beneath the jacket bespoke her passion, both for business and for pleasure.

"How soon can we get the secure line hardwired in?" he asked.

"Tomorrow. Mr. Thomas is taking care of everything. I want to be certain that he is rewarded for his efforts to make this transition as smooth as possible."

"Another plus for this area. The people seem friendly and accommodating."

The image of Ellen promising to come here later popped

into Adrian's mind. "Indeed. Thankfully, when the Addisons' renovated, they did it up right. I'd hate to think of the distraction of having everything newly wired and plumbed."

Selena planted a finger on his lips, a seductive smile stealing onto her lips. "I wouldn't have recommended the house if it wasn't a *new* older home. The amenities of new with the ambiance of old. It has the right feel to it, don't you think?"

"Absolutely." Although privately, Adrian failed to comprehend how a house could have a feel. It either suited his purposes or it didn't. He could work well anywhere that was wired sufficiently to run his computer software enterprise. At least with regard to working on a project offline. His direct access to client files had to be through a segregated, security-enhanced line.

"Where's Peter?" he asked, glancing up the stairwell to the second floor landing in anticipation of the answer.

The tilt of Selena's mouth fell. "In his room, where else?"

The sarcasm put a damper on the chemistry between them. But then Peter was a walking damper to most. Sometimes the boy could be as sweet and considerate as his mother had been, but when his mood was dark and his temper unchecked, it was too easy for Adrian to dislike his own son, in spite of his soul-deep love for him. Only those who knew Peter's good heart and sensitive nature felt at ease around him.

Such was the nature of Asperger's Syndrome. The autism-related disorder impaired Peter's social and communication skills. His son had difficulty reading tones or body language, taking everything literally. His cluelessness to others' feelings

often came off as lack of empathy, as offensive as his outbursts
of anger and frustration, while his high level verbal skills
manifested itself in formal speech patterns that made him
seem even more out of touch with others. Thankfully, Peter's
case was not as severe as others, but it was still enough to
keep Adrian on edge, struggling to see beyond it to the beautiful child whom he wanted the world to know and love.

"Chip off the old block, eh?" He wished that saying it
would make it so.

Selena leaned into Adrian, tilting her face to his. "Hardly."
She slipped her fingers under the perfect Windsor knot of his
tie. "*This* electronic hermit, I can do something with." She
caressed his lips with hers. "I can do *lots* with."

The innuendo dimmed Adrian's concern that Selena
and Peter were an *east is east and west is west, and never the
twain shall meet* pair. Selena had already done so much with
Adrian and his business. Since he'd hired her on, she'd recre-
ated his rather plain image for the covers of GQ and Forbes,
and grown his private security services into a public corporation. She'd taken him out of his office and into the world
of politics and finance he'd shunned because of the constant
social demands he'd seen in his parents' lives. He'd eventually moved from Cape Cod to the security-sensitive hub of
the Washington, D.C., area.

"As for Peter, I'm checking on your alma mater. I was
thinking the experience would broaden his world beyond a
computer screen and books." Selena looked as though she
expected Adrian to be overcome with joy.

He wasn't. "Edinburgh?"

The Edinburgh Academy had been his mother's choice for his schooling, ideal in that it was near her family, but a poor fit for Adrian. Like his son, he was more at home with a hard drive than other people. And while life had forced him out of his primarily solitary world, it did not necessarily mean that he was at ease there, especially on the trips that had him skiing on the Alps or diving in the Mediterranean with members of the world's "Who's Who." Granted, he'd been accomplished at those endeavors since childhood. That was in his competitive nature. But the social scene was not. His son was the same way.

"I don't see Peter at Edinburgh," he stated flatly with a shake of his head.

"The boy is smart enough, Adrian, and we both know he needs to become more social. Even the birds force their little ones from the nest at some point."

Ah, but at what expense? If Adrian had let them, the taunts would haunt him to this day, even though he was as financially successful, if not more so, than those social wonders who'd made life unbearable for the more introverted sorts. And while he was inclined to strangle his son at times, Adrian was always committed to protecting him. He couldn't do that an ocean away. It would be hard enough with Peter nearby.

"He will become more social," Adrian replied. The therapist insisted that he would. The communication skills and anger management that did not come naturally for those with Asperger's Syndrome could be learned. Adrian gave Selena a placating peck on the cheek. "But it will be closer to home where I can keep an eye on him and his therapy can continue."

"Amen to that!" a voice sounded from the next room.

"It's a relief to know that you agree with me, Mrs. Duffy." Adrian wasn't certain who was more astonished—himself at being overheard or the housekeeper, who'd inadvertently admitted to eavesdropping from the dining room.

Selena grabbed Adrian's arm and ushered him into the office, closing the door after them. "And I thought this house was big enough for the four of us."

Peter wasn't the only one who didn't adapt well to change. The sooner Selena realized that Adrian's son and housekeeper were as much a part of his life as his fiancée would be, the easier it would be for all of them.

He took the curvaceous woman in his arms and gave her a proper kiss, full on the mouth. Although stiff at first, Selena melted against him as his kiss deepened. While Adrian's pulse quickened in natural response to her sensual appeal, he knew exactly what he was doing. Selena had been her own worst enemy when she taught him the effect that he could have on women. How to disarm them with charm. Not that his attraction to her wasn't genuine, he thought in answer to an unexpected pang of guilt. A man would have to be blind and bloodless not to be taken in by Selena's brains and beauty. Adrian was neither.

But neither was he so consumed by her appeal that his brain shut down during a kiss as it had with his late wife. A disturbing thought . . .

As he drew away, she sighed, snuggling her head into the curve of his neck. He inhaled her exotic perfume, and was plagued by yet another thought. As wonderful as Selena was, he did not feel the connection, the oneness that he'd shared with Carolyn. Perhaps that would come with time.

"There, now," he mumbled into the softness of her up-swept hair. "We all want what's best for Peter, don't we?"

"Of course. I was just trying to help."

Adrian couldn't see her pout, but he could hear it.

"I wonder if I'll ever make a good mother. Everything I do seems to be the wrong thing when it comes to Peter."

"Nonsense. The fact that you're trying so hard shows what you're made of." At least, that's what Adrian hoped.

Mrs. Duffy had always been the closest thing to a mother to Peter since Carol's passing. Adrian could understand the resentment on both their parts toward Selena, but he also knew them to be fair-minded. They would accept Selena, once they came to know her intentions were for Peter's best interests. Everything, it seemed to Adrian, was a matter of time. It just couldn't happen soon enough to assuage his need for harmony and order.

His gaze wandered to his computer screen where an even stronger desire beckoned. He wanted to get back to the security project he was working on. He was on the verge to hacking into Putnam Laboratories' computer system to test the effectiveness of their security, and the idea was as stirring as the woman snuggling against him. Especially since he was trying to break into a security system that he'd set up and maintained.

But first, he needed to take care of security here, even in Piper Cove. When corporate and state secrets were at stake, no precaution was too much.

"Oh, I ran into our neighbor at the club café earlier," Adrian said, stepping away from Selena. "She said she'd be over this afternoon to take a look at the project and talk it over with Mrs. Duffy."

Selena bristled.

Realizing he'd stepped off the fine line separating the territories of the two women of the house, Adrian added, "Unless you have some specific ideas for the grounds. All Mrs. Duffy cares about is her herb and flower garden."

"As a matter of fact, I do have a few things in mind."

Adrian wandered over to the computer.

"I want a gazebo and think we need to connect . . ."

He couldn't dial into the security system to fix anything without the protected line, but he could try tapping in through European carriers to hack in. His fingers were a blur over the keyboard. First France, then Germ—

Selena raised her voice behind him. "Earth to Adrian. Are you listening to me?"

"That's up to you two to work out. I still haven't quite gotten through—"

Before he could finish, Selena walked out of the room with an exasperated huff. "You are just as bad as Peter!"

Good, Adrian thought, scanning the computer screen. Now he could concentrate.

CHAPTER FIVE

E llen stood on the open porch with Mrs. Duffy, surveying the yard leading down to the creek behind the Sinclair home. "Actually you could use the closed-in part of the back porch as a greenhouse to get a good start for next year," she suggested.

The Addisons had closed the area in for a laundry room, but shelves could be put up to keep the plants out of the way.

"The southern exposure is perfect for that," Peter observed from the spot in the yard just off the kitchen that Ellen had marked for a combination formal and herb garden.

"You're absolutely right, Pete . . . er," Ellen amended, recalling the boy's penchant for formality. "So, do you have an interest in landscaping?"

"I mostly know about herbs and flowers." Affection softened his sober features momentarily with his glance at the older woman. "Mrs. Duffy started my interest when I wasn't much more than a toddler."

"And he's read every book written on herbs and flowers since," the housekeeper said proudly.

Peter Sinclair was a strange duck, but any kid who had an appreciation for plants was A-okay in Ellen's book. He'd followed her around like a shadow as she had taken photos of the house and grounds, watching intently, asking questions. He was fascinated by the software that could take out the old shrubbery and replace it with new in 3D. "Well, if you have anything in particular that you'd like in the garden, let me know. In fact, once I lay it out, your input will be more than welcome."

Peter nodded.

"And I have your list of musts," she added for Mrs. Duffy's sake. Not that she had to. Ellen sensed that if Peter wanted candy canes planted, the housekeeper would give it a try.

Behind them the kitchen door opened and Selena Lacy emerged, dressed to kill in a pantsuit tailored to her impossibly perfect figure. "I'm sorry. I was held up on the phone," she said, more matter-of-fact than apologetic. "Problems in D.C. Adrian's getting ready to head back."

"Are you going with him?" Peter asked.

Selena smiled, if one could call a grimace that. "Of course, Peter. Your father needs me." Ignoring Mrs. Duffy's sniff to the contrary, she turned to Ellen. "Now, for you."

Ellen swallowed the wry *Honored, your highness* that sprang to her mind. Maybe this was how a heavy-duty player in the nation's capital acted. No time for anything but business.

"I want a gazebo," Selena announced. "Adrian and I want to be married in it this spring, so you'll need to design some sort of covered walkway from the house to it. Perhaps an arbor? The last thing I'd need is pigeon doo on my designer dress."

"Seagulls are more likely culprits in these parts," Ellen said, stifling a snicker at the picture she conjured of Selena on the receiving end of a bird bomb. What was it about this woman that brought out Ellen's ornery side? At Selena's pointedly annoyed look, she acquiesced. "An arbor's a good idea. Not sure how well established we can get the vines by spring, though."

"Then we'll use artificial or weave in real vines. Money can make anything happen, Miss Brittingham."

"Almost anything." It couldn't buy happiness. At least not for the kid, whose gaze had lost its earlier sparkle. What kind of a woman would tell a kid that his father needed her in a tone that suggested he didn't need the kid? "Anything else you had in mind?"

"Do something about that drab waterfront," Selena replied with a dismissive wave of her hand toward the creek bank.

"Can do." Visions of pink, red, and white hibiscus, iris, red-spiked lobelia, and marsh marigold danced in Ellen's mind's eye. "Anything else?"

"No, but I'll call you if I have any other ideas." Selena glanced at her watch. Ellen couldn't see the make, but from the diamonds sparkling around its face, she guessed it to cost a bundle, maybe two. "Mrs. Duffy, the men will be here tomorrow to wire the house for security. If you have any questions—"

"I'll call Mr. Sinclair, of course," the housekeeper assured her with a stubborn lift of the chin.

With a dismissive glance, Selena turned and walked toward

the back door. "You have *both* our numbers," she called over her shoulder.

There was definitely another channel to this show, Ellen mused. One that did not bode happily ever after.

"I thought moving here was going to be different." The accusation in Peter's voice drew her attention back to where he wiped his hands on his jeans, as though he'd dirtied them.

"Now Peter, you know your father cannot work from here until he has secure lines installed. I'm sure it's an emergency."

"There's always an emergency," Peter ground out, his face now dark with anger. "Father could take me with him. I'll be working there some day."

"Of course you will, dear," Mrs. Duffy said, concern grazing her face. "But there's so much to be done here to set up both house and office. And I shouldn't like staying here alone right off."

Peter's sullen gaze cracked for a second revealing his willingness to do anything for Mrs. Duffy. "I'm going in to see what's happening," he announced.

Ellen stepped aside as the boy lumbered up the steps and stomped into the house, the door slamming behind him. "Check you later, Peter," Ellen called after him.

Mrs. Duffy turned to her, an apologetic look in her gray gaze. "You must forgive Peter. He quite often forgets his manners. That mind of his seizes on something he's interested in, and everything else ceases to exist." She sighed and stared at the yard beyond. "He has a mild case of Asperger's Syndrome. It makes him a bit of a loner, socially-challenged, and wrapped up in what interests him to the point that nothing else matters. He loves his father fiercely, but has such a hard time showing it . . . at least in an acceptable way. Of course, he's much better than he used to be, thanks to therapy. But things that we take for granted—like saying hello or recognizing the meaning behind a tone change or body language—he's had to be taught. But if he could say what's in that big heart of his . . ." The housekeeper shook her head in despair.

"Like his emotions are in a cage," Ellen observed.

Mrs. Duffy's face lit up. "Yes, that's the very thing . . . except for the anger. The anger always gets out. But it's the child's frustration at not being able to communicate like the rest of us or do something as simple as catch a ball. Something like his brain doesn't get the same signals . . . or the signals aren't as clear as they are in others." She shrugged. "I don't pretend to understand it all. I just know that Peter is a special, gifted child with a heart as big as all outdoors and isn't so good at showing the gem he really is."

"God made each of us different," Ellen said. "I'm sure He has a special plan for Peter."

"And it's my prayer every night that Peter find that plan and see that he's not a little nerd, as herself calls him."

"What?" Ellen thought Selena was self-centered, but not that insensitive.

"Oh, not to his face, mind you, but I've heard her use the term." As if they might be overheard, Mrs. Duffy motioned Ellen toward the designated herb garden site. "She made Adrian over—window-dressing if you ask me—but he's adjusted to it well enough. Being smitten with her helped, though—" She broke off with a second thought. "Well, it's none of my business," she said. "But if she tries the same with Peter . . ." She shuddered, all the while swelling with resolve. "She'll have to go through me to get to the lad."

Ellen couldn't help but chuckle at the mad hen effect. "In that case, Peter is safe."

"I only wish I could protect Adrian from the schemer." The housekeeper caught her breath, eyes widening. "And now I've said far more than I should. But you've got such a warm and open way with you, well, I forgot myself."

"I'll take that as a compliment." Ellen winked. "And what you say is safe with me. I'm just hired help."

"Indeed, you're more than that, Miss Ellen," Mrs. Duffy declared. "You're a breath of sunshine."

Adrian watched out the window as his longtime housekeeper gave Ellen Brittingham a big hug. When Mrs. Duffy took to someone, she did so with all her heart. That sterling judgment of character had never been wrong in all the years that Adrian had known the woman . . . until Selena. He turned away from the window, replaying the call that had come in earlier from the FBI.

"Sir, we think you should see this evidence for yourself. The perpetrator is definitely one of your own."

Not just one of Adrian's own staff, but Mitch Knittel. Disbelief would not allow the affection and respect for his best friend and partner in Alphanet to wither. There was no way that Mitch would risk everything to sell a stolen list of credit cards. Granted, selling credit card numbers to thieves who would use them to make untraceable internet or phone purchases could be lucrative, but that kind of thing was child's play for someone of Mitch's skill. He'd certainly never have been caught, even by the FBI's finest cyber-detectives.

And he didn't need the money. Adrian's former college roommate had always been a man of simple tastes. While Mitch's Bethesda townhouse was outfitted to the hilt with technologically advanced everything, Mitch put the majority of his earnings into stocks and bonds, which made him even more money.

They'd both become millionaires within two years of starting the company. The charge simply made no sense.

"Are you ready?" Selena asked, breaking into Adrian's troubled thoughts.

"Yes. But I'm waiting on Peter. I'm taking him with us."

Selena hesitated, carefully choosing her words, lest she make obvious what Adrian already knew: Peter made her uneasy. "Do you think that's wise? It could get ugly with Mitch."

"Nonsense. I don't believe that there is substance to any evidence that suggests my partner is pilfering credit cards for profit. It's insane."

"And what is Peter going to do while you work at disproving Mitch's guilt? Eleven-year-old boys, even bookworms like Peter, get bored after awhile. I have a feeling we're going to be more than overnight with this."

Adrian's resolve wavered. Peter would be disappointed.

"Besides, it's hard to tell what our schedule will be. You know he doesn't do well with unexpected changes."

Like the time the lad stormed through the office, bouncing off the walls of the corridors dividing it into private workstations like a crazed soccer ball and bellowing his discontent all the way into the stairwell leading to cafeteria below.

"I thought with the move that it might do him good to keep him close."

"Closer than Mrs. Duffy?" Selena challenged.

Adrian flinched inwardly from the truth in her words. It was easy to see why Selena was so successful in promoting the company services. She made sense. Her offense and defense were equally prepared for the win. Mrs. Duffy was closer to Peter than Adrian could ever hope to be—perhaps the only real stabilizing force in his son's life.

"I see your point." He wished things were different, but there it was.

At the report of Peter coming down the steps like an elephant in combat boots, Adrian braced himself for the inevitable confrontation.

"Peter," he said, as his son came into the room, backpack slung over his shoulder and pale cheeks flushed with anticipation.

"I've had second thoughts about your accompanying us. As Selena pointed out, it could take me more than an overnight to deal with this issue."

The brightness in Peter's gaze faded as he shifted it to where Selena had taken a seat behind Adrian's desk. Accusation rushed in to take its place. "*She* doesn't want me along."

"If I knew we'd be back tomorrow, Peter, I'd love to have you with us. But you know how impatient you are when your father and I are involved in business."

"And *you*," the boy said, nailing Adrian next with the cold blue of his eyes, "will do whatever *she* says." He slung down his backpack. Loaded with books, its impact with the floor was as explosive as Peter's humor. His temper visibly escalating, his breathing more rapid between clenched teeth, Peter kicked his backpack and backed out of the office entrance. "I *hate* her."

"Peter!" Adrian started after the boy as he stormed toward the back of the house. Selena intercepted him, grabbing his arm.

"It's okay, Adrian. I'm used to his outbursts."

The flip side of Selena could be as insensitive as Peter, or at the least, so focused on herself that she was impervious to another's feelings. Adrian sighed. "I'll join you momentarily . . . after I tell Peter and Mrs. Duffy good-bye."

Maybe that's why he'd insisted on waiting until spring to marry. To be certain that they stood a chance of making it as a family. He'd promised Carol that Peter would always come first. Selena fit the bill as a business associate just fine. That, combined with her feminine attributes, made her a good wife prospect, as well. But Peter had to accept her, or it would never work.

Mrs. Duffy met Adrian on the way out. "What is it, Adrian?"

The housekeeper had earned the right to call Adrian by his given name, since she'd worked for Adrian's parents long before coming into his employ when Peter was born. "Peter came out of the house like a shot and took off for the water."

"Selena and I have to go back to D.C., at least overnight. He wanted to go, but it's just not practical at this point, Duff." He looked past the housekeeper to where Peter sat on a weathered wharf protruding into the creek, shoulders slumped.

"I'd say from the look in your eye that there's more to this business problem than Peter's tantrum."

The woman could read him like a book. Adrian lowered his voice as a large, black dog lumbered into the yard from a fenced orchard on the Brittingham farm, barking at Ellen as she put out markers along the creek bank.

"The FBI claims it has proof that Mitch has been selling stolen lists of credit card information from our bank client to a small time crime syndicate that brokers the numbers for fraudulent use."

"Like people buying the card numbers for a pittance and buying thousands of dollars worth of merchandise over the phone?"

"Or Internet," Adrian said.

"Blessed be." Her gaze widened at the magnitude of how much a bank's credit card list could translate into.

"But it's small time compared to what Mitch could do, if he so chose. Although, to think he would do anything dishonest is preposterous. But," Adrian added, "it may take me some time to prove his innocence."

"He is, of course. Mitch hasn't a dishonest bone in his thin, little body."

"No, he doesn't," Adrian agreed, his gaze on Ellen.

After getting a thorough head rub and greeting from her, the Lab noticed Peter and started his way.

Adrian tensed. His son didn't take to people touching him without warning, and while the dog seemed friendly, it was likely to agitate Peter if it nudged him the same way it had Ellen. Only if he was forewarned of affection did the lad accept it with any kind of grace.

"Land sakes!" Mrs. Duffy exclaimed as the dog approached the boy.

Adrian headed for the two, but before he could reach Peter, the huge dog braked and seemed to lock gazes with the boy. Peter stiffened.

"Marley, come back here," Ellen shouted, making her way toward the dock as well. "Not everyone loves you as much as I do."

Ignoring Ellen, Marley gradually walked up to where Peter sat and dropped down on its haunches, tail wagging expectantly. To Adrian's astonishment, his son failed to recoil as he'd done when introduced to his first—and last—puppy. Adrian found a home for the pup the next week.

Peter peered over his glasses at the dog as it flattened against the dock and inched closer and closer, head held low, large brown eyes inquisitive.

Adrian slowed and held up his hand to keep Ellen from rushing the two. He didn't know why *pet the beast* kept running through his mind, but it did. Perhaps he wanted to see that Peter was capable of spontaneous affection, even if it wasn't directed at his father.

Peter remained frozen, his hand on the dock, as the dog nosed closer and closer. Its nostrils twitched as the animal familiarized itself with the boy's scent.

"He doesn't bite, Peter, but Marley might knock you over with love," Ellen warned softly.

In response, Peter hooked one arm around a piling, but the hand the dog approached never moved. Nor did the dog . . . until Peter spoke.

Adrian couldn't make out what he said, but the dog stretched out as far as his thick neck would allow and rested its chin on Peter's hand with a heavy sigh.

"I've never seen him do that," Ellen remarked at Adrian's side.

"Nor I."

"I meant the dog."

"I meant the boy." Adrian matched the quirky smirk of humor tugging at her lips. "Peter's never taken to animals."

"Marley's never resisted smothering anything that breathes with love . . . and slobber, lots of slob—"

Adrian clutched Ellen's arm, cutting her off as Peter slowly pulled his hand out from under the dog's chin and touched Marley's head, tentatively at first. Marley wriggled closer and stopped.

"He's such a suck-up," Ellen observed at Adrian's side.

"Amazing," Adrian said, as Peter ran his hand over the animal's sleek head.

With a groan of sheer pleasure, the dog shifted its weight and rolled over on its back, baring its belly for more. . .

"Marley!" Ellen shouted.

And dropped off the edge of the dock into the water with a splash that sent Peter vaulting to his feet in panic.

Ellen raced forward. "It's okay, Peter. He's okay," she assured the boy as Marley bobbed to the surface and began paddling toward the creek bank. "He might be a klutz, but he was born to swim. His feet are even webbed."

Peter watched in mixed wonder and disbelief as the big Labrador bounded out of the water and headed, tail wagging, toward them.

"Brace yourself, kid, we're going to get a shower."

To Adrian's surprise, Peter did just that, crossing his arms over his face and peeking between them as the canine shook free of excess water. Once he'd forced a rub of approval from Ellen, the animal turned to Peter and sat down as though waiting for the boy to initiate contact.

Once again Peter let down his guard and gave the dog a head rub. "You are the most uncoordinated animal I've ever seen." And he chuckled.

"How much for the dog?" Adrian asked.

Ellen swung a disconcerted look at him. "What? Marley's not for sale. Not for a kazillion bucks."

"Marley." Still anxious, Peter eased down to a squat and held out his hand. "Pleased to meet you, sir."

Marley obliged with a paw-shake as though he understood every word that was being said. But more importantly, the fact that this boy needed a special approach.

"Tell you what, though," Ellen said. "I can bring Marley with me when I come to work here. And Pete can visit us anytime, as long as Mrs. Duffy says its okay. Oops," she added, popping her hand over her mouth. "I mean *Peter*—"

Peter looked up from petting the dog, thoughtful. "I suppose that since we are neighbors, it can't hurt to call me Pete . . . if you want."

"You could be called worse," Ellen shot back at him, grinning. "Pete, it is."

She was as amazing as her pet in getting past the wall of Peter's personality. Adrian was still in shock from Peter's seeming interest in her motorcycle the other day, and now the double whammy of his son's response to the dog and Ellen.

"Well, I'd best be on my way." Adrian nodded to Ellen. "I can see that Peter is in capable hands, what with Mrs. Duffy and good neighbors. Good-bye, Peter." He extended his hand to his son. The therapist had told him it was best to have Peter initiate any affection.

The return handshake held none, nor did his son's somber gaze. Like staring into intense nothingness. Adrian beat down his disappointment. If there was a God, He had a twisted sense of fairness.

CHAPTER SIX

The Bethesda building that housed Alphanet Security Corporation was a tower of glass and concrete, completely modern in design. Silent, Adrian stood in the elevator between Mitch Knittel and Selena. Mitch had been released on bond with orders not to access a computer of any sort. At the ding of the elevator bell, the three emerged onto the fifth floor where a spacious lobby of soft grays and rich burgundy hues served as the hub of the offices—the executives on one side, the cubicle stations for the rest of the staff on the other, and the boardroom behind it. Since it was after hours, everyone, save a janitor, was gone for the day.

Once inside his office, Adrian pulled off his sport coat and dropped into the plush burgundy leather chair behind his desk. "So what happened?"

They hadn't discussed the matter in the limo on the way

back to the office after posting Mitch's bond. Now, in the privacy of Adrian's office, it was time to dig into this travesty, assess the damage, and remedy the situation.

Mitch took a seat in one of a pair wingback chairs facing the desk, his face haggard, bemused. "I don't know, A." Mitch liked to shorten names to one syllable so much that one would think the introvert rationed his speech. "No one has access to my station."

Yet someone had retrieved the files from one of their banking clients on Mitch's computer, using his password and leaving a sloppy trail that practically shouted, *Look at me!* The fraud had hit in at least four databases that Alphanet was contracted to protect.

"Nor access to my banking information," Mitch went on, utterly miserable. "Not that the $250,000 *payoff*"—he bracketed his sarcasm with his fingers—"is small change, but, honestly, it's not worth my career. It's clearly a set-up, but why? I'm a nice guy. My mother taught me to be polite."

"You do have direct deposit through payroll," Selena suggested. "Perhaps someone got the information there."

Adrian toyed with a pen from a desk set given to him by an appreciative client. "Everything is encrypted. No one is allowed to share a password with another. We can surely start there, although Claire Devlin has been our comptroller from the beginning."

"Unless someone cracked her password as well," Mitch said, slumping down in the chair. His rumpled shirt and trousers looked as if they'd been slept in, but that wasn't unusual. "If I could just get in the system, I'd get on that cracker's trail like ugly on an ape."

When Mitch and Adrian had hacked into NSA's files as college freshmen, they, too had been crackers, a term that now applied to those who hacked into systems to cause havoc or for financial gain. Although, at the time, Adrian and his partner had been kids who did it just to see if they could. No harm had been done, unless one counted the message they left in the system that its security was crap. Now, the law had grown ruthless with crackers, no matter how innocent their objectives.

"Don't worry," Adrian assured him, "I'll do this personally."

It had taken them a lot of hard work to build this business and convince their clients that they were ethical hackers with the client's security in mind and not the same two kids who'd played in the defense department's files for fun. When this got out, and it would, Alphanet's reputation would take a severe hit.

"What about the Bright Star project?" Mitch asked. "I'm a Red Team leader."

"I'll have to take over." The thought of getting actively involved in the war for control of cyberspace was a shot of adrenalin to the weariness of a long day. Adrian and Mitch had flipped for the opportunity to participate in the cyber war games.

"Just as well," Mitch had said, beaming from the victory of the toss. "You're the pretty face of the company. I'm the grunt." It wasn't completely true, of course. Adrian did a good share of the work, but focusing on expanding the business had taken a big chunk out of his station time.

"You have some major PR to do, Adrian," Selena pointed out as though reading his thoughts. "The press will want a statement. Perhaps——"

"That's what I hired you for," Adrian cut in, impatient. He hated public appearances in good times, which this was not.

"All I need is for you to make the initial statement," Selena said with the tenacity that made her such an asset to the company. "I'll write something up, although you usually come across as the man of the hour without my help."

Adrian nodded. *So much for spending more time with Peter,* he thought, gaze drifting to the photo of Carol holding their infant son. Business was business, and this was not an ordinary situation.

"Once you've assuaged our clients here, I want you to head for the UK and France," he told Selena.

"I take it I won't be seeing much of you." Pulling a ripe pout, Selena walked around the desk and started massaging Adrian's shoulders.

Her touch was gentle and meant for affection, but under the circumstance, it annoyed him. Adrian shrugged her attention off with an apologetic smile. "Sorry, dearest, but that isn't helping. Thank you for the effort."

Mitch slammed his fist into the palm of his hand. "Man, if only I could get in——"

"But you can't, Mitch. You can't even use a PlayStation until you're cleared." Adrian's fingers tightened around the pen. "And you *will* be cleared."

Undaunted by his irritation, Selena perched on the edge of the desk, her legs crossed so that Adrian couldn't help but appreciate the tease of her short, straight skirt. One of her high heels dropped off her ankle, dangling playfully from her toes.

But he was in no playful humor. "Take some time off . . . go to the islands for some deep-water fishing," he suggested to his crestfallen partner. Fishing was Mitch's only other interest. "But keep in touch. I may need to ask some questions."

Mitch shoved his unruly red hair, always in need of a cut, off his temples and proceeded to rub them. He always did that when he was thinking, as though the action organized his thoughts. "I need to bring you up to speed on Bright Star . . . before the press hounds descend."

Mitch was right. The news was likely to break tonight. From that point on, anyone coming in or going out of the building was food for the press frenzy. The idea made Adrian cringe. Thank goodness the security at his new home would be up and running by the time he returned.

"You look like you need a good night's rest first," Selena told his partner.

For the first time since they'd arrived, some of the old Mitch's wry humor surfaced. "Nah, I had plenty of time to nap waiting for you two to get up here. And those guys at the FBI were pretty amusing. I challenged their top net guru to figure my password out and watched him sweat it out all day. No one could break that password, A. Not even you."

Adrian grinned, imagining the tech's frustration. They both knew any password could be broken . . . eventually. But theirs would challenge an uber-hacker—the best of his trade—and his best software. Everyone at Alphanet was required make them ten digits or more long, have both letters and numbers, and have nothing to do with their personal life or business location.

"Looks like we're going to pull an all-nighter," Adrian said in resignation. "But it won't be the first time, eh?"

"Yeah, you go on and get your beauty sleep, Selena. I'll keep A out of trouble."

"Like you kept yourself out of trouble?" Selena snapped.

She did like to get her way, which, tonight, included dinner at a high-end steakhouse down the street.

"That was a cheap shot," Mitch replied, "but I can take it."

Adrian met Selena halfway. "You're welcome to stay and order pizza with us." It had been just a matter of time before his companions started in on each other. Mitch never really liked Selena, even though she'd done wonders in promoting Alphanet. *"It's like you can't see past those big brown eyes of hers, you know?"* he'd said on more than one occasion. Selena called Mitch "Geek the Red" behind his back. He called her "Slima."

"You can count on A and me to get to the bottom of this," Mitch continued. "It'd take more than a half-baked credit card thief to get away with messin' with the big boys."

Selena lifted a condescending brow. "Meanwhile," she said, sliding off the desk, "this big girl is going to save your . . . *reputation*." From her emphasis on the word, it was not what she was thinking.

"We all will . . . by working together." Adrian's tone was intended to whip the two antagonists back into place. "So, your office or mine?" he asked Mitch.

Selena leaned over and gave Adrian a kiss on the cheek. "I'll leave you boys to your pizza and fun. See you in the morning, darling."

His mind already on to ferreting out possibilities, Adrian stood and gave her an absent hug. "Sleep well."

As for him, he would not. Not until the perpetrator of this set-up had been found and prosecuted to the fullest extent of the law. It was not just his business at stake. It was his and Mitch's reputations.

This was a fine fix. Ellen straightened from mixing compost and topsoil in the back of a pickup truck and wiped the sweat from her brow. It had taken her two weeks to get back to Adrian Sinclair with her completed proposal, and he'd wanted her to start immediately. That meant she and Carlos were the only ones available, since Pop had the regular crew working on another major project. All week long, she'd noticed when she dropped off the mail at her parents' home that Pop was totally wiped out from the late summer heat. More than he should have been.

Ellen glanced over to where Carlos was digging out the

beds around the large Victorian home. She was going to have to put her foot down, even if it meant crushing Pop's spirit. His *want-to* simply didn't match his *able-to,* and he was going to kill himself if they didn't cut back somewhere. He'd ordered more field stock and was gearing up to sell fall flowers, pumpkins, and nursery plants for the do-it-yourself clientele.

And Ma was no help. She *kvetched* about Dad working too hard, but when Ellen suggested that they sublet the labor for the Sinclair job with her design, Bea was adamantly against it.

"This one, you should do yourself. And don't wear those ratty clothes." Ma hated Ellen's worn out jeans that she wore on the job. "You look like a man."

"I'm not making a fashion statement, Ma. I'm working," Ellen had argued.

"It wouldn't hurt for such a handsome man to notice you."

Bea was in matchmaking mode. The moment she'd heard Adrian Sinclair was back home from his sudden trip to D.C., she'd carried over an apple cake, one of her many culinary specialties. Before the visit was over, she'd wangled a lunch invitation from Mrs. Duffy, during which the two cooks exchanged recipes, and Ma got the lowdown on Adrian's marital status. Widowed, engaged, but *not* in love, according to Mrs. Duffy. Armed with that information, Ellen's mother researched Peter's condition on the internet and presented Ellen with printouts that were totally unnecessary.

Knowing that she'd be working around the boy, Ellen had already read what she could about Asperger's Syndrome, which was pretty much what Mrs. Duffy had already told her. Pete was an exceptionally bright boy who frustrated and angered quickly, was physically awkward, and had trouble communicating his feelings.

Yet he could talk incessantly about things that interested him, like flowers and herbs. Already he'd visited the Brittingham home at Ma's invitation to offer an opinion on her private garden, whereupon, she'd fed him home-made chocolate chip cookies and sent him home with a bag full.

And the kid was a computer wizard, which came as no surprise given his father's business. Ellen's grasp of computer technology had come about on a need-to-know basis only. Sitting for hours at a computer as Adrian Sinclair and his partner did would drive her nuts. In the two days that she'd been on the job, she'd seen the two men twice. Add that to the fact that the office light remained on well into the wee hours of the morning, and it looked to her like they were glued to the thing.

Not that Ellen had been spying, but some critter had set Marley off barking in the middle of the night and, upon rising to check on things, she couldn't help but notice the light on across the field where country darkness usually prevailed.

Mrs. Duffy had confided that the thin, shy, red-headed guy now staying with the Sinclairs had been accused of computer crime and Adrian was helping him prove his innocence. If one of her friends was in similar trouble, Ellen would burn the midnight oil for them, too.

"Marley!" Laughing, Pete raced around the side of the

house with Ellen's dog hot on his heels. In the boy's hand was a faded red Frisbee, the Lab's favorite toy. "Go get it, boy," Pete said, giving the disc a sling.

Marley was on it with his usual lumbering grace. Suddenly he launched into the air and grabbed the Frisbee between his teeth. Cheeks flushed, Pete clapped his hands. "Way to go, Marley. Good boy."

"Hey, Pete," Ellen called out to him. "You remembered to put sun lotion on, didn't you?" The youth's fair complexion and freckled nose had become pink from staying outside since Ellen and Marley arrived for work yesterday. "I don't leave home without it."

"Mrs. Duffy made me slather it all over," the boy replied with a distasteful grimace. "Number forty."

"That should do it." Marley returned the disc to Pete, but the boy ignored the dog, walking to where Ellen stood in the bed of the truck. "Need help?"

Ellen snorted. "Now that would go over great. Me working my client's son and charging the client for it."

"I'm bored. Mitch and Father are busy, and I've read every book I have at least once. The only good news is that Selena is in Europe." He shoved his glasses up on his nose. "Besides, I like planting and growing stuff."

Ellen motioned him over. "Knock yourself out, then. Because the soil is so sandy here, I'm mixing in compost to help hold the moisture."

"Aerobically decomposed remnants of organic material," Pete rattled off. "Do you make your own?"

"We use too much for that. Although Ma has her own compost heap by the shed."

"Mrs. Duffy and I wanted to have one, but Selena complained of the stench and said the neighbors would report us for some breach of neighborhood association rules."

Selena didn't strike Ellen as much of a naturalist. "It can get pretty rank," she admitted.

The slamming of the storm door on the porch drew Ellen's attention to where Adrian's partner stepped out and stretched. Upon seeing them, he broke into a smile and approached. "Hey, Pete, how's it going?"

Evidently she was not the only one who was sanctioned to use the nickname.

"Fine. I'm helping Ellen mix compost into the topsoil."

"Ellen," the redhead said, extending his hand. "Mitch Knittel here."

Ellen wiped her hand on her coveralls, self-conscious of the dirt under her nails. "Pleased to meet you Mitch. I hear you've been putting in long hours."

Mitch nodded. "And I hear from Mrs. Duffy that you're the lady to talk to about fishing."

"I've caught my share." Ellen had given Mrs. Duffy some fresh-caught flounder over the weekend. A body would have thought she'd delivered gold, the way the housekeeper raved over the gift. "What kind of fishing are you looking for?"

Mitch's teeth flashed white. "This is the white marlin capital of the world, isn't it?"

"It's been called that." Ellen jumped down from the truck,

leaving Pete to continue mixing the compost and dirt. "But if you're after game fishing," she said, taking another shovel from the back, "I'd go down to McMann's or one of the bay-side wharfs and charter one of their boats. Big fish means big bucks though, if you don't have your own boat," she warned. "Me, I take my houseboat onto the bay and fish with all the comforts of home."

"Houseboat?" Mitch echoed in surprise.

"Yeah, I live on a houseboat just down the creek. It's fine for fishing the river and bay, but I'd never take it oceanside unless I wanted to sink her."

"I hear you ride a Harley, too." There was admiration in Mitch's gaze.

Ellen felt color rising up her neck. "Guilty," she said. "Except in really bad weather. Then I *schlep* my tush from the boat to my parent's house and hunker down."

"Cool. How about joining A and me for supper tonight? You pick the place."

"I . . . well, I . . ." She hadn't seen that coming.

"Me too?" Pete asked hopefully.

"Sure, why not?" Mitch said. "My treat. Maybe we can even get Mrs. Duffy out of the house. I feel like I've been cooped up forever. You don't have other plans, do you?"

"Other than a shower and leftover barbecued chicken, no, but—"

"Good," Mitch exclaimed, cutting her off. "It's a deal then. A and I could use a break and who better to show us where to eat than a local?"

Wait, had she said yes? Evidently so. "You can't beat Mc-Mann's for good food either. It's nothing fancy, just a bar and a seafood grill, but most of the charter boat captains hang out there, too. So you can eat fish and talk fishing, too."

Mitch, with his mop of hair, faded tee shirt, and jeans would feel right at home. Pete would be fascinated by Rose McMann's trophy case and pictures of past fishing tournaments. But Ellen didn't know about Adrian or Mrs. Duffy. Although she could see Mrs. Duffy and Rose hitting it off on the cooking front. What Rose couldn't do with seafood had no business being tried. But Ellen hadn't seen Adrian in anything but dressy clothes . . . too smart for the dockside. "How about if we pick you up around six-thirty?" Mitch asked.

"Six-thirty sounds good." That would give her two hours to clean up and kick back for a few.

Mitch looked at the shovel Ellen held. "How about if I help you? I'm not supposed to be in there with the big A right now. He's in a classified area," he explained, easing the shovel out of her grasp.

This was on the far side of weird. She'd made an exception for Pete, figuring a kid would get bored quickly and that would be that. Ellen grimaced. "It doesn't seem right to put my client's son *and* guest to work and still charge the man for it. I'd really rather you—"

"Come on, Elle. Help me out here. I'm bored crazy."

Ellen glanced at Pete, who was intent on his task, and back to Mitch's expectant look. "Okay, so long as you explain to the boss man that I did object. You can start spreading the mix in this dug out bed. Fill it a little higher than the yard level."

"You're the boss."

Disconcerted, Ellen returned Mitch's grin and pivoted toward the cab of the truck where her plans lay on the seat. As she picked them up, her thoughts scrambled toward the evening. Maybe she should recommend one of the fancy restaurants instead. The Baylander was really nice and Ocean City had dozens of upscale gourmet places.

But how in the world would she ever keep her mother from reading more into this outing with the Sinclairs than it really was?

CHAPTER SEVEN

Adrian sat in a cushionless wooden booth overlooking the sunset on the bay at McMann's Wharf and tried not to stare at Ellen Brittingham as she teased Peter into a smile. He'd never seen her hair loosed from the single braid she usually wore. To say it was brown hardly did it justice. There were hints of red and gold in its silken thickness, brought out by the dying sunlight shining through the picture window.

"Planting bulbs upside down. And I thought *you* were the expert." Ellen made that little snorting sound that seemed to embarrass her. Adrian found it charming in a mischievous sort of way. "I'm going to have to dock your time for that, kid."

"It was a simple mistake to make," Peter replied in his defense, stoicism returning. "And Mrs. Duffy said that they would have come up eventually."

Ellen leaned on one elbow, pointing a playful finger at the boy. "*Eventually* being the key word here."

"Give it up, Pete," Mitch chuckled. "She's got you."

It was hard for Adrian to believe that Bea Brittingham and Ellen were related, except for the genuine heart aglow in their hazel eyes. Bea reminded Adrian of a throwback sixties mom in a housedress and apron, while he'd yet to see her daughter in anything but jeans, tanks, or tee shirts, and those baggy coveralls that made her look almost girlish.

The moment Mitch had arrived at the Brittingham home to pick Ellen up for dinner, Bea met them in the yard and invited Mitch, Adrian, and Peter into the house for appetizers.

"Just a tidbit to tide you over," she said, leading the pack like a mother hen. "I've been experimenting, and you can be my guinea pigs."

It would have been rude to refuse. And the pastry-wrapped sausages and cheeses were delicious. Ellen's father Edward motioned for them to take a seat in the large country kitchen and family room. With the Weather Channel playing on a television in one corner, he'd swapped a few fishing stories and prompted Mitch to ask Rose McMann about a few more.

"Although Pumpkin here," he said, nodding to Ellen with fatherly pride, "brought in that eighty-five pound white there over the fireplace. She didn't have more'n thirty or so pounds on the fish, but she had more fight. Had to strap her good in the cockpit, but she brought it in all by herself."

Feisty, Adrian thought, stealing a glance at the woman beside him as she handed off some ketchup to Peter. And wholesome, yet, given the Harley factor, not quite the poster girl-next-door. "Ever try that, Pete?" Ellen pointed out some people on Jet Skis skimming over the sparkling water beyond the docks. "I've got a couple at my disposal, if you want to explore some of the creeks and waterways around here. The water is really warm now."

Peter shook his head. "I'm not very athletic."

"What's to be athletic over? You just sit on them and go. It's not like water skiing. Ever see that Disney character Goofy on water skis? Well, that's me," she told him. "All arms, legs, and no coordination."

"I somehow doubt that." Adrian didn't realize he'd spoken until she turned that enigmatic gaze upon him.

"Trust me, Sinclair, it's not a pretty sight," Ellen replied. "But you and Pete can borrow them anytime you want to go."

"Would *you* go with us?" Peter asked. "Not that I've decided to go," he added hastily.

Adrian was floored. That Peter had spent the last two days outside, romping with a dog, had been incredible, but his consideration of a water sport was nothing short of a miracle. He'd all but given up on getting Peter away from his books and computer, given the volatile temperament associated with Asperger's.

"Sure. Maybe Sunday afternoon after church. I'm working at the youth center Saturday." She glanced at Adrian. "If it's okay with you, of course." She squirmed in her seat the same as she'd done earlier at her parents' home. "I mean, I can take Pete, if you're busy."

"You'll owe yourself a break by then, A," Mitch put in.

Now Adrian knew Mitch was putting two and two together and coming up with five. Ellen was fascinating and friendly, but Adrian was engaged to a very lovely lady who shared the same interests.

"Why don't you go?" Adrian suggested to his partner.

"Because I hope to be out on the ocean wrestling with a big fish."

"Here you go, lady and gents," a jean-clad waitress announced, before Adrian could reply. She placed a tray of steamed orange-red hard crabs on the table along with mallets and knives in front of Ellen and Mitch. "Your crabcakes and shrimp basket are coming up," she added for Pete's and Adrian's sake. "And Rose says she'll be out after you're finished."

Ellen took up a knife and gave Mitch a wicked look. "Ready to get down and dirty?"

"With you, anytime," Mitch shot back. When Adrian ignored his probing glance, he motioned to the heap of steaming crabs between them. "So where do we start?"

"Just follow my lead."

Adrian had seen hard crabs picked before . . . at someone else's table. Watching Ellen pull the back off, cut off the legs and knuckles and scrape chum from the shell of its ribs was part fascinating and part repugnant. But with two more slices of the blade, she exposed open compartments filled with white crab meat of the sort that made up the two fist-sized cakes the waitress brought him.

"Now," she said, flipping out a loose piece of backfin, "under this top piece, you'll find a thin membrane of shell that will open up these." She removed the shell with her blade and flexed the piece open, revealing more tidy little compartments of meat.

"Cool." Peter, who'd watched her every move, picked up a mallet. "So what is this for, beating the claws?"

Ellen wrinkled her nose at him. "You can, but I don't use them." She took one of the crab claws and laid it on the table. "I put my blade on the whiter underside, just above the pincers, and press down hard enough to crack it, but not cut all the way through." Once she'd cracked the shell, she snapped it the rest of the way. "Voila," she said, producing the darker claw meat.

"I'd rather use the hammer," Peter said, taking up one of the claws.

"Whoa, whoa," Ellen warned him. "You don't just hammer it or you'll be picking crab shell out of your teeth. Make a strategic hit with the edge of the mallet in the same place where I put the knife."

Peter hammered the piece of claw, driving shell into the meat just as Ellen had predicted.

"That's okay," she encouraged. "You have to do it a few times till you get the right feel for how hard to hit it."

And so it went. Peter took more interest in picking the crab meat than in eating the shrimp he'd ordered. Although most likely it was the surgical approach that appealed to him, Adrian observed. At times, when he separated them with the same precision that Ellen did, he nearly beamed.

"This is the dessert of the crab," he told Adrian with a newfound authority. He handed one of his triumphs over. "Try it, Father. It's sweeter than the other meat." It was all Peter promised, but that his son had cracked the claw just for him struck an emotional chord in Adrian, one that had rarely been played. "It's delicious, Peter," he said after drawing the meat off the shell with his teeth and eating it. "Quite delicious."

"Want another?"

"Absolutely. You're getting to be a pro." Adrian would eat all that Rose McMann could supply to keep that glow on Peter's face—a glow directed at him.

Peter didn't answer, but his enthused nod said all Adrian needed to hear.

Ellen changed from her dress slacks and top into a black tank swimsuit after the Sunday church service. The jury was still out on whether Peter was actually going to show, but she was going to be ready, just in case. He'd seesawed with uncertainty ever since she'd mentioned the outing, but as of last night, his father's promise to join them seemed to have cinched the deal.

She wished she'd been able to talk the boy into attending her Sunday school class as well, but one step at a time. Too much change too fast could throw Peter into a psychological tailspin. Or he might put the brakes on totally. It was just that Ellen saw so much potential for joy in what appeared to be an isolated, mundane life at a computer or in a book.

The kid wasn't getting a chance to be a kid, but had isolated himself in his own little world where he felt safe. Then there were the undercurrents between Peter and his father. And any kid in pain put her in pain . . . until she could do something to help.

After nuking a cup of this morning's leftover coffee in the microwave, Ellen grabbed a fitness bar and stepped out onto the front deck to savor it and the view spread ahead of her. Granted, most of it was marsh with trees rising in higher spots, but it was green and alive with wildlife. There was even a late summer splash of color here and there—red cardinal flowers and purple Joe Pye weed. Any number of birds from thrush and warblers to duck and heron made their homes here, as well as raccoon, white-tailed deer, the occasional fox, and of course marsh rabbit, an Eastern Shore delicacy more commonly called muskrat. Cooked off the bone, the meat tasted like a spicy beef, but when served with the head, it could turn the heartiest of appetites. Ellen's was one of them.

The chime of Ellen's cell phone jerked her back into the reality of the modern world at large. She checked the caller ID. Ma.

"Hi, Ma, what's up?" she asked.

"I've called Mrs. Duffy, and she's coming over this afternoon for a cookout. Adrian and Peter are joining us, too, after your outing. Now, which swimsuit are you wearing?"

Ellen groaned. That Selena Lacy was in Europe on business put Ma in full matchmaking mode. "The pink-trimmed tank, not the turquoise-trimmed one." They were both identical, aside from color. "I'm still not sure Peter will even go through with this."

"Of course he will. You can talk him into doing anything. Irene said so."

And Ellen wasn't certain that Irene Duffy wasn't Ma's co-conspirator. As if a guy like Adrian Sinclair would even look at her, Ellen mused. He was just grateful that his son was coming out of his shell.

"You are a Pied Piper, I believe," he'd told her again after dinner the other night. Peter and Mitch were playing a pinball machine at the other side of the small dockside restaurant and bar. "You've done more to animate my son than I have in a lifetime."

The admiration in his gaze made Ellen feel all gooey inside, but the sadness in Adrian's voice tugged at her heart. Pete wasn't the only one locked in a shell. Granted, it was a different kind, but Adrian Sinclair had built walls around himself, as well. He was polite, even charming, but Ellen sensed that there was a part of him that he held back. Even from Selena.

"What are you going to wear after you get back?" her mother asked. "Please don't put on jeans and a tank top. How about that cute skirt I bought you in New York? And wear sandals, not sneak—"

"Uh-oh, I think I see someone coming," Ellen said, cutting her mother off. Ma meant well, but *back off* was not in Bea Brittingham's vocabulary.

Ellen made out the orange Corvette approaching in a small cloud of dust on the long lane that connected the creek front to the main road. "Yep, it's them. Gotta go. Bye."

She snapped the phone shut and rose as Adrian pulled up at the dock. Clad in swim trunks and tee shirts, he and Peter got out of the car and approached the *Sassy Sparrow*. It was the first time she'd seen the man in shorts of any kind, and he did them justice. Nice legs, broad shoulders . . . Okay, maybe she *should* sic Ma on Adrian on her behalf. Except he was engaged, she wasn't his type, and Ellen didn't play games . . . especially with someone else's man.

"Hey, Pete! Ready to rumble?"

Peter dug into his pockets and produced a pair of earplugs. "I guess so." He glanced dubiously at the two Jet Skis tied next to her houseboat, one Ellen's and one borrowed from Josh and Alex. "But I want to show Father your house first."

Peter had joined her for peanut butter and jelly sandwiches one evening after work and was intrigued that she lived on a boat.

"Peter, I doubt Ellen wants us trekking through her home."

"Nah, it's fine," she assured them, all the while mentally checking to be certain she'd put her clothing away when she'd changed. She had. "Welcome aboard the *Sassy Sparrow*."

"Is there a story behind the name?" Adrian's brow hitched with expectation, but it was his eyes that cause the hot flash igniting within her. Suddenly she felt naked.

"Kind of," she admitted. "Scripture says that God sees everything, even the sparrow when it falls. Sometimes I feel like a sparrow, little or nothing in the scheme of things, and barely able to stay in the air. But I know He still watches over and loves me."

"And the sassy part?"

Ellen shrugged. "What can I say? God knows I have a sassy streak a mile wide. But I'm a work in progress. Want a soda or something? I have some lemonade made."

"No, thank you. We just had lunch."

Ducking slightly, Adrian followed Peter through the sliding door into the salon. The helm was to their right and beyond it a breakfast bar and galley. On the left, or port side was a queen size convertible sofa and dining set with swivel chairs.

"Do you live here year-round?" Adrian asked.

"Pretty much. If it gets really bad, I tie her down good and head for the house. But it's cozy . . . all I need."

"And she can fish from the comfort of her home," Peter added, hopping onto one of the bar stools. "Isn't that incredible?"

"Quite frankly, Peter, I think our neighbor is incredible."

Something pinged from Adrian's gaze into Ellen's. Something startling.

"The bedroom is in the back and there's a waterslide off the deck. Oh," Peter went on, his eyes sparkling with excitement. "There's a place to ride and steer on top too."

"A bridge," Adrian informed him, following him past the

closet door, where the pair of cotton underwear that she'd worn to church that morning hung on the knob.

Her stomach sinking, Ellen snatched the underpants off display as her visitors went out on the stern deck. It was just a pair of Fruit of the Looms, but her skin fired with embarrassment as she shoved them into the closest drawer. Mrs. Duffy probably wore some just like it. *That* realization made Ellen feel even more inadequate.

But what did she want? Frilly little silk things like Selena probably wore? A Victoria's Secret gal, Ellen wasn't. No, she'd have been happier if she'd just put away her granny drawers in the first place. Oy! She gave herself a mental smack. Now she was conversing with herself and neither one of her was making sense.

CHAPTER EIGHT

Peter held on to Ellen's waist tight enough to cut off her wind if not for the mandatory lifejackets they wore. Since she was more experienced, Adrian had suggested that his son ride behind Ellen until he got the hang of it.

"It's been a while," he'd explained with a sheepish smile not in keeping with his power-player image. He was like two men in one, and one of them was a lot like his son.

Once out in the bay, Adrian gave the Jet Ski full throttle and pulled ahead of them. His lifejacket failing to disguise a toned chest and waist, he zigzagged and circled back toward Ellen, who took it easy for Peter's sake. Even in the calm and at a moderate speed, there was plenty of bounce in the ride over the rippled water.

"What do you say, Pete? Should we give him a run for his money?"

He heard her in spite of his earplugs and nodded, the arms around her tightening even more.

Ellen gunned the engine. The Jet Ski lurched ahead, hammering crests of the water and their backsides with each rapidly successive impact. "Kind of use your legs to cushion the ride," she shouted over her shoulder. "Like riding a horse . . . posting."

She demonstrated, but Peter was still taking the worst of the ride instead of the best. She slowed the motor down. "I have an idea. Why don't you drive?"

"No, thank you," the boy grated against her.

"You might enjoy it more, if you had control of the Ski. I'll be right behind you."

"No, thank you. I'm *fine*." Anger tinged the declaration, probably fired by embarrassment. Not that Peter had anything to be ashamed of. Her first time on a Jet Ski, Ellen had held on for dear life as well. The difference was, she got a thrill out of it. She wasn't so sure about Peter.

"Is everything alright?" Adrian shouted, coasting up alongside.

"Sure," Ellen said. "Follow me."

With Peter's arms still clamped around her, Ellen headed for the narrow white sands of Isle of Wright Wildlife Refuge. Maybe he'd enjoy the nature walk. After all, they were exploring.

The moment Ellen beached the Jet Ski, Peter was off. He pulled the earplugs from his ears. "Where are we?"

"This is a small wildlife park. I thought you might enjoy exploring here."

"Oh." There was a decided lack of enthusiasm in his manner. Having left his glasses behind, he squinted at the gray-green beach grass and scrub trees beyond as his father pulled up on the sand behind them and cut his engine.

"Quaint little beach."

"*Quiet*," Peter added dryly.

"Pop and I used to dig clams here. The bay is full of them."

"Dig," Peter repeated, bewildered. "As in the mud?"

"Yeah. Come on, I'll show you." Ellen made certain her Jet Ski was secure on the sand, draped her lifejacket on the handlebars and waded into the water. "You just dig in with your toes, since I don't have a rake on me."

In no time, she felt something cool and hard in the water. Reaching down, she dug out a clam and held it up for Peter to see. "See?"

"I knew that boats with rigs dig clams at sea," the boy told her, matter-of-fact.

"They live in the sea bottom wherever, but not many commercial boats dig around here. Mostly locals dig them for personal use."

Peter waded in beside Ellen, intent as he moved his feet around. Suddenly his face lit up with satisfaction. "I found one!"

Ellen laughed. "That makes two for the chowder pot. If you want to get more, I guess I can knot my tee shirt and use it as a bag. But watch out for the jimmies."

"The what?" Peter asked.

"The crabs. If you feel something move, back off quick.

Although I think if you make a ruckus, crabs'll move away from you."

In an instant, Peter was out of the water. "In that case, I'll make sure."

He walked into the brush growing along the beach and found a dead branch. After pulling off its smaller limbs, he had himself a small pole. "I intend to use this to clear the way and save my toes," he informed her, somber as judge. "Father? Would you like to try?"

Adrian, who'd stood aside after beaching his craft and stripping off his lifejacket, watching his son as though seeing the boy through new eyes, nodded. "Why not? I love a good clam chowder." With a grateful expression directed at Ellen, he stepped into the water. "Aren't you glad that Selena found this place, Peter?"

"Yes." Peter didn't look up from his concentration on the task at hand. A moment later, with a satisfied twitch of the lips, he dug up another clam.

The mention of Selena shouldn't have bothered Ellen at all, but it did. And that troubled her even more.

God, I want to help this kid, nothing more. I am not going to let myself be attracted to Adrian. Just his car. No matter what Ma says or how goofy he makes me feel inside. So would You help me turn off whatever it is that keeps hitting my buttons? Please?

After the first dozen or so clams were in the makeshift bag, Adrian abandoned the water and came up on the beach where Ellen sat, keeping an eye on the Jet Skis.

"Mind if I join you?"

"Pull up a piece of beach and make yourself at home," Ellen said. "I'm just keeping an eye on the Skis. I don't want to have to walk to the highway and flag a ride home."

"Good thinking."

"Yeah, I learned the hard way. Pop and I went hunting in an aluminum skiff on one of the islands and thought we had it secure. When we got ready to leave, the tide had come in and taken the skiff out. Pop had to strip to his skivvies and swim in cold winter water to get it."

"You *hunt*? With *guns*?" Adrian stared at her as though she'd just said she killed puppies.

"Well, the duck and geese won't exactly fly to my feet so I can whop them on the side of the head with a ping-pong paddle," Ellen quipped. If the grannie drawers hadn't made Adrian think she was Neanderthal, the fact that she could hold her own with a gun and bring home game for the table surely did. But she was who she was and made no apologies. "Sometimes I use a bow with deer. We usually bag our quota and get them dressed and packaged for the local shelters."

"You are an amazing woman."

"I mean, the Bambi population ruins crops, if it's not kept in control by hunt—" Adrian's words caught up with her. "*Amazing*? Like, you don't think I rub snuff and have missing teeth? Or carry a club when no one's looking?"

"Don't be absurd. I've hunted wildfowl in Scotland," Adrian told her. He grimaced. "But I don't get away from the computer much."

"Speaking of which, have you had any luck in clearing Mitch of his charge?"

Adrian sighed. "I've worked on little else. Whoever did this somehow accessed our network with his password and established remote access, then deleted the program once they'd gotten what they wanted from our client."

"The list of credit cards?" Uncharacteristically nervous, Ellen rubbed her arms, warm from the sun. "Man, that's scary."

"I found traces of the program, but not enough to find out who put it there or where the list was accessed from. It has to be someone on the inside, someone who saw him type his password. That's the only way we can imagine it happened."

"Sharp eye," Ellen observed. "I can hardly remember my passwords, much less figure out what someone else is typing. Although I did see a show on TV about crooks with binoculars who watched people at ATMs punch in their pin numbers." Ellen looked away from Adrian's flexing biceps, lest she be tempted to touch them. What was it about this guy? She couldn't keep her eyes off him.

"I can't imagine who would do such a thing inside the company. We're a small tightly knit group . . . have known each other for at least three years, many of us longer."

A clam landed a few feet away from them on the sand. Peter held up the tee shirt-bag, starting to bulge with his catch. "We can make a lot of chowder," he called out to them. "I'm going to get a few more."

"I think Pete's more of a landlubber than sailor," Ellen remarked.

"I never know what will appeal to him." The sadness—no, hopelessness—in Adrian's voice was heartrending. "Selena thought moving down here, away from the office, might afford me more time to spend with him, that we might find more to do together. But we are so different."

"I don't know about that." Ellen mimicked Adrian's position, resting her chin on arms folded over her knees. "You both are bright, more introverted than extroverted from what I can see." A puzzled frown claimed her face. "Although . . . you dress and act like James Bond. Are you really comfortable like that? I mean, your usual dressed-to-the-nines ensemble looks hot in this summer heat, and I get the feeling it's not you."

Oops—runaway mouth strikes again. Ellen didn't dare look at Adrian. She knew he was studying her. When was she going to learn to put her brain in gear first? *Likely never,* a small voice responded.

"No, it's not," he admitted. "But I am the face of the company. It's a PR persona. Such is the price I paid for going public and international." He made a half-laughing sound. "Sometimes I feel as though my baby grew into a monster, and I can't get it back into the cage."

"I hear you." Ellen knew exactly how he felt. "You feel trapped in something that you like, but it no longer makes you tick. It just drains the life out of you."

At Adrian's silence, Ellen ventured a peek and fell into the blue pools of his gaze.

"So landscaping no longer holds your heart?"

"Yes and no. I love the design, but the inventory, running the crew . . ." She retreated her gaze to the sun-glazed bay. "I want to work with the kids at the community center. That's where my heart is. With kids. I mean, I could still do the landscape planning. I love that part, but—"

"You're a natural. I must say that. Peter is a different child around you."

"It's probably all there is to do around here," Ellen demurred, more than the sun heating her face. "What about you?" she asked, eager to escape the penetrating attention. Every nerve she had was ringing *tilt*. "What would you do if you could wave a magic wand and make it happen?"

"I'd go back to Mitch and me, in the basement of the old house Carol redecorated, working security checks, legitimate hacking. Now we develop and sell security software, have to keep it updated, as well as monitor the security of our clients."

"So why not sell the big business and start over?"

"Why don't you?"

Ellen screwed up her face with dismay. "It's complicated. My folks depend on the business. They started it. It's like *their* baby, not really mine."

"And you haven't the heart to ask them to sell it," Adrian said, as though reading Ellen's thoughts.

She nodded.

"You are like my late wife in many respects . . . wonderful with kids, thoughtful to a fault." Adrian's whimsical smile faded. "*Faithful* to her death."

The way he said the word *faithful* didn't sound so hot. For a change, Ellen chose to remain silent. How did one reply to a remark like that?

"Carol refused to terminate the pregnancy, as the doctors suggested, to get therapy for the cancer. By the time she'd delivered Peter, it had metastasized. She held on till just after his third birthday."

Ellen couldn't imagine how the woman dealt with knowing that she was going to leave a loving husband and beautiful son behind. She prayed she never would have to face such anguish, such test of faith.

"I've yet to reconcile why the God she believed in allowed her to die. She was beautiful, inside and out."

"Bad things happen to good people, Adrian. Scripture says it's the result of sin."

"Don't give me that," he snapped. "She was faithful till her last breath. Sin didn't kill her. Cancer did."

"I didn't mean that it was *her* sin," Ellen said. "But I believe that all things that lead to death are either as a direct result or, in Carol's case, part of the ripple effect of sin." At his skeptical look, Ellen ventured on. What did she have to lose? "I believe that the world was once perfect as God created it. Just like the Garden of Eden."

"Aren't those just stories?"

Ellen recognized a half-hearted protest when she saw one. There'd been a time when her spiritual judgment had wavered. She'd wanted to believe, but logic had cast doubt over what she knew in her heart to be true. And that was what she now sensed in Adrian. He wanted to believe. But bitterness and grief wouldn't let him.

Her mind spun. How did one explain a lifetime of searching and finding in a few short minutes? Because that was all she would have. Adrian only gave her that much out of his polite upbringing.

"It's obvious when a suicide bomber blows himself up on a bus," she began, "that a sinful act is the cause of innocent people dying."

"*That*, I'll give you."

"But Scripture says sickness is a result of sin—not necessarily that of the victim's," she stipulated. "Some scholars believe that illness has resulted from an imbalance of nature, which has been compounded by poor stewardship and unhealthy lifestyles and diet throughout time. Some theologians believe the imbalance began with the Flood. And there are some scientists who agree that something caused an upheaval in nature."

"Actually there are Flood stories in every culture."

Ellen glanced up to see Peter emerging from the water. "Exactly, Peter."

"And this caused Carol's death?" Adrian drawled. "The Flood."

Peter hiked his brow at Ellen. "Mother died of cancer," he said flatly.

Great, now she had both of them to contend with.

"Alright then, I'll give you that environmental problems and man's poor choices can cause illness," said Adrian.

"Everyone knows that," Peter chimed in. "It's the by-product of progress. Food additives, chemicals sprayed on our produce—everything causes something these days."

Okay. By-products of progress *and* an unbalanced nature from the sin-caused Flood, Ellen reasoned. "In the end, it all boils down to faith, which I have." She glanced at her sports watch. "Wow, we'd better get going. Ma wanted to have supper at six, and we'll need to shower and change before the cookout."

That much of a concession was enough for one day. Only God knew if it would somehow offer solace to the pain Adrian carried in his heart. Ellen prayed it would.

Adrian's Jet Ski skimmed the water's surface beneath him, hammering into each crest. It was a rough, body-slamming ride, but the physical beating was far preferable, even a welcome distraction to his spiritual trauma. He had no reason to doubt Ellen had read some scientific validation of Scripture into the historical Flood, but his skepticism was spawned more of anger than of logic. Anger he thought he'd tucked away. But being with Peter, seeing his wife's eyes sparkle in his son . . .

Maybe this isn't what Adrian wanted at all. Had he been subconsciously avoiding Peter as Adrian's mother had suggested?

God in heaven, that was the last thing Carol would expect of him. A blade wedged in his throat at the very idea that he'd let his late wife down.

God in heaven?

His ambiguity soured Adrian even more. He had contempt for God, yet there was a part of him that called out to Him when he was in pain. And he had been in pain for a long time. It came from nowhere to strike at him from within, and it was as raw as it had been the day his wife passed.

The cry was from habit, he decided. Not reverence. That had died with Carol. And left a hole in his spirit, like the one she'd left in his heart.

Immersed in the ride toward home, Adrian tried to let go of the emotions battering him from the inside, out. He wanted more than anything to be close to his son, to care for him as Carol would have him do. As he *wanted* to.

He glanced over his shoulder where Ellen and Peter brought up the rear. Ellen waved. Peter, punch proud of his shirt full of clams, let go long enough to point toward the entrance to the creek that led to their home and resumed his death grip. Adrian simply didn't know how to connect with the lad. There were times when he wondered if the boy was capable of returning feelings. Picking up a tissue that he'd dropped exacted the same flat-line "Thank you" as giving him a new, state of the art computer.

Yet, deep within, Adrian knew better. Aside from his son's awkward, seemingly obligatory hugs, there was more of a response. It was suppressed by the nature of the syndrome, but it was there, hidden in the boy's eyes. In a place where only one who knew and loved him could see it. He needed to know his son better. Whatever the cost.

Ahead, the *Sassy Sparrow* gently rocked in the outgoing tide. Ellen's earlier declaration of faith flashed through his mind.

That God watched over her just as He did the most insignificant of living things. A part of him wished that he could believe in a God who really cared for sparrows. That he could find even a portion of the peace and serene acceptance of God's will Carol had enjoyed. He'd tried to support her, prayed with her because that seemed to give her strength and comfort. But inside, his anger at the Father she almost looked forward to seeing gnawed at his spirit and eroded his own faith.

The roar of Ellen's Jet Ski startled him as she sailed past him and headed up the creek. Ruddy-cheeked, even smiling—or was it a grimace—Peter risked a wave. Adrian reveled in it and followed. When he saw Marley racing along the shore ahead of them, he understood Peter's smile. Marley had raced into Peter's heart carrying a Frisbee and a soulful look that begged for play.

Adrian gunned the Jet Ski and closed the distance. He wouldn't mind seeing how far past his property the creek went. His pulse surged with a sense of adventure and pleasure in the freedom of skiing over the water, the wind and mist in his face. He'd definitely been an all-work-and-no-play Jack of late.

Perhaps Mitch was unwinding just like him at the moment, reeling in a monster of a fish. Adrian hoped so. He couldn't imagine the frustration his partner endured, framed and unable to participate in his own vindication. But Adrian tried to remind himself that today was for play, not for dwelling on past or present problems.

CHAPTER NINE

E llen cast a landscaper's eye from the water's view of the Victorian gingerbread trim adorning the Sinclair home. Nestled among verdant oak from which the lawn terraced down to the water, it was nothing short of elegant. The gazebo, which Selena had purchased prebuilt, stood like a gatehouse halfway down the shallow slope. Once painted in the same cream, green, and red of the house, it would appear as though it had been there forever. If not for the electric and phone wires connected to the house, the place might have looked this way a hundred years ago.

"Will Marley come into the water?" Peter shouted behind her as they headed upstream and around the bend in the creek.

"He's born and bred to it."

Past the Sinclair property, the creek wound snakelike to the left. The moment Ellen cleared the rushes that obscured the view beyond, she knew she was in trouble. The water barely covered the muddy bottom and there were no brakes on a Jet Ski.

"Hang on, Pete!" she called out, bracing herself as the momentum of the vehicle carried them into the shallow water and onto the mud. Ellen slammed onto the handlebars, cushioned by the lifejacket. Peter's shoulder crunched against her, his head wedged under her left arm. Miraculously they held their seats.

"Thank you, Jesus," she prayed, as the engine stalled.

Who knew the creek had filled in since the last time she'd been this far up? Instead of admiring the scenery, she should have paid more attention to the low tide. She'd never have done that on her bike. *Look where you're going* was always the rule.

"You okay, Pete?"

She felt his nod. Adrian throttled down a distance behind them. She fought Peter's death-grip to stand up and waved him off. "We're aground!" Of course, he couldn't hear her, but he could see.

"What now?" Peter asked, as the Jet Ski began to wobble on its rounded bottom. "Should we walk to shore?"

Ellen tried to maintain their balance, her attention fixed on Adrian. He cut the throttle and went into a turn, a perfectly natural thing to do. But common sense did not apply to a Jet Ski. Having lost a good deal of its thrust in the water, the ski became unwieldy and predictably pitched him into the creek.

"Dad!" Before Ellen could stop him, Peter slid off the Jet Ski and lunged toward Adrian in a panic.

With the sudden shift in weight, Ellen went over into the same mud, which grabbed at Peter's legs and feet.

"Dad!"

"Peter, stay where you are. I'm fine . . . for landing in a mud pit," Adrian added in distaste. He pulled himself upright, mud clinging to his legs, arms, and swim trunks. "Ellen?"

"Finer than frog hair," she said, gaining her feet in the muck. Ellen grabbed the handlebar of the tilted, grounded Jet Ski. There was nothing to do but push it off. "Adrian, are you still afloat?"

"In one sense of the word, I suppose."

"Pete, you think you can help me push off?" she asked. No sense even trying to start it. She just hoped the Ski hadn't sucked up too much of the marsh mud when they ran aground.

"Sure, but what about Da . . . Father?" he corrected himself hastily.

Ellen had never heard him call Adrian, *Dad*. But before she could comment, the boy pivoted, plucking one foot from the nearly knee deep mire, and lost his balance. Ellen lunged forward to steady him, but the mud was no more accommodating for her than him. Peter fell on his backside with an unchildlike expletive. Ellen splashed face down on her hands and knees, all of which sank into the bottom.

"Aw, man," she complained, straightening and wiping the dark brown, decidedly pungent marsh mud from her arms. "Some people pay good money for mud baths."

"That's one way to look at it," Adrian chuckled.

"This stinks!" Peter struggled to his feet, covered from the waist down in the brownish-green slime. "I *hate* mud." He shot a dour look at Ellen.

"Sorry, man. I don't like it either. Thank goodness, it'll wash off, huh?"

Without answering, Peter trudged through the mud to the front of the grounded Jet Ski.

"I never would have dreamed the marsh would have filled in like this," Ellen remarked, taking a place on the other side. "This time last year, Pop and I took the skiff at least another half mile inland."

"I'm *not* blaming you," Peter ground out.

Ellen met his dour gaze. "Well, *I* am." She placed her hands on the Jet Ski and handlebar, matching Peter's hold on the other. "Ready on three. One, two, three . . . go!"

She pushed for all she was worth. With no one on it, the ski moved easily on the slick bottom. Too easily. Momentum carrying the top halves of their bodies farther than their muck-entrenched feet, both Ellen and Peter splashed face first as the vehicle slid ahead of them.

Ellen didn't even comment this time. As she righted herself in the now thigh deep muck, she gave Peter a hand. "Is this the perfect end to a perfect day or what?"

"Are you two alright?" Adrian asked.

"Yeah, for mud daubers—wasps that live in mud nests. Nasty critters," Ellen explained. His resulting bemused look was an improvement over Peter's scowl. "Try to push your Ski into deeper water so it'll start. So," she turned to to Peter, "I have a plan. You game?"

"I guess I have to be, don't—" Peter's dour expression brightened as he looked beyond her. "Marley!"

Sure enough, the Labrador had plunged into the marsh and half-swam, half-hurled himself toward them, parting the rushes in his enthusiasm.

"Mud and water is as good as it gets for him."

Peter never took his gaze from the dog. "At least *he'll* be in his element."

Marley was no help whatsoever. The dog swam, splashed, and leapt in the water, having the best of times, while Ellen used the natural floatation of the wobbly Jet Ski to keep her from sinking too deep in the muck and pushed it into shallow enough water. Once there, she flattened on the water surface and flutter-kicked, pushing the Ski the rest of the way toward Adrian.

"Just doggy-paddle or crawl on the bottom, Pete," she called back, upon realizing that Pete had fallen behind. Between Marley's antics and Pete's awkwardness, he spent more time bogged down than moving. "Use the buoyancy of the water. Like Marley. You can do it."

"I keep getting stuck in this *muck*," the boy snapped.

"Peter, it's not Ellen's fault," Adrian chided.

"I didn't say it was," he argued back in frustration. "It's simply the most accursed situation!"

Accursed? Ellen caught Adrian's eye and suppressed a

giggle. What a word for an eleven-year-old! Although it pretty well summed up the situation. She pulled a straight face.

"Yes, it is," Adrian agreed. The twitch at the corners of his mouth betrayed his own humor. "Suppose we focus on getting out of this muck, shall we?"

"I *can't* get the hang of this," Peter objected, stumbling in the marsh. "I'm *not* a marsh dog."

"Then why not allow your *Dad*," he emphasized, "to help you." Adrian's gaze connected with his son's, and Ellen felt something inside of her melt.

Peter nodded, solemn, trusting. "What do we do?"

"I'm going to hold you by the waist and you half-float, half-crawl like Marley is doing until we get to my Jet Ski. Then you hold onto it, until Ellen's is free and clear."

Adrian helped free his son of the mud. "There we have it. Now crawl-swim a little further and rest on your belly if you have to until I catch up."

"Okay, Dad."

Adrian plucked one leg free, then the other, moving tediously forward so that he could support his son. "I like your calling me Dad."

The boy nodded. "I've been considering it for some time. Most of my schoolmates called their fathers *dad*, but Grandmother—"

"I'll deal with Grandmother, if that's what you want to call me. *Father* is too formal for us, don't you think?"

"Absolutely." As he gained confidence, the boy moved as

much on his own as he did with Adrian's support. Marley, moved along Peter's side, doing his share to coach.

Ellen moved slowly, but surely toward the deeper water. She marveled at the father helping his uncoordinated son through the water. Kind of like she imagined God helping her sometimes. She laughed to herself. Looks like God saved the day after all. Only He could have pulled something really terrific out of this muck.

Ellen's Jet Ski refused to start. Finally, Adrian insisted that Ellen take Peter on the working Jet Ski, and tow the other with Adrian holding on behind it, floating in its wake. Marley, weary of swimming, made his way to dry land and ran parallel to them.

"Alright, Dad?" Peter yelled over the noise of the engine.

Dad. Adrian could kick himself for never making the suggestion before. He'd been *Daddy* once, when Carol was alive. After her death, Adrian's parents had kept Peter while Adrian built the business. To his shame, Adrian couldn't even be certain when *Daddy* disappeared and *Father* took its place. It had seemed natural, since Adrian addressed his father with the same formality.

If Peter called him *Dad* once more, he might be able to float above the mud-clogged Jet Ski.

Back at the Brittingham dock, Ellen gunned her ski up on the floating ramp. Her father ran down to the water and hooked the ski to the winch, pulling it the rest of the way up and securing it, while Adrian and the disabled one floated nearby.

"We look like mud daubers!" Peter announced, turning

full circle for Ed Brittingham to see the mud the boy now wore like a badge of honor.

"That you do," Ed laughed. "You need a good hosin' down before you're fit for a shower."

While Peter filled Ed in on the details of their escapade, Ed and Ellen hooked a line to the disabled craft and winched it in. Adrian swam to a ladder on the dock and climbed out.

"One might think you had a good time, Peter," he teased, as Peter showed off the bundle of clams that had been tied to Ellen's rig.

"Of course I did. Didn't you, Fa . . . *Dad*?"

Adrian stepped up and gave his son a hug. "Never better. Cleaner," he said, with a playful glance at Ellen, "but never better."

To his delight, Peter returned the hug and then broke away. "I'm going to show the clams to Mrs. Duffy. Is she here yet?"

Ed nodded, his weathered face crinkling with a grin. "Yep, her and Bea are up at the house talking about cooking like two cacklin' hens." He turned to Adrian as the boy ran off. "Looks like they'll be talking about clam chowder next. You know how to open clams?"

"What?" Adrian pulled his attention from where it had drifted. Ellen stood under a dockside shower, washing away the mud, the turn of her long legs toward the stream of water all but mesmerizing him. "Er . . . no. Perhaps you'll show me." If the man didn't toss him off the property for ogling his daughter.

"We'll make a Shoreman outta you yet, Sinclair. But I'll

wait till you've changed," he said, glancing at his watch. "The missus likes things to run on her time."

"We've got an hour, right?" Ellen called to her father as he started for the house.

"Just shy of one. I'll get the grill started," he replied, without looking back.

Ellen motioned toward the shower. "It's cold water, but if you want to get the worst off before heading home to change—"

"I'll just put some towels over the car seats." He extended his hand to her. "I can't thank you enough for today."

She laughed, snorting. "Yeah, right. The mud bath was complimentary."

That startled look of embarrassment when she made her characteristic snort tweaked something inside of Adrian. It was endearing.

"I'm serious, Ellen. You gave me a chance to get closer to Peter. If it takes mud, so be it."

"*So be it,*" she mimicked, grinning from ear to ear. "I love the way you guys talk. You sure you're not a spy or something?"

"Just a humble white hat—that's a legitimate hacker in case you didn't know."

"Well, take it off and enjoy yourself." She started toward the *Sassy Sparrow,* then turned. "Need towels?"

"There are some in the car, thank you." What was this sudden urge to hug the woman in gratitude? Not the spontaneous type, Adrian walked, instead, over to the Corvette and spread out the towels that Mrs. Duffy had packed for them.

Upon sliding into the driver's seat, he glanced at the houseboat where Ellen had entered. For the first time in a very long time, Adrian actually looked forward to a social evening.

Peter emerged from the house, flanked by two mother hens and stuffing a chocolate chip cookie in his mouth.

"Do use the shower in the utility room," Mrs. Duffy pleaded as the boy climbed into the car. "It will catch at least most of the mud."

"We were in it up to our *necks*," Peter said.

"As if that's a surprise." Bea Brittingham rolled her gaze heavenward. "*Oy*, that girl will be my death. Always the daredevil."

"It really was an accident," Peter said in Ellen's defense.

"I'm sure of it. She's a walking accident, my Ellen." Bea poked her head in the open car window. "She needs a keeper, if you get my drift."

Adrian did. "I don't know. It was quite the adventure, eh, Peter?"

After a moment's silence, Peter nodded. "I think since I'm calling you Dad, that you should call me Pete . . . like Ellen does."

"Pete, is it?" Mrs. Duffy challenged. "And is that just for a privileged few, or does that include me, *Master* Sinclair?"

Peter arched a brow at her. "May I call you Duff, like Dad does sometimes?" he asked, impish.

Mrs. Duffy was no less delighted than Adrian had been. She crumbled like a shortbread cookie. "Well, just between us three . . . at home, that is," she stipulated.

"Dinner will be ready in one hour, with or without you," Bea warned. She gave Peter an affectionate tweak on the cheek. "See that your father is on time, sweetie."

As Adrian pulled out of the drive, Peter donned the glasses he'd left in the car and turned to him in all seriousness. "I'm not *really* her sweetie. She calls everybody that." He frowned. "Or something like *bubble-lah*."

"*Bubeleh*, not bubble-lah," he replied. "I think it's a Yiddish term of endearment."

Adrian smiled within and without. His son's horizons were growing faster than he could keep track. Seeing it was a thrill like none other.

CHAPTER TEN

As Adrian pulled into the tree-lined lane leading up to his home, he spied one of the garage doors open. Inside sat the Mercedes purchased for Selena by Alphanet.

"Oh, no," Peter groaned, echoing Adrian's spontaneous thought.

Adrian overrode his bolt of dismay. "This doesn't change anything. I'm sure Mrs. Brittingham won't mind having one more for the cookout—"

"*I* mind," Peter objected. "*She* ruins everything."

"Selena will be a pleasant surprise." Even if Adrian hadn't expected her back until next week. Perhaps in the less formal environment, Peter might warm toward her as he'd warmed toward Adrian. "Just give her a chance, Peter."

After he parked the Corvette next to the Mercedes, Peter climbed out and stomped into the house.

"Do you have a towel to dry and wrap in after you rinse off?" he called after the boy.

"I forgot."

"I'll get you one . . . and your robe."

Tossing the dirty towels into the basket beside the washer, Adrian made his way into the kitchen. He'd actually been cleared of the mud, being towed like a barge behind the Jet Ski. But the marsh bouquet had followed him home.

Selena, looking exotic in a flowing tropical sundress, met him in the central hall. "Hello, darling! Are you surprised to see me?" She stepped up to embrace him when the smell of marsh mud checked her. "What in the world is that stench?"

"I believe it's called *eau de swamp*. We've had quite a day, Peter and I."

"Oh?" she said slowly, as though not really sure she wanted to know.

"Ellen invited us to go Jet Skiing and—"

Selena *harrumph*ed. "The *landscaper*? I'd hardly think her your type, Adrian."

Where did *that* come from? Still, Adrian felt his face flushing, as though his body knew something his brain did not.

"Selena, you are above that. The thing is that Peter . . . *Pete*," he amended with a delighted cock of his lips, "actually went along. It was all for his sake. And you should have seen him! Oh, there was a bit of anger—"

"Surprise, surprise."

"But I think . . . no," Adrian said on second thought. "I *know* he had a good time. Even when we were stuck in the mud." He gave Selena a short account of the day, ending with the muddy ordeal. "He called me Dad . . . and asked me to call him Pete."

"Won't your mother love that," Selena drawled, reluctantly intrigued.

"I love it." Adrian grabbed her in a bear hug. "And I owe it all to you, darling."

"Oh?" She wrinkled her nose in distaste.

Adrian couldn't blame her and backed away. "For insisting we move down here . . . away from the business. I had a good time as well. And the Brittinghams are great people. You'll like them. Very down-to-earth. Mrs. Duffy is over there now." He was babbling with excitement. No wonder his fiancée looked at him askance.

"You mean we're *alone*?" A feline smile slowly spread on her face, and Adrian felt like a fish in a bowl. He'd nearly succumbed to Selena's charms once. Thankfully, a phone call from Mitch had interrupted them before it was too late. Call it old-fashioned, but he did have a son. And a housekeeper. And Carol's memory. Perhaps that was his salvation as well as his curse. But Selena never seemed to give up.

"Peter is in the utility shower," he told her.

The smile waned.

"But we are invited for a cookout at the Brittinghams as soon as I shower and change," Adrian added.

"But, darling," Selena pouted as she swayed toward him, placing her hands on his bare shoulders, "I'd hoped that you and I might go to dinner, somewhere romantic, on the water . . . perhaps with dancing."

"Peter is expecting—"

"He can go. Mrs. Duffy can bring him home." She ran her

fingers up the taper of the trapezius at the back of his neck. "You did spend the whole day with him . . . and I haven't seen you in over a week."

"It would be rude not to go when they are expecting us," Peter announced from the kitchen entrance to the hall. Wrapped in one of the soiled towels, he nailed Selena with a hostile brown gaze, then shifted it to Adrian. "I knew she'd ruin everything," he said flatly.

"Pete, Selena would be delighted to go with us, wouldn't you, darling?"

Selena crossed her arms at Adrian's pleading look. Finally, she relented. "Of course. It will be fun."

"So she can ruin that, too?"

"Peter," she cajoled, "how could my going with you possibly ruin anything?"

Peter clamped his mouth shut. His now glittering gaze moving from Selena to Adrian. "This is great," he ground out. "Just *great*." With that he bolted toward the stairwell and up the steps like an elephant on a rampage. Light of foot, the child was not. Tactful seemed beyond hope.

"There you go, Adrian," Selena said as Peter's footsteps thundered up another flight to the third floor rooms he'd claimed for his own suite. "The boy doesn't want me to go. Heaven knows but what he'd lose that temper of his in front of our neighbors and embarrass—" She closed her eyes. "I don't think he'll *ever* accept me as his mother."

"He will . . . in time." Adrian drew her to him. "I promise, darling. Your leading us here has opened doors in Peter that have been shut since his mother's death. The change is just what he needed. When he realizes that, he'll be grateful." He kissed her forehead. "I promise."

Selena laid her head against Adrian's chest, the touch of her soft golden hair seductive in its own right. "Well, I don't suppose he can like me any less, so things *have* to get better."

Her breath warmed his skin. The scent of her French perfume wafted up into his nostrils, dislodging the stench of marsh mud, and curling like little fingers around his brain. Urgent signals hailed from it, causing Adrian to tense in a concerted effort to stop them from tripping a baser reaction beyond the reach of his will.

"But you go on with Peter. Maybe I can go over your notes and see what progress you've made in vindicating Mitch." She pulled away from him slowly and raised a gaze to his that would warm a statue. "And I can tell you later how my trip went. Exhausting, but all good, of course."

Her trip! Adrian groaned in silence. She'd been in Europe trying to save his company and this was how he treated her? He sighed heavily.

"No, I'll call Mrs. Brittingham and ask if we can drop Peter off for the barbecue."

Selena shook her head. "No, Adrian. As Peter said, that would be rude. You go with him. We can discuss business later."

It was tempting. But there was too much at stake at the moment. His business and the careers of his people—including his best friend's and his own.

"No, we can go to the Lighthouse Sound. It's a lovely restaurant overlooking the water." Adrian grinned. "It's not Rose's, mind you—"

"*Rose's?*" Selena repeated, bewildered.

"A crab shack on the docks. Almost like stepping back into the fifties. Wood booths, pinball machines . . ."

Selena's expression was less than impressed.

"Ellen took Mitch and me there so that he could charter a boat for today."

"The landscaper again?" She propped her hands on her narrow waist. "Should I be jealous?"

"Don't be ridiculous. Ellen is a friendly girl-next-door. And she's been great for Pete." The moment the referral to Peter was out, Adrian wanted to reel it back in. Selena felt badly enough about her inability to relate to Peter without rubbing her nose in it. "Actually, it's . . . it's more her dog that relates so well with him."

"A *dog.*" Selena pivoted abruptly away. "Stop stammering, Adrian, before you trip into a hole too deep to escape."

"Good advice." He headed for the steps before he did just that, taking them two at a time. He hated to disappoint Peter, especially given the new ground they'd broken. But he owed Selena his attention, as well.

Adrian walked into the master bathroom and turned on the shower. It was easier to run a business than it was a family. At least he had *some* control in the business. As a family man, he was sinking in farther and farther over his head.

CHAPTER ELEVEN

"Okay now, this might not be kosher among the professionals, but it works just the same."

Ellen's father balanced one of the large clams on its back by holding the tip of an Old Hickory butcher knife on the bill. "Now just giver 'er a tap like so . . ."

He struck the handle of the knife, driving into the clam's mouth as she'd seen him do time and again.

"Work it around to the side and twist. Tight-mouthed little buzzards, but they're worth it," he grunted, using his fingers to pry it the rest of the way open. Inside was the shiny muscle. "And just scrape it into the bowl."

"Can I try?" Peter asked.

"Maybe if I hold the clam with a pair of tongs and Pop guides you with the knife," Ellen stipulated.

After the day they'd had on the water and a meal of barbecued chicken with side dishes prepared by Ma and Mrs. Duffy, Ellen wondered how the boy could hold his eyelids open.

Grabbing the barbecue tongs off the grill, she took the seat next to Peter and adjusted her skirt, part of the outfit that Ma had surreptitiously laid out in the houseboat, while Ellen was Jet-Skiing. Wearing the casual, feminine outfit was easier than arguing with her matchmaking mother.

Not that wearing it advanced Bea Brittingham's cause. Adrian had to switch feet at the last minute. Mitch had arrived just as Adrian and Selena were preparing to bring Peter back for the barbecue, so his partner came in Adrian's place. During the meal, he'd regaled them with a great story of the one that got away—a white marlin that, according to Mitch, *had* to have weighed two-hundred pounds. Ellen didn't know if he fished like a Shoreman, but he certainly could stretch a tale like one.

"Go to it," Ed told the red-haired man. "The boy dug enough for a good mess."

"A what?" Peter asked.

Her father winked at the boy and ruffled his hair. Peter only slightly shied away from the physical affection. "Enough for a meal . . . a healthy pot of chowder."

"And fritters," her mother suggested. "I could fry some fritters, too."

"Then *I'll* make the chowder," Mrs. Duffy announced. "I can't have you doin' all the cookin' in the neighborhood."

"Would that be *Irish* clam chowder?" Bea asked.

"*Boston* clam chowder," the housekeeper replied. "Thick with milk and potatoes—"

"Ow!" Mitch cut Bea off. "Sonuva—*m . . . motherboard*," he amended quickly, drawing their attention to where he'd nicked his hand with the knife.

"Mine's almost open," Peter told him, pride beaming in his gaze. With Ellen holding the clam with tongs and Pop guiding the boy's hands, they'd opened the clam's mouth. Now Peter struggled to finish the job with his fingers. Growling through clenched teeth, he gave it all his effort and succeeded.

"Good job, Pete!" Ellen high-fived him.

"I think he's got a knack for it," Pop said. "A little practice, and he'll be a regular Eastern Shoreman."

"Doesn't digging them make me at least half of one already?"

Peter's expression was so serious, Ellen had to laugh with the others. "Add wallowing in the marsh, and you're at least three quarters," she teased.

"Bubeleh, you were one of us the minute you walked into our hearts," Ma called out to him. "Such a *boychik*," she bragged to Mrs. Duffy. "What a surgeon, he'll make."

"I don't think I'd like being a surgeon," Peter said, screwing up his face. "I get queasy at the sight of blood."

"She was just kidding, Pete." Ellen had already discovered that Peter had trouble determining the difference in straight and kidding tone. Ma would settle for a lawyer or engineer. She glanced at Mitch. "You need a bandage?"

"Nope, it's not bleeding. Just scared me," he said with a sheepish glance.

"What's *boychik*?" Peter asked.

"A boy genius," Ellen explained.

"I'm learning all kinds of new . . . oops!" Peter missed the bowl for the clams, sending his prize sailing from the shell to the lawn, where Marley promptly gobbled it down. "Hey, that was *mine*, Mutt," the boy complained. But Marley got a head rub just the same.

"Sorry, Pete, Marley lives by the Finders, *Eaters* rule," Ellen laughed.

"I'm a bit confused," Mrs. Duffy ventured, uncertainty blending with the deepening pink of her round cheeks. "I didn't think Jews ate clams and such."

Bea brushed her embarrassment aside. "They're *traif*—"

"Not kosher," Ellen translated for Peter.

"But when I married Ed and moved down here," her mother continued, "I became more Gentile." She shrugged. "What can I say? There's no Messianic Jewish community nearby, so I didn't have a lot of choice. I even go to the Methodist church."

"Yeah, but Ma showed the ladies how to do a Messianic Passover Seder when I was a kid, and they're still doing it."

"It's all about combining my two loves," Bea said. "Jesus and cooking."

"Guess you could say Ma and I are Christian mutts, a little of this and a little of that, but all for Jesus." Pop's loving glance in Ma's direction became one with hers. Ellen felt its warmth within her chest.

"So that's the secret to that chicken . . . Jesus and kosher salt," Mitch said, distracting her. "Man, Adrian doesn't know what he missed. That was the best meal I've had in . . ." Hammering the knife into the shell with his hand gave him time to backtrack. "Aside from Duff's," he amended. "If I don't get back to work soon, I'm going to need to buy larger clothes."

"Why don't you move down here, too, Mitch?" Peter glanced up from lining up his knife on the clam. "You could work from home like Dad. We've got an extra bedroom. And you're more fun than Selena."

"I don't see that in the plan, Pete. But you can bet I'll be visiting. This is the next best thing to having a place over Starbucks in the city."

"Small wonder the lad doesn't turn into a coffee bean," Mrs. Duffy sniffed, casting a fond glance Mitch's way. "It's what he lives on."

"That can't be good," Ma chimed in.

Mitch didn't stand a chance against *two* mother hens.

"So, where are we going to have the clam chowder and fritters—here or next door?" Ellen asked.

"*Here*," Peter declared. "I caught them, so I should get to choose, right?"

Mrs. Duffy's resistance melted into a chuckle. "Very well, then. If it suits Bea and Ed, that is."

Ma shrugged. "What's not to suit? Maybe even Adrian can make it this time." She aimed a pointed look at Ellen.

"And Selena," Ellen added, dodging it. Next thing she knew, Ma would have her in a dress. When was her mother going to get it in her head that Adrian was spoken for, as in *off limits*?

Peter slammed a clam down on the other end of the large wooden picnic table, startling them.

"Hey, man, what're you trying to do, give me a heart failure?" Mitch exclaimed. "What's wrong?"

"Nothing! Just nothing!" The boy shoved off the bench to his feet, looking as though a dark cloud had enveloped and crushed him. "I gotta go to the bathroom," he said to no one in particular.

Mrs. Duffy followed the boy with an aching heart-on-her-sleeve gaze. "Blessed be, I hope Adrian knows what he's doing not only to his son, but himself."

"You ain't the only one, Duff," Mitch agreed.

Ellen held her breath, praying that Ma didn't jump on the bandwagon. For a change, she didn't. But *I told you so* was written all over her demeanor.

Lighthouse Sound at the Links offered a warm elegance with its cathedral ceiling braced with massive natural wood beams. Seated near one of the tinted windows, Adrian and Selena sipped good wine over a seafood specialty for two. With the sundown, the skyline of Ocean City came to life across the bay with lights that glimmered on its dark blue water. A pianist played softly in the background. When the waiter, clad in formal black and white, offered to pour Adrian a second glass, Adrian covered it with his hand.

"Thank you, no."

Selena cocked her head at him, large gold triangles dangling from her ears and sparkling in the candlelight. "Are you going to be a party pooper?"

"Sorry, darling. I had no idea that having so much fun on the water could be so exhausting."

"We could have cuddled up over a bottle of wine and carryout back at the house, you know."

The suggestion in her dark gaze was exactly why Adrian wanted to be anywhere but alone with her. Though he nearly chuckled as he considered that the reason rested more on his exhaustion than Selena's temptation. Now there was a switch. He braced himself for her lecture on his mother's strict Presbyterian upbringing being so dark ages.

As though reading his mind, at least part of it, Selena smiled. "Okay," she said. "How about if *I* cuddle up with the wine and you cuddle with me on the sofa when we get home?"

"If you don't mind my dozing off." Adrian stifled a yawn. "Sorry."

"We really need to settle on a day in May." She swirled the wine in her glass. "Weddings do take time to plan. Did I tell you I found a gown in Paris?"

"Yes." Adrian smiled. "Over the phone and again on the drive over."

"Well, I can't help it if I'm excited over getting married to the most fascinating man I've ever met."

Selena was an exquisite picture, her heart-shaped face aglow, her ripe, red lips in a tempting curl. So why was Adrian seeing another woman in his mind's eye—spunky, laughing, turning long, muddied legs to a stream of water from the outdoor shower?

"I wasn't fascinating until I met you," he reminded her. "In fact, I was something of a dull boy . . . a nerd."

Selena walked her fingers across the linen tablecloth until her hand covered his. "But such a handsome . . . and *fascinating* nerd."

Her sultry laugh usually conjured images of silencing it with his lips, but instead he saw Ellen as she extracted herself from the mucky bottom of the creek. Her unbridled laugh had even infected Peter.

This was not good. Not at all. Perhaps the marsh mud and fumes had rendered him fickle, something Adrian had never been. Selena was his fiancée and deserved his full attention. "Would you like to dance in the moonlight?"

The burst of pleasure in Selena's gaze was all the answer he needed. Adrian rose and helped her from her chair. Once they stepped out onto the patio where the live music was piped, she melted into Adrian's arms.

"You are the light of my life," she said, laying her head on his chest. "I know you're exhausted, so after this, I'll finish my wine while you get the check. Have I ever told you I love you?"

"Not enough times for me to really believe it. Square pegs and round holes rarely mesh well."

"Words to knock a woman off her feet," Selena teased. Adrian swung her around and dipped her. If he couldn't dazzle her with words, he'd do so with dance. When the song ended, he escorted her back inside to their table and summoned the waiter for the check.

"What are you doing?" Selena asked, her gaze narrowing at the cell phone he fished from a jacket pocket. "Calling home to see if the crew has arrived."

She leaned forward. "But this is our night—"

"I just want to tuck Peter . . . Pete," he said grinning, as he punched the speed dial number, "in."

"Well, you misdialed, darling."

Adrian glanced up, surprised. "What?"

"You dialed twenty-one, not twelve," she pointed out, annoyed.

The phone screen showed that she was right.

"Right. Sharp eye."

He backspaced and redialed. "Hello, Mrs. Duffy. How was your evening?"

A short conversation revealed that Peter was already asleep. He hadn't even made it home. Mitch had to get him out of the car. A good time had been had by all.

"Tomorrow night?" Adrian caught Selena's eye. "How does clam chowder and fritters sound tomorrow night at the Brittingham's?"

"Fritters." Her tone was a flat no. "You know I don't eat fried foods, darling." Her gaze sharpened ever so slightly. "So does Mrs. Duffy, for that matter."

"I couldn't very well refuse two nights in a row," Adrian said after he'd accepted the invitation and hung up.

Selena's silence spoke louder than words. She could refuse. She wouldn't, but she wanted to.

The waiter brought the check, pre-empting Adrian's re-assurance. He placed a hundred dollar bill in the leather folder and handed it to the man. "Excellent service. Keep the change."

"Thank you, sir," the man said, his smile widening even more when he saw what Adrian had left him. "Come back again soon."

When they reached the parking lot, Selena broke her silence.

"The next time I return here, you'll be picking your teeth with straw," she muttered as he opened the Corvette door.

"They are good people. You'll enjoy them." Adrian slammed the door and walked around to the driver's side. "You picked this neck of the woods as I recall," he reminded her, once behind the wheel.

"I had no idea our neighbors were so . . . obsessive."

"They are doing this for Peter. He dug the clams. It's *his* night."

"Oh, alright." She wriggled the diamond he'd given her in front of her face. "But back to a wedding date. Adrian, I really need time to plan everything."

"Speaking of planning, how about if we plan a party here after school starts? It would be a chance to meet the community. Perhaps an open house?"

Adrian's mother loved to have open houses, especially on the holidays. While he hadn't participated much in the gatherings, he loved the festive atmosphere.

"*We* meaning *me*?"

"Well, I suppose Duff could—"

"I'll do it," Selena cut him off, folding her arms across her chest.

"Why not a harvest affair? Better yet, a costume party at Halloween."

The smile pulling at Selena's lips told him his idea was growing on her.

"I'll have invitations printed immediately. Halloween will be here before we know it. But you'll owe me."

Adrian glanced her way. "Oh?"

"We spend Labor Day at the yacht club in Annapolis. Just us."

Adrian winced inwardly. He and the FBI had closed the back door the mysterious hacker had installed in his client files, but he was no closer to finding who'd put it there than he'd been at the start. And he was working in Mitch's place on the Air Force contract. . .

"I promise that I will *try*."

"Adrian."

"It depends on how much progress I make this week. Otherwise, all your outstanding efforts abroad to smooth things over may be in vain."

Selena didn't argue because she knew he was right. But by the look of it, the cold shoulder she turned his way wasn't going to warm anytime soon.

For some reason, Adrian almost found it a relief.

CHAPTER TWELVE

Even though it was a simple meal of clam chowder and fritters, Ellen's mother pulled out all the stops when she heard that Selena Lacy was coming. Gran's china graced the dining room table along with the linens, which had to be starched and pressed. Pop even changed from his work clothes into khakis and a polo at Ma's insistence. In the family room portion of the country kitchen, he and Mitch, who'd come over early with Pete, nodded on and off in their respective chairs to the white noise of the Food Network on TV.

Clad in denim capris and a sleeveless yellow top, Ellen wrapped the last service of Gran's silver in a linen napkin and slipped on a silk-rose napkin ring that Bea had made to match the china. Clean denim was good enough for clams, she'd insisted when her mother tried to get her to wear a sundress.

Ellen wasn't much on putting on the dog, but she had to

admit, the table was gorgeous. The rose and Queen Ann's lace centerpiece was the crowning feature. Ellen had picked the wild Queen Ann's lace from the ditch banks along Piper Cove Road on the way home from work, and in no time, her mother had combined it with her carefully tended roses for a work of art. Selena ought to feel right at home with all this elegance.

"Bea, those roses. I just can't take my eyes off of them," Mrs. Duffy marveled as she stirred the chowder. She'd been working on it all afternoon, while Ma prepared home-baked bread and the mix for the fritters.

The two reminded Ellen of clucking hens happy to share the same hen house. Upon hearing Marley barking, she glanced out the kitchen window to see Adrian's Corvette pull up in the yard. Her heart did a cartwheel. Color like a sunset and those custom alloy wheels gave it a style all its own. Of course, the hunk who climbed out and walked around to open the door for his fiancée wasn't bad either.

Selena emerged from the vehicle, her blonde hair curling over her shoulders instead of in the usual upswept do. Navy capris tapered down to where matching three-inch espadrilles were tied about her ankles, while a nautical-themed top showed off a Barbie torso. It just wasn't natural to look that perfect.

Ellen gave herself a mental slap as her mother and father went outside to meet their company.

"So herself decided to come after all," Mrs. Duffy observed beside Ellen. "Peter and I were hoping for one of her convenient migraines."

"You are bad," Ellen chided, pinged by her own guilt at

having thought the same. Not about the migraine, but that Selena wouldn't come. But she had, and gracious was going to be Ellen's middle name. "Uh-oh."

Having spied Marley making a dead-straight run for the newcomer, Ellen abandoned Mrs. Duffy and raced outside to intercept. But she was too late. Marley nosed Selena, rubbing against her as though she were a long lost friend.

"That monster should be kept on a leash," Selena exclaimed, brushing her hip where Marley's affection had left a wet spot.

"You just looked so good, you made him drool." Selena's cool stare brought color to Ellen's cheeks. "He's just too friendly for his own good. I'll put him in the utility room."

"Why?" Pete demanded. "Marley and I were playing Frisbee."

"I believe it's almost time for dinner, Pete," Adrian intervened.

"Your dad's right," Ellen chimed in. "Why don't you come with Marley and me and give him his treat? He loves playing catch with them."

"Why don't you put *her* inside," Pete grumbled under his breath.

"I'll show you to the powder room so you can freshen up," Bea announced, diverting attention from the disgruntled boy and taking Selena under her wing at the same time. "If you live in these parts, Miss Lacy, you'll learn to expect big, friendly dogs. The next time you see that big galoot, just point your finger at him and tell him 'Sit!' He'll settle right down."

"I'll keep that in mind," Selena replied in a voice as stilted as her shoes.

Once Marley was quarantined in the utility room, contented with the dozen or so treats that Pete tossed him, Ellen poured refreshments while her mother served deep-fried vegetable appetizers to her guests, now seated in the front parlor.

"Let me help you with that, dear." Mrs. Duffy started to pick up the tray with the glasses on it, but Ellen stopped her.

"You are our guest, Mrs. D. You want Ma to skin me alive? Get in the parlor with everyone else."

With a crestfallen look, Mrs. Duffy preceded Ellen into the front room. Adrian was seated on the sofa with Selena close enough to him that one dose of salts could have worked the both of them. With all the other seats taken, the only one left was on Selena's other side. Mrs. Duffy took it with a doleful glance at Ellen.

"These olives are delicious, Mrs. Brittingham," Selena told Bea. "What is this coating?"

"A sharp cheese breading," Ma said. "But Eddie did the actual cooking. Since he got the new turkey fryer for Father's Day, most of the frying is done outside with that. Saves such a mess in the kitchen!"

"I nearly set the garage on fire the first time I used it," Pop confessed. "Of course, I wasn't fool enough to have it in the garage, but just outside," he explained. "Had too much oil and putting the turkey in caused it to overflow." He chuckled. "Singed my eyebrows and scared the bejittles out of me."

"Speaking of which, you'd better get started with the fritters," Bea reminded him.

"I'd best check on the chowder." Mrs. Duffy popped the last of the appetizers on her napkin in her mouth as she rose.

"Stay," Bea said. "I can do it."

Ellen handed Pete the last of the drinks watching the two women square off like black gum against thunder, neither of which would give an inch.

"Now you know I'm more at home in the kitchen than the parlor, and you said to make myself comfy."

"Next week, Mr. B is going to grill tuna steaks," Mitch spoke up as the two women left the room behind Pop. "Compliments of my outing yesterday."

"All this fried food—" Selena waved her hand at the appetizer platter that Ellen's mother had placed on the coffee table.

We rednecks like our fire and grease, Ellen wanted to say.

Adrian nipped the temptation in the bud. "Actually, Mrs. Brittingham is quite the gourmet," he told Selena. "Mrs. Duffy practically drools over her assortment of recipes."

"Darling, I should hate to know what Mrs. Duffy's cholesterol is. I worry about your diet sometimes."

"I worry about tofu and bean sprouts." Mitch helped himself to a napkin full of the appetizers. "Get a good whiff of that stuff, before it's buried in spices and sauces, and tell me it's good for me."

"This from the man who thinks a loaded pizza is a balanced meal," Selena shot back.

"Selena is right about the fried food, though." Ellen couldn't believe she was defending the barbed Barbie. "We really don't do much frying any more because of Pop's heart and cholesterol problems. But on special occasions, like when *someone*"—she glanced fondly at Pete, who stared with a bored look out the window—"catches a record lot of clams . . . well, it's fritters or else."

Pete practically beamed. He didn't need to know that Pop had purchased extras for the meal. "I want to go fishing with Mitch the next time he goes out."

"Not until you weigh as much as the fish," Mitch teased. "Mine would have pulled you over the side, squirt."

"So what kind of foods do you like, Selena?" Ellen asked. "I'll bet with all your travel, you've tasted all kinds of exotic fare."

"I do try to eat the local foods of the country that I'm in . . . for dinner, at least. I love Middle Eastern and Indian cuisine. But I try to keep breakfast and lunch organic and whole grain. Are there any organic farms around here?"

"Sure. There's one about five miles from here. They sell their produce at the local Food Mart. There's also a place where you can buy grain-fed beef and chicken in Delaware. And, of course, you can buy them directly from one of the nearby farms. You kind of have to know someone to get your meat that way."

"And something tells me you do." Adrian smiled and Ellen's stomach flipped like a fish out of water.

Bea showed up in the doorway between the parlor and dining room. "I think by the time everyone is seated at the table, the fritters will be finished. I hope you're hungry because we have clam fritters, clam chowder, homemade bread, corn on the cob, and fresh field greens."

As Adrian rose and helped Selena up, she put her hand to her temple. "I hate to be such a baby, but I'm starting to see light specks."

"Migraine?" Adrian guessed.

"Must have been the cheddar cheese on the olives." She gave Bea an apologetic look. "I didn't want to say anything, but when you told me it was cheese coating, I feared the worst."

"Nonsense," Bea pooh-poohed. "I've heard of cheese causing migraines. Why don't I get you an ice pack and you can lie down in the guest room? Maybe we can nip it in the bud. Do you have any special medicine for it?"

Selena nodded, all the while rubbing her temples. "It's at home."

"Do you want me to go get it or would you rather just go home?" Adrian asked.

Selena leaned into his broad shoulder as though relief rested there and sighed. "I really should go home. You know how debilitating these can be for me."

"I'm truly sorry, Mrs. Britt—"

Bea cut Adrian off. "Sorry, *schmorry*. She's sick. What's to apologize for, except that I should have asked if anyone had any dietary problems?" She turned to Ellen. "Sweetie, you see everyone seated while I fix two platters to go for Adrian and Selena."

"Sure, Ma." But Ellen didn't miss the exchange between Pete and Mitch. Both rolled their eyes heavenward. She wasn't sure if it was in disbelief of Selena's excuse to leave or a thank you prayer. "Alright, you guys, to the table. Mush!"

"You don't have to do that, Bea" Selena objected, walking in the circle of Adrian's arm through the dining room after Ellen's mother. "I'm ruining your dinner party. Please, just join the oth—"

"I'll have your food ready to go in a jiff. No cheese." Ma's tone said the rest.

End of story.

Selena was going home with those fried fritters, like it or not.

CHAPTER THIRTEEN

Freshly showered and changed from work clothes into clean jeans and a tank, Ellen rolled into the parking lot of the Piper Cove Country Club on her Harley and pulled into a convenient spot next to Sue Ann's convertible. With the Labor Day chaos behind them and school back in session, the lot wasn't even half-full and the pool area was quiet.

Alex is here, too, Ellen noted upon spying her car, and more than likely Jan had hitched a ride with one of them. Ellen had been working all morning at Piney Banks, filling in for Pop while he kept a doctor appointment.

Upon entering the coffee shop, Ellen found Sue Ann and Alex at their usual booth in the back.

"Hey, where's Tink?" she asked, sliding in next to Alex. "I wasn't supposed to pick her up, was I?"

"She didn't call me," Alex said.

"Me, either. I thought she'd come with you on that little ol' two-wheeler of yours," Sue Ann drawled.

Ellen flinched at her Harley being called *little*. But everything was a *little ol'* this or *little ol'* that with Piper Cove's resident southern belle. "I don't think she called me. I had no messages."

"That's strange. Jan's never missed a *sundae* meeting." Scowling, Alex took out her cell phone and punched the speed dial. "Of course, it could have slipped her mind. Some days, Tink doesn't even know what day it is."

"Sugar, if that's cause for alarm, call 911," Sue Ann declared, "because I have a dickens of a time telling the days apart since I stopped working at the realty."

"That was ten years ago, Sue Ann," Ellen teased. "Ever hear of a calendar?"

Sue Ann didn't have to work. She not only had a nice annuity from the sale of her family's real estate business, but she'd married the richest man in Worcester County. Ma never let Ellen hear the end of how she should pay more attention to Sue Ann, and how imitating that accent and sashaying around in figure-tailored clothing could make Ellen a *femme fatale*.

"No answer," Alex whispered, hand over the mouthpiece. "Hey, Tink," she said after waiting for the tone at the end of the answering spiel. "Alex here. Where are you? It's a Sundae meeting on Wednesday. Call ASAP. Bye-bye." Alex hit the red button, ending the call. "I don't get it. She said she was coming when Josh and I saw her Monday at the Food Mart."

"Aw, isn't that cute. Two lovebirds grocery shopping together." Ellen patted her hand over her heart.

Sue Ann fixed her attention on Ellen. "Sooo . . ."

That one-syllable crescendo put Ellen on interrogation alert.

"Tell us all about your new neighbor over *they-ah*." With a Mata Hari–slant of perfectly lined blue eyes, she drew Ellen's attention to where Adrian Sinclair sat with Hugh Thomas of Atlantic Realty and Joe Phillips, the co-owner of the Baylander Hotel and Restaurant and brother to Jan's current beau.

"He's very nice." Heat began to prick at Ellen's neck, gaining momentum toward her face. It wasn't as if she had anything to hide from her buddies. "And very engaged, like I told you before. Not that it makes any difference to Ma."

Alex chuckled. "Bea's been matchmaking?"

"*Oy*, you wouldn't believe. Not that I'd have a chance, even if Selena wasn't a bombshell in spiked heels. I'm more Pete's type."

"Pete?" Alex echoed.

"His eleven-year-old son. Cute kid. I took to him the minute I met him. So did Marley."

"Marley takes to fire hydrants, Ellen."

Ellen made a face at Sue Ann. "Like I was saying," Ellen continued, "even if I had a chance against his fiancée, it's shot now."

Sue Ann wriggled in anticipation. "Tell us."

It was almost worth sharing the ordeal in the mud weeks earlier with Sue Ann and Alex just to watch their faces contort in sympathy. And it was funny . . . for the most part. In a warped way that appealed to Ellen's admittedly strange sense of humor.

"Ugh," Sue Ann exclaimed, waving her hand in front of her nose. "I hate the smell of marsh. Martin says it reminds him of home. I say it's one step up from a sewer."

"What did your mother say?" Alex asked, giggling.

"Ma sneaked aboard my boat while we were gone and laid out this skirt and *frooffy*"—Ellen flicked her fingers around her neckline imitating ruffles—"blouse for me to wear. But once that man got away from me, he *stayed* away."

"No!" Sue Ann protested in jest. "You mean you dragged him through the marsh, and he ran when he got back to solid ground? Well, I do declare. Go figure."

"Actually his fiancée came home and nixed the deal," Ellen explained. "I've seen him a couple of times since, but we've both been busy."

From what Ellen could gather from Mrs. Duffy, it wasn't going well with the investigation of Mitch's security breach. Mitch had become so wound up and gotten on Adrian's nerves so much that he'd left to visit his parents over Labor Day. It was just as well, since Adrian and Selena had gone to Annapolis, leaving Pete behind.

So Ellen and Pop started a bike kit with him. It was just a little dirt bike, but Pete had practically lived in the garage since they started it. Pop claimed he needed it for scooting around the fields. Ellen wasn't so certain it wasn't just to perk up a little boy. Either way, it was a good investment for the both of them.

"It's hard to imagine someone like him, up to his neck in

mud," Alex said, drawing Ellen back into the conversation. She cast an appreciative glance in Adrian's direction. "He's so continental."

"He traveled a lot as a kid, and his mother's Scottish . . ." Ellen's voice drifted off as she caught his reflection in the plate glass wall. He wore a lightweight jacket, open neck shirt, no tie, pale slacks. Maybe blue like his eyes. It looked like his group was getting ready to check out.

"Sugar, you've got *your* man," Sue Ann chided Alex. "Let Ellen have her dapper little mud dauber."

Falling in with the girl mischief, Ellen leaned forward, voice lowered. "I tell you, he looked good . . ." Pause. " . . . in . . ." Another pause. " . . . mud."

The three of them burst out laughing. A loud snort escaped Ellen's nose. She hated that! "I swear," she said, covering her nose belatedly with her hand. "I'm gonna look into surgery on this *schnoz*—"

Sue Ann kicked her under the table.

"Wha—" Ellen saw that the men had gotten up from their table and approached hers.

With flawless poise, Alex extended her hand behind Ellen. "Mr. Sinclair, hello. Hello Joe, Hugh."

Ellen pivoted in her seat to face them and, removing her hand from her nose, she saluted. "Gents, you look like you might be up to mischief." A good offense beat a defense any day. Although, if he'd had any doubts that she was a fool before, they were affirmed for sure now.

"Actually Adrian and I dropped by here for lunch," Hugh explained. "And we ran into Joe and joined him."

"I just enrolled Peter in the Berlin Academy this morning," Adrian told Ellen. The tick of his jaw spoke volumes. He was obviously concerned.

"Now that is one of our *finest* private schools," Sue Ann observed, as if she were Mother of the Year.

"Think he'll like it?" Ellen knew this kind of thing was always hard on a new kid, but one with Pete's social problems would have it rougher. Part of her wanted to hop on her bike and head for the school to protect him. The other half wanted to hug Adrian till the furrow on his brow disappeared.

"It's that or sending him away, so I'm sure we'll both be pleased."

He didn't seem certain. Or was something else bothering him? Ellen wondered.

"Yeah, well, I think you'll be pleased in the Rotary, too. We do a lot for the community, especially the kids. After Pete adjusts to some new friends, maybe I can get him to come to the community center."

A flicker of appreciation registered on Adrian's face, striking a kindred chord in Ellen. They were definitely on the same page—Pete's.

"I volunteer there all the time, along with Ellen, and Alex's husband Josh," Joe spoke up, "so we could keep an eye on him for you."

"Ellen is a regular Peter Pan," Alex said, adding a playful, "I think it's because she's refused to grow up herself."

Adrian laughed. "So I've seen. I'm lucky to have her and her parents as neighbors."

"And Marley." Ellen batted down a sudden feeling of uneasiness at being the focus of Adrian's attention. She just didn't know what to do with it.

He laughed again. "And Marley."

That lyrical quality of his voice was gorgeous. Even if he was only talking about a dog.

The waitress came to her rescue. "Sorry, I'm late, ladies. Grandma needed help in the kitchen." She looked anxiously around the group. "Oops, sorry for interrupting."

"It's okay, Candy," Hugh assured her. "We were just going. So we'll see you three next Monday evening?"

"As president, I gotta go," Ellen replied. "And these ladies better back me up."

"President?" Adrian asked, clearly impressed.

There went her composure. "Yeah, they were desperate," she quipped. Her throat was trying to close on her.

"Desperate?" Joe objected. "She's a great president."

Besides, *Pete* was the one she should be thinking about.

"Where's Miss Jan?" Candy asked, pen poised over her order pad.

"Right here. Laggin' and draggin', but here," Jan said behind her. The petite blonde dropped on the seat next to Sue Ann.

"Where have you been?" Alex chided, after the men had left. "We were about to go looking for you."

"Did you walk over from the Food Mart?" Ellen asked. "I could have swung by and picked you up. What gives?"

"Well, when you three have gotten the mother hen out of your systems, I'll tell you." Jan leaned wearily against the back of the booth. "Scott and I went to a show in Dover last night and then I went straight to work at the bakery. I hadn't slept all night, so I laid down in the break room after work and overslept."

Ellen bit her tongue. Knowing Scott, they were at Dover Downs more to gamble than to see a show. *Lord, Jan needs a good man more than I do. I have no trouble waiting for Mr. Right, but this guy is such bad news.*

"Should I come back when you're ready to order?" Candy asked, reminding them of her presence.

"I'll have a burger, no fries or chips." At the astonished looks aimed at her, Jan shrugged. "I haven't eaten anything since dinner last night, other than pastries at work. I need protein, not more sugar."

"Mark it, Candy. You are watching years of tradition go down the drain today over a guy," Ellen complained.

"And a small shake . . . chocolate." Jan stuck her tongue out at Ellen. "There, it's not a complete break."

Sue Ann turned to Jan after placing the rest of their orders. "Just how long are you going to try to run with the big bad dogs? Till you make yourself sick?"

"So you think Scott's too rich and successful for a poor working girl to keep up with? Is that it, Suzie Q?" Jan folded her arms across her chest. "I knew I should have just gone home."

"Jan, honey, you know that's not what Sue Ann means," Alex said.

"I said *bad* dogs, not rich ones," Sue Ann snapped, impatient. "*You* are too good for his likes."

"Yeah," Ellen put in. "We're only annoyed at Scott because we love you and he doesn't."

"But he *does* love me. He takes me to nice places—places I could never afford. And he's fun . . ." Jan trailed off, shaking her head. "You all don't understand. I've never had a guy like him interested in me. *Me*, from the wrong side of the tracks. He makes me feel classy, important . . . like Sue Ann or you, Alex."

"Well *thanks*, Tink." Ellen's smile belied the sarcasm in her voice. She knew that Jan wasn't putting her down, but pointing to the fact that Sue Ann and Alex had both been born to privilege, not to working class families. And no one could resist that plea in Jan's gaze.

"Sugar," Sue Ann said, drawing Jan into her arms. "You are as classy and important as any one of us." Mischief tugged at the corner of her mouth. "Maybe even more so than me."

"So, what did I miss? Wasn't that your new neighbor?" Jan said, turning the heat off herself and on to Ellen. "How's the *landscaping* going?"

"The landscaping," Ellen mimicked Jan's suggestive tone, "is going just fine. I'm almost through. Just a few more plants on backorder." She heaved a sigh. "As if that's not enough,

Pop's decided to reopen our old roadside stand for fall and is stocking it with fall flowers and pumpkins, gourds, and specialty relishes and preserves. And him at the doctor's this afternoon!"

"You've got to have a heart-to-heart with your folks, Ellen," Alex told her. "Let them know how you feel about cutting back."

"And how your Pop has to cut back," Jan said.

"I know, I know. I just want to finish out the season. Then we'll talk." Getting Ma to go along with selling the nursery would be simple. They could easily live on what the land would bring. But Pop loved his family farm.

Sue Ann pulled a napkin holder into the center of the table and waved her hands over it. "Let me look into your future," she said in one of her best fortune-teller drawls. But as she peered into the shiny stainless surface, she let out a little squeal. "Why didn't someone tell me my lipstick had faded? And all those men saw me like this!"

"Great, my future is a fading mouth," Ellen quipped.

Sue Ann brushed her friends' laughter aside and pulled a straight face. "I see good things ahead," she said, "but you are going to have to listen to your heart, Ellen Brittingham. It knows more than you do about work and about love."

Ellen smirked. "Well, don't give up your day job, Madame Suzie Q." She laughed with the others, but not inside. The truth was, Pop's situation was tearing her heart apart, and when Adrian was around, it practically broke itself.

CHAPTER FOURTEEN

Adrian drove across the Route 90 bridge and onto Ocean Highway, which ran the length of Ocean City's beach strand. After enrolling Peter in the academy, he'd felt obligated to take Hugh Thomas to lunch. The realtor had gone above and beyond to see that Adrian and his family blended into the new community. But primary on his mind was the meeting he'd set up after lunch—the one with the FBI agent in charge of the security breach investigation.

Adrian slowed, searching the stretch of food places, beachwear boutiques, and tee shirt and souvenir shops for the sign to Seacrets, where he was to meet Agent Rick Statler. He spied the weathered board sign with Seacrets, Jamaica U.S.A. painted on it. It looked as if it had been salvaged from a wrecked ship on a Jamaican beach, hardly what Adrian had expected, even though Ellen had told him a bit about the fun and exotic nightclub and hotel the night they'd gone to Rose's restaurant. After parking he walked toward the entrance along the sand-strewn pavement past a rickety, abandoned rowboat. All around, island-style shacks were interspersed among palm trees and coral walls. It definitely fit the advertisement of Jamaica, U.S.A.

As Adrian walked through the door and into the open air lobby, a man in a business suit rose from a bench. Adrian recognized him instantly from previous interviews regarding the investigation. Agent Statler looked more like an accountant than an FBI agent, but when they shook hands, Adrian caught a glimpse of his firearm.

"Mr. Sinclair, good to see you again."

"You, as well, Agent Statler . . . barring the circumstances, that is." He didn't hold ill will toward the man. Just the helplessness he felt. Whatever Adrian had traced or uncovered went straight to the FBI, but nothing came back from them to complement his findings.

The hostess led them into an enclosed section of the massive complex of buildings. Constructed to look like a ramshackle spread of huts, some featured courtyards, while others were accented with old brick and wine bottles mortared together. From what he'd heard, this was one of the largest nightclubs in the country, spread over several blocks of valuable real estate on the bay. It had even expanded with a small hotel, which he'd seen off the parking area. Truly, it looked as though Caribbean pirates had made their home here. As Ellen had suggested, a must see for Peter.

"Will this be alright?" the waitress asked after Statler had requested a private area for a business discussion.

"This is perfect, thank you," Statler said, sliding into a dark plank booth that overlooked a small, sandy cubicle of palm shrub, hanging with ferns beneath a skylight.

"My name is Kerry, and I'll be your server. What can I get you drink?"

"I'll just have a soda. Thank you, Kerry," Adrian replied.

Statler pointed to the menu. "I'll have coffee and some of those Phantom Fries. And water. The doctor says I don't drink enough water."

Once Kerry disappeared behind a black-painted swinging door, they had the place to themselves, except for an elderly couple on the opposite side of the sandy square, seated at a window overlooking the narrow beach. Beyond the beach was a dock and several markers, a couple with Jet Skis moored off them. Once again, Ellen came to mind. Adrian could see her with Pete, slicing through the waves in the bay . . . before the mud bath.

"I asked you to confide in no one about this meeting because you definitely have a mole inside your firm."

The image of Ellen vanished. "Do you know who it is?" *Not Mitch,* Adrian thought as though to make it so. *Surely not Mitch.*

"Your partner is still under consideration, although . . ."

"Although what? What do you have?"

"We traced the backdoor access to a little old lady in Florida who used the internet to sell her hand-knitted goods.

Definitely not our perp. From there, we traced it to a group of teen hackers in France, one specifically. But I think the kid was being used by someone bigger."

"An uber-hacker?" Masterminds like that usually used young hackers to do their dirty work.

"We think so. But the trail ran out there."

"Kid wouldn't talk?"

"Kid *couldn't* talk. He was hit by a bus on his motor scooter in Paris."

Adrian's heart sank. "Accident?" he forced himself to ask.

"I don't think so, but there's no way to prove it." Statler shrugged. "The kid could have had bad luck, but it's a strange coincidence that he was hit so soon after being taken in for questioning."

Now Adrian was queasy.

"Why would Mitch put a backdoor in his own computer for these people?" *These people.* Adrian had no idea who his enemy was—who Mitch's enemy was.

"That is why we asked you to tell absolutely no one." Statler leaned forward on his elbows. "We think Mr. Knittel was set up as a diversion. Either that, or he's as diabolical as he is brilliant."

Adrian scowled, following Statler's lead to the obvious conclusion. "So if it's not Mitch, who set him up?" A dozen or so faces flashed through his mind, men and women that he'd hired. Adrian had done background checks on all of them. They were all good people, people who'd worked for Alphanet Securities for at least five years. Like family, closely knit with warped senses of humor, and often, odd fashion sense. "Have you any other suspects?" he asked.

Statler sat back as the waitress returned with their beverages and the fries.

"Here you go, gents. Do you want vinegar with your fries?" she asked, her voice as bouncy as her ponytail.

"Vinegar?" Statler echoed, surprised.

"Malt vinegar as in for fish and chips," Adrian said.

Statler shook his head. "I'm a ketchup man, myself." He reached for the condiment on the table.

Once Kerry disappeared again, Statler looked up from dowsing the thin, straw-like fries with ketchup. "It has to be someone from your company who travels abroad to work with your European clients."

Adrian's mind clicked through its files. "That would narrow it down to four people, myself included."

"Oh, we've checked you inside and out."

Adrian stiffened, though he'd suspected as much. By now, they had no doubt checked everyone in his organization right down to the brand of underwear they wore. Still, he disliked the idea of anyone looking into his private life. "How far have you gone? Is my home wired?"

"We've checked you out thoroughly." From Statler's tone, that was as much as he cared to reveal. "And your family has been cleared."

"My family?"

"Your parents, in particular. Your father was in the Foreign Service. They have many international connections."

Adrian tamped down a flare of anger. It would do no good for either of them. Statler was simply doing his job. As the owner of a security-based company, he would have done the same thing. "Exactly what is it that you suspect the perpetrators are after?"

"You are involved in a top secret operation with a defense contractor for the U.S. Air Force."

"The cyber war games?"

"Bright Star," Statler said, revealing more specific knowledge of the project. "Someone with the access codes to those games could really do some damage, both on the inside and on the out."

Adrian took a sip of his soda without tasting it. The new battlefront in the war on terror, as well as on other threats to the United States, was cyberspace. Anyone with knowledge of the government's technology could circumvent it for sinister purposes or set it back by damaging the files. Or simply get a leg up on the latest technology to track them. "Do you think they've already been in the government network?" Just the idea tied a knot of frustration in his stomach.

"Not without the codes, which you and your partner have taken steps to keep from your hard drives."

They were on a portable hard drive, which was not integrated with any system. But if the hackers had implanted a program to record all keystrokes on Mitch's station, including his password . . .

No, Adrian had addressed that first. After meticulous checking, no such program had been found. But knowing that it could be hidden in his DLLs—the dynamic link libraries—he'd shut the system down and reinstalled the software from scratch. It was a costly and timely process, but the only option to know for certain that a rogue program no longer existed.

That might not hold true for long if they didn't identify the mole.

"So what do you want me to do?" The agent hadn't driven down just to tell him that there was a mole in Alphanet Securities and that it likely wasn't Mitch, after all. Nor were they going to tell him whom they suspected.

"I want you to let us install security cameras and wires on all your locations."

"You mean you haven't?" Adrian couldn't help the sarcasm. He felt as if he were being slammed from both sides—the authorities on one, and the enemy on the other.

"We *are* monitoring your business offices with your own system per your consent," Statler conceded. "But not your home office."

"I'm the only one who works from my home," Adrian objected. "I thought I was cleared."

"Selena Lacy accesses your main system from there. We have records of her logins."

Adrian snorted. "Surely you don't suspect my fiancée? Besides, she's in the sales/public relations area, not in the programming."

"She has access." Statler stuffed a ketchup-drenched stack of fries in his mouth.

The idea was preposterous. Selena didn't have the security clearance to get into the programs Mitch and Adrian worked with.

Unless she'd had Mitch's password. Anyone could have logged in as Mitch and gotten through to secure sites.

You dialed twenty-one, not twelve. Her words that night at the Lighthouse Sound restaurant when she'd identified the exact numbers he'd speed-dialed from across the table echoed in his memory.

But even if she had seen Mitch type in his password, Selena was promotion and sales, through and through and used computers only to facilitate her own work. "Could someone use her without her knowledge?" There was a tinge of understanding in Statler's tone. But Adrian recognized that the man was a pit bull in disguise, determined to protect national and corporate security above all else. On the one hand, Adrian was grateful, but on the other—

"Selena is a very sharp businesswoman. I doubt she could be used . . . but I doubt even more that she has the knowledge to do what you're suggesting. To get inside, plant a program, steal the credit card list and try to find the codes. The two seem unrelated. Why call attention to oneself by dabbling in credit card fraud?"

"Unless the credit card theft is a diversion," Statler replied, echoing the same unsettling answer that popped into Adrian's mind the moment he'd asked the question. "Does she know where you keep the codes?"

Adrian nodded. "In my safe . . . when I'm not using them.

She doesn't know the combination." Could she have seen the combination like she'd seen his misdial on the cell phone? Adrian tried to think back. He didn't think she'd ever been present when he'd opened it.

He shook off the gathering suspicion. "It must be someone else."

"So tell me all you know about Kowalski and Burnett." Statler pushed away his empty plate.

"They handle our clients in Northern Europe—Holland, the Netherlands."

"But they travel back and forth from the main headquarters in Bethesda," Statler stated, rather than asked.

Adrian nodded. He wished he'd never gone public. Never expanded beyond the U.S. The business had taken on a life of its own, and his life with it. He hardly knew his only son. In truth, Adrian hardly knew himself anymore. At first, it had been novel. Now, the created façade was wearying. It was not who he was, nor who he wanted to be. At least not anymore.

CHAPTER FIFTEEN

Ellen tried not to scratch her neck as she sat at the head table during the Rotary Club meeting at Clamdiggers the following week. Ma had purchased a shirt with some kind of stiff ruffle around the neckline that was driving Ellen nuts.

"It's all the style," her mother said, fixing Ellen's pant-suit jacket so that the blouse wasn't rumpled. "It's a tuxedo blouse, or some such thing."

And now Bea sat in the audience with Pop, eyeing Adrian and Selena as if she could separate them with her scissors-sharp gaze. Ma never came to the Rotary meetings, unless Ellen counted the one during which she was sworn in as president.

Yes, Ellen could have refused to wear the blouse, but it would have upset her mother. It just wasn't worth it. Not that Ma was controlling. She simply smothered Ellen with good-intentions. Kind of like Marley when he drooled.

"So, the SonShiners football team needed jerseys," Joe

Phillips, the club treasurer told the group, "and that accounts for the donations' number. Any questions?"

Ellen rose and approached the podium when there were none. As she took Joe's place, her stomach clutched as the moment she'd been waiting for neared. "Does anyone want to motion we approve Joe's report?"

The motion was made, seconded, and approved. A mix of pride and dread battled in Ellen's chest. Her pride came from the community center having grown to the point that it needed more than a volunteer administrator. And it could pay a modest salary. The dread part was that she couldn't take the job.

A particularly nagging itch surfaced on her chest, but rather than pull a Marley and scratch for everyone to see, Ellen willed it away and brandished a smile. "And now for my report on the SonShine Community Center. Thanks to the hard work of the kids, everyone's support, and a very welcome grant," she said, glancing at Reverend Ingerman who'd helped her get the paperwork through, "I am pleased to announce that we now have a job opening for a director at the center . . . a *paying* job opening."

Sue Ann, Jan, and Alex jumped to their feet almost as fast as Ellen's mother with applause. Before long, everyone in the restaurant was standing and clapping. It was overwhelming. Ellen opened her mouth to speak, but a blade of emotion caught in her throat. *God, not now. I can't be a wimp in front of all these people.*

"Thank you, thank you," she said in a loud voice. "But give yourselves a hand, too, because without your support and the hard work of the volunteers and kids, we wouldn't have anything to celebrate but a vacant car dealership building."

Still, the enthusiasm carried on, even after the meeting was adjourned. Ellen found herself surrounded by friends and members.

"I'm so proud of you, Pumpkin," Pop said, bear-hugging her from behind. "Just wanted to let you know that Ma and me are leaving," he added in a whisper. "I'm a mite peaked."

"Love you, Pop," she said, giving his cheek a quick good-bye kiss over her shoulder.

"You know, you should take the job, Brit," Joe said from across the table.

"Yeah, the first thing I'd do is double your salary," she shot back.

"Maybe you should," Pop said, surprising her that he was still behind her. "Take the job, that is. It puts a look of pure joy on your face every time you mention it."

Ellen pivoted in disbelief of what her ears told her. "Pop, do you hear what you're saying?"

Eyes already crinkled by time, weather, and an ever-present good humor, he winked. "We'll talk later."

"But—" She said as he turned and waded through the milling group. What *was* he talking about?

"I know something you don't," Josh Turner teased in a singsong voice.

Ellen raised one brow, all the while refusing to allow her heart a little song and dance. This just didn't make sense. No way Pop could run the business without her. No way. It would kill him. Nearly had, until she took over the business end.

Ellen fixed a puzzled look on the woman Josh held around the waist. "Alex?"

Alex shrugged. "Don't look at me. Whatever it is, I had nothing to do with it." But a telltale twinkle in her eyes said otherwise.

"Lying is against the Big Ten, you know," Ellen warned.

"Hey, Brit," Scott Phillips shouted over the after-meeting din. "You're looking hot tonight. What's with the frills?"

Disconcerted, Ellen met his glazed gaze. It wasn't that she had never been complimented, but this guy was either high from the drinks he'd been chugging down, on something, or both.

"I think your friend has cleavage," Scott marveled to Jan, who gave Ellen an embarrassed, apologetic look.

Ooo kay. Ellen gave herself a few seconds to rein in her anger. Scott couldn't help that he'd never seen her in ruffles, but there was no excuse for being a jerk. If not for Jan's pleading gaze, there would be no mercy.

"Scott, look at the time," Jan exclaimed, shoving the man's watch to his face. "Don't the races start soon?"

What *did* she see in him? Ellen wondered as Jan drew her inebriated companion away with a last apologetic glance over her shoulder.

"He might be good looking and have lots of money," Ellen whispered to an equally concerned Alex, "but crap in a shiny package is still crap."

"Couldn't have put it better myself," her friend replied.

"Sugar, I just love your matching bag and shoes," Sue Ann

told Selena Lacy as she drew Selena and Adrian into the cluster around Ellen.

Ellen had asked Sue Ann to sit with the newcomers to make them feel welcome earlier.

"I bought them in Italy," Selena informed her with what Shore folk called *airs*. Ellen stiffened as Sue Ann's gaze sharpened. Sue Ann had more money than Midas, but she had no tolerance for a richer-than-thou attitude.

"Well of *co—ahse*," she replied, squeezing two syllables out of the last word. "I have a set just like it. I left the bag home. Didn't have time to change purses." Sue Ann turned a shapely ankle on display. "So much for the claim of *limited* quantities . . . unless you and I bought the only two sets made!" She laughed. "Besides, sugar"—she gave Selena a hug—"imitation is the highest form of flattery."

Ellen minced a smile, holding her breath. Susie Q could tell someone where to go and make them look forward to the trip.

"I tell you, I almost lost my breath when Fendi nearly took Prada under, back in the nineties," Sue Ann went on. "Who are they with now?"

"LVMH, I think," Selena replied, failing to hide her astonishment behind a façade of sophistication.

Score one for the country bumpkins, Ellen thought. And while she was one and proud of it, Sue Ann could swash her buckle on both sides of the social dividing line as the occasion demanded.

"Fendi, LVMH . . . Are we talking shoes or cars?" Ellen exclaimed.

Sue Ann and Selena laughed simultaneously.

"Sugar, Fendi is only one of the world's top designers in fashion." Sue Ann winked at Ellen. "See why we love her so much?" she said to Adrian and Selena.

Ellen shrugged. "No wonder I'd never heard of it."

"Selena was telling me earlier that she and Adrian are going to have a combination costume party and open house on Halloween and asked me to help them put together a guest list," Sue Ann announced, as though they were the best of friends.

That was the beauty of Susie Q. Once her point was made, she forgave and forgot just as quickly.

"If anyone knows who is who in these parts, it's Sue Ann," Ellen told the couple.

Not that Sue Ann was at all like Selena. She could don jeans and an old shirt and slap on paint with her less affluent friends in a beat of her big heart.

Sue Ann waved a dismissive hand, bedecked with enough stones to start a mine. "Don't be silly. Look who's queen tonight." She gave Ellen a perfectly wicked wink and slipped her arm through Selena's. "So while Ellen holds court, why don't I introduce you to some of your prospective guests, sugar?"

"Adrian?" Selena called over her shoulder, still off-balance as Sue Ann shepherded her away from the cluster.

"Go on," he replied. "I'll catch up in a moment."

"Oh, let him be," Sue Ann said. "You know how men hate this kind of thing. He can hang out with the guys . . . and Ellen."

Ellen shot Alex a pleading look. "Go put a leash on her," she mouthed.

"On it," Alex mouthed back.

"On which one?" Adrian asked Ellen as the women left the group.

"Which what?"

Suddenly his meaning dawned on her. Heat suffused Ellen's face. "Um, Sue Ann, of course. She's such a trip."

Adrian swallowed her with that disconcerting gaze of his, part intense study and part something that made her itch even more than the blouse. "Now that I have you to myself, may I buy you a drink?"

To myself? Ellen glanced about, surprised to see that the group around her had dissolved into smaller ones engaged in their own conversations. Like too much chocolate, this was not good. It was sinfully wonderful, but not good for her in the long run.

"Sure," she replied. "Soda, fully leaded."

Up went that perfect hedge of a brow over his left eye. "Fully leaded?"

"As opposed to unleaded, as in diet," she explained.

Adrian laughed and slipped his hand behind her back, sending a giddy awareness up her spine. "One fully leaded soda coming up."

Ellen groaned in silence, praying she wouldn't babble or make a fool of herself now that she was one on one with a man who could turn her world topsy-turvy. Either Ma had more influence than Ellen gave her credit for, or God had one weird sense humor.

"Actually, Selena needed to be brought down a notch," Adrian said after buying her a fountain soda in the bar side of the establishment. He could have said more, much more. But a gentleman wouldn't.

Ellen shrugged. "Maybe she was nervous among all these strangers and just rambled on about what she knew best. I mean, that's what I'd do."

"Perhaps." It was a generous thought.

But then, everything about Ellen was generous. In coming to know her, Adrian had begun to see just how petty and self-absorbed Selena was. Although the idea that Selena might be involved in his business problems still seemed far-fetched. She had little to gain and everything to lose—her job, her future as his wife. It made no sense.

A twinge of guilt niggled him. Although he'd not exactly been eager to set the date Selena wanted so much, Adrian couldn't honestly tell her why. She was smart, beautiful, and desirable; yet something set off a panic button each time she broached the subject. In fact, it had been Selena who had brought up the subject with her customary pragmatism. They complimented each other as business partners. And Peter needed a mother. . .

"Hey, Brit!" A short, stocky man with a round, smiling face called out to Ellen from the TV end of the bar. "You and your buddy there want to team up for a game of darts?"

Ellen cut a perfectly impish gaze up at Adrian. "Adrian, meet Tony Richardson, our illustrious state's attorney. He is scared witless of playing shuffleboard with me because I skunk him all the time. Tony, this is Adrian Sinclair."

Adrian shook the other fellow's extended hand. "Pleased to meet you. And I could be persuaded to play a game, if the lady is willing." Darts were his *forte*, given the hours spent at local pubs during his university days.

"I'm not that good at it, but I'm willing," Ellen replied.

But before they could pass out the darts, Selena approached with a middle-aged gentleman. Adrian tensed upon seeing that he wore a collar of the clergy.

"Adrian, I have someone we need to speak to. This is Reverend Ingerman of the Faith Community Church."

Tall, with a thick shock of salt-and-pepper hair, Reverend Ingerman shook hands with Adrian. "Congratulations, sir. I understand you two are planning a spring wedding."

"Yes," Adrian said, hoping his hesitation hadn't been too noticeable. "Yes, we are." It felt as though he were lying. He managed a smile as Selena slipped a possessive arm through his. Did one fall *out* of love?

"I thought I might set up an appointment for us after the holidays to speak with the reverend," Selena told him. "What with the decorating and festivities planned, I'll be frantic. I did tell you that I spoke to your mother and that she and your father will be down for our house-warming bash."

"It must have slipped your mind." Adrian didn't mean to sound trite, but he was annoyed. Annoyed at this business muck. Annoyed at Selena's rush to marry. Annoyed at Selena. And annoyed at himself because he no longer saw his situation as clearly as he once had.

"Which is why I've decided to hire the House of Scoglio to decorate. I want everything to be perfect for them, and Gino is a genius."

Adrian had never heard of the man and had been doubly embarrassed when Selena made the announcement earlier in front of Ellen's decorator friend Alex. Alex evidently was familiar with his work and graciously endorsed it.

"What's to decorate?" Ellen pulled a teasing grin. "A few fake cobwebs and some orange and black cutouts, and you're done."

Selena gave Ellen a patronizing look. "That might do for a *children's* center, but this is for an adult social event, Miss Brittingham. And while Gino is at it, he might as well see what he can do with the house itself. I've been at my wit's end as to how to make it more stylish."

The reverend retrieved a card from his jacket pocket and handed it to Selena. "Well, then, when you've survived the decorating and holidays, call me at this number and we can start planning the main event. Mr. Sinclair," he said, turning to Adrian. "I hope I'll be seeing you and your fiancée in my church soon."

Adrian recoiled inwardly. Whether it was from his mistrust of God and church or the idea of a forever with Selena, he couldn't be certain. Perhaps it was both—

"I think we should be leaving, too. I have to drive back to Bethesda tomorrow," Selena said, leaping on the opportunity the minister's departure presented as though it were a life ring. She leaned her head against his arm with a sigh. "Won't it be wonderful when I can devote my full time to being Mrs. Adrian Sinclair?"

Adrian glanced at her, a bit startled. They'd not discussed her quitting the business. He'd come to depend on Selena's PR abilities. Not that she'd used it tonight. She cast about disdain like it was candy. Between the prospects of marriage, church, and an increasingly manipulative fiancée, it was all Adrian could do not to run from it all.

Instead, he bade a reluctant goodnight. "I'll take you up on the dart game another time," he promised Ellen and Tony. Adrian had actually looked forward to the challenge.

"Give my love to Pete and Mrs. Duffy," Ellen called after them as he escorted Selena from the room.

Her love. Adrian pushed open the door to the parking lot for Selena to precede him. Ellen was full of heart. It showed in everything she did.

Once outside, Selena took a deep breath of fresh air. "Thank goodness that's over. I feel like I just stepped out of Sheriff Andy's Mayberry. Or was it that other show? *The Dukes of Hazzard?*"

When had she become so . . . so haughty? Why hadn't he seen this before? Adrian didn't have to think about the answer. He'd always been with her among her associates, dancing to her tune. All for the benefit of the company—

Drawing a mental line, Adrian tightened his grip on her arm. "Better get used to it, darling. This is our home now." He leaned over and gave her a short kiss on the cheek. "And I can't thank you enough for bringing our family here."

The bemused look on Selena's face almost made Adrian smile. It was, perhaps, the first time he'd ever seen her speechless.

CHAPTER SIXTEEN

The crowd thinned so quickly, Ellen didn't get to say goodbye to Sue Ann or Alex and Josh. Tony cajoled her into losing three out of three games of darts and she hadn't seen them leave. But what could she do? Say no to a longtime friend who'd had a rough day and needed some company for a while? As for losing—and Ellen hated to lose—how could she concentrate on anything with Pop's mysterious parting words echoing in her mind?

Ellen headed home as fast as her Hog would carry her. She had to find out just what Pop had meant.

Maybe he wasn't thinking clearly. An ache squeezed Ellen's chest. He got confused, more of late. Last week, he'd made a duplicate order. Fortunately Ellen caught it and stopped it in time. So far, God had helped her help him keep the lucrative business he'd founded on his family land—his legacy.

Meanwhile, she'd hired kids from the community center to help Ma run the produce stand till after the fall flowers and pumpkin/gourd stock was gone. It had been the only way Ellen could take care of the office *and* help Pop oversee the jobs in the field so he wouldn't overtax his heart.

Face it. There was just no way she could handle the community center job, too.

Is there, Lord?

All things were possible.

Ellen winced. *Okay, God, is that You or my memory of Your Word? I don't want to confuse my will with Yours. And You know how bad I want this.*

To that, there was no reply. Just the roar of the Harley as she gunned down the dirt lane toward her parents' home on the creek. To her surprise, the front lights were on, as well as the country kitchen light in the back where Ma and Pop spent most of their evenings. As Ellen coasted up to the rear porch, Marley bounded out to greet her.

"Down, boy," she commanded. Marley dropped on his haunches, his tail wagging at warp speed. Ellen put down the stop on the Harley, draped her helmet over the handlebar and gave the dog the scratching of his life—behind the ears, over the ears, under the ears—chin, too.

"You are one big lump of love," she chided, pausing at the porch door long enough to dig out a doggie treat.

As she stepped into the kitchen, she was taken aback by a chorus of "Surprise!"

Ellen checked her step, blinking as the overhead light came

on. The indistinct figures outlined by the TV lamp materialized into familiar ones. Alex and Josh were there. Sue Ann in
her Prada heels. The only one of the bosom buddies missing
was Jan. Although *what* Jan was missing still eluded Ellen.

"It's a sundae night," Alex announced, pointing to three
half-gallons of ice cream sitting on the table amidst every
topping imaginable.

"Aw, you guys!" Ellen felt her throat tighten with emotion.
"This is great. A little overkill, considering the community
center's success was the result of many, many hands—not
just mine—but great, just the same."

"Who says it's about the community center's success?"
Pop asked from where he got up from his worn, green easy
chair.

Confusion grazed Ellen's thoughts. "Well . . . what is it for
then?"

Ma put a handful of spoons on the table and turned, pinching Ellen's cheeks. "It's for your heart's desire, bubeleh. Your
new job as the director of the community center, what else?"

"But—" Ellen looked at Pop, a grayed, slightly bent reflection of the strapping man he used to be. "What about the
nursery?"

"We're closing it, pumpkin. We're gonna finish the jobs we
have underway, and that's it."

"Don't you think it's time we retired?" her mother asked.
"It's your time now."

"But the land . . . how—"

"Josh made us an offer we couldn't refuse," Pop explained.

"We keep the house and its creek front, and he develops *Brittingham Shire* with the rest he's buying from us." Pop shook his head. "Sounds right fancy, doesn't it?"

Ellen was speechless. Inside she jumped and squealed with delight, between pangs of anxiety and utter disbelief. How had all this come about without her having the slightest hint? She cut her gaze to Alex and Josh.

"Don't look at me," Alex told her. "I knew something was up, but I didn't know what until we were on our way over here."

"Can I keep a secret or what?" Josh said with a Cheshire cat grin. "And as chair of the SonShine board of directors, I've been authorized to offer you the job."

"So say something, sugar," Sue Ann prompted, waving her hand at the gallon containers on the table with mock impatience. "*Before* the ice cream melts."

"Did *you* know?" Ellen asked Sue Ann as her mother ushered her to the head of the table. A sign had been hung on the chair reading SonShine Community Center Director.

"I know now," Sue Ann replied. "And that's all that counts."

"I . . . I just can't believe this. I mean, I'm ecstatic and all, but—" Ellen took a deep breath. "I just can't believe this!"

"Jan sends her love and congratulations," Sue Ann told her, dropping into a chair nearby. "She did us a favor by *not* joining us with Scott."

"Josh, you dip the ice cream," Bea said, handing him a scoop. "Alex, you man the chocolate sauce."

Alex stirred the small crock of hot melted chocolate with an ecstatic, "Umm."

"Sue Ann," Bea continued. "You're in charge of the fruit and nuts."

"That's appropriate," Josh teased.

Sue Ann poked her tongue at him.

"Now I see why you won Miss Piper Cove . . . when was it? Nineteen—"

The former beauty queen cut him off. "Oh, shush, Josh Turner. You know I don't do dates. Never will."

Pop slid into the chair next to Ellen. "And in case you're worrying about a pay cut, the nursery in Pittsville is looking to hire out their landscape design. So's the one in Salisbury."

Freelance design. Just what Ellen had hoped to do when she went to college for her degree. Until Pop's heart attack forced her into running the nursery and the field crews, too. Ellen gave him a big hug.

"You've thought of everything, haven't you, Pop?" She could imagine him calling all the local nurseries and checking them out for her.

"Your Ma and I tried to," he replied. "We just want you to be happy, pumpkin."

Unable to hold back any longer, Ellen bolted up from her chair and gathered her mother and father together in a group hug. "I *am* happy. I'm so happy, I can't stand it."

"All's you need now is a husband," Ma sighed through building tears of joy.

"Ma—" Ellen groaned.

"Someone nice, like Mr. Sinclair."

"Ma!" Now Ellen was horrified, even though she wished it were so. But wishing and reality were like east and west— never the twain to meet.

Sue Ann waved a spoon in front of her. "You know, I think he's kind of stuck on Ellen. He looks at her like he could just eat her up."

Heat spread like wildfire to Ellen's face. That's just what it felt like when she fell into his gaze, but—

"A ready-made grandson would be nice," Bea said. "And word is, things aren't so blissful on the engagement front."

"No?" Sue Ann's face brightened. "Do tell."

"That *woman*—" Ma said the word just like Mrs. Duffy, as if it left a bad taste in her mouth. "—has been trying to get Adrian to set a date for over two years, but he keeps coming up with excuses, so I hear."

"Ma, she's made a date with the minister after the holidays to *set* a date," Ellen said. "This is crazy. I don't need a man."

"But he needs you," Bea replied. "And Pete needs you, not *her*."

Pete. Just the mention of the kid's name melted Ellen's heart. "Pete will have all the support from me he needs, but that doesn't mean marriage, Ma. Now I don't want to spoil this by talking about Adrian and Selena."

"Ellen's right," Alex said, the voice of reason. "Even if Selena all but told me that my decor style wasn't sufficiently *haute* for her taste."

"She *what?*" No wonder Adrian was embarrassed.

Sue Ann mimicked an aloof pose. *"I'm looking for a certain . . . effect."* Scrunching up her face, she added, "And I was nice to her, but only because Ellen asked me to be. That woman is as phony as a three-dollar bill."

"Mrs. Duffy says Selena is going to send Pete away as soon as she says, 'I do.'" Ma sniffed in disapproval. "It's breaking her heart."

"Okay, who wants what?" Josh spoke up. "I've got chocolate, vanilla, and strawberry getting soft fast."

Ellen gave him an appreciative smile. "I'll have a banana split. Ma, do we have—" She broke off as her mother put a dish of sliced bananas on the table.

"One banana split, coming up for the lady of the hour." As Josh heaped a dip of each flavor over sliced bananas spread on the bottom of one of Ma's ice cream dishes, Ellen's thoughts centered on Pete. Adrian would never allow Selena to separate him from his son, no matter how smitten Adrian was with Selena. Yet, even as the thought registered, Ellen remembered the way Adrian had talked about how much he and his company owed Selena. Gratitude in itself could be mistaken for a lot of powerful emotions.

Like love.

Oh, Lord, I can't have love and Adrian in the same thought. I just got my dream—and thank You for willing it to be so—and it's nuts to want another one.

Isn't it?

"One dip of pineapple, one of strawberries," Sue Ann said, adding to the dish Josh had passed her.

"Hot chocolate . . ." Alex dribbled the warm dark topping over the center dip.

"And nuts." Sue Ann sprinkled on a heaping spoonful of chopped walnuts.

"Who's doing the whipped cream?" Ma asked, taking out two cans of topping from the fridge.

"I will!"

Everyone turned to see Jan standing in the entrance . . . alone.

Looking like the cat that swallowed the canary, she walked into the country kitchen and took one of the containers. "After all, this is my specialty."

"Where's Prince Charming?" Sue Ann asked as Jan made a perfect tipped swirl atop each topping coated scoop.

"I left him asleep in his car at his condo and bummed a ride from the Food Mart with my manager." Jan shoved the heaping dish of delight toward Ellen. "To the best youth center director ever born!"

"Hear, hear," the others chorused.

"Now you eat, I'll make sure the others catch up with you," Josh told Ellen.

As Ellen indulged, she watched as her friends continued to make their respective sundaes, laughing, joking, and most of all, loving each other the way they had since high school. All for one, and one for all.

God, I am so blessed with both family and friends. And bless the Sinclair home, too. Please, Lord . . . for Pete's sake.

CHAPTER SEVENTEEN

"You talk about a Halloween nightmare. Just try *my* house!"

Pete paced the floor back and forth past the kitchen table in the Brittingham kitchen, red-cheeked from his run across the field in the nippy, fall air. He stopped long enough to pick up an applesauce muffin, still warm from the oven.

Ellen had seen him hightailing it across the field without his bicycle. Curiosity piqued, she'd come up to the house to see what was up.

"I had all my books and computer stuff exactly where I wanted it and that dumb designer comes in and changes my room all around. I can't find anything, *including* my science project. It's *his* fault—not mine—that I couldn't turn it in." The boy bit into the muffin as though he wished it were the decorator's calf. "What was wrong with our house in the first place?" he mumbled and chewed at the same time.

"Here, dear," Ma said, handing him a glass of milk to wash it down before he choked.

"I'll never get my project finished now," he lamented after taking a couple of undignified gulps. The milk left a mustache, which he promptly licked off. "And Dad's going to send me to that boarding school if I don't do well. That's *Selena's* idea."

Bea cut a sidewise glance at Ellen, nodding as if to say, "I told you so."

"So what do you have to do to finish the project?" Ellen asked. She couldn't do much about the threat used to get Pete to apply himself, but she might be able to help him with his immediate dilemma.

She'd hardly seen Adrian since the Rotary meeting. When she laid the special-order landscaping stones for Mrs. Duffy's herb garden, he'd remained confined in his office. One of Gino Scoglio's staff, not the decorating icon himself, skulked around, taking pictures and notes as though the house existed just to vex him. Mrs. Duffy had echoed Pete's complaints at every opportunity.

Pete burped. "Sorry," he said with a sheepish grin. "Anyway, I was supposed to collect an assortment of different tree leaves and write which kind they are and information as to how they grow. I had *twelve* different species."

She grinned. "Well, you've come to the right place for tree leaves. I can help you get that many in no time."

A glimmer of hope sparked in the boy's gaze, then died. "But I have to write something about each one, maybe get some pictures—"

"What, you think a landscape artist doesn't have books on trees?" she challenged. "Not to mention the Internet info highway. We can pull pictures off the Internet of the trees in summer foliage and put them next to the fall leaf."

"Grand! But it's due tomorrow."

"It's only four o'clock," she said, glancing at her wrist-watch. "We can take the Harley back to the woods and get all we need before dark."

"I think I've got a blank scrapbook around here somewhere," Ma thought aloud. "Would that work for your paper?"

"It would be awesome." Enthusiasm sparkled in Pete's eyes.

"And I'll call Mrs. Duffy and ask if it's okay for you to have supper with us," Ma said. "How's that, bubeleh?"

Pete stopped in midstride toward the door. "I wish you were my family."

Ellen cuffed him on the back of the head. "Hey, we're neighbors. That's almost as good in these parts."

"You still have earplugs?" he asked. "Can Marley go too?"

Ellen pulled on her jacket and picked Pete's up from off the rack by the door. "Yes," she said, tossing the boy his coat. "And yes. Wild horses couldn't keep Marley home."

Three hours later, Pete worked on the laptop while Ellen placed the various leaves they'd collected on the galley table in the houseboat. They'd decided to work there since she had everything needed to pull off the project aboard. "Now don't copy the information word for word," she cautioned as she carefully glued a dried leaf in place on the scrapbook page.

Pete gave her a droll look and threw up his hands like Ma. "What, do you think I don't know what plagiarism is?"

"And you think you're not family," Ellen chided. "When you pick up a Brooklyn accent, I'm going to run blood tests."

With a half-yawn, half-grin, Peter turned his attention back to her laptop. The toll of being in the woods until almost dark with the temperatures dropping, the warmth of the cabin, and a belly full of fried chicken and potatoes smothered in what he'd dubbed *burnt* gravy—gravy made from browning flour in an iron skillet—was beginning to show.

"You know, I don't trust that designer guy."

Ellen wiped the excess glue off her fingers. "Oh? Why not?"

"He's got his nose in everybody's business. Fa . . . Dad threw him out of his office this morning. I've never seen Dad so angry . . . or grouchy. He gets mad at everything."

"It's probably the security problem and his business."

"Yes, well when I tried to throw *Al-fa-redo*"— the way Pete rolled his eyes and said the name almost made Ellen laugh— "out of *my* room, I got yelled at. It's just not fair. My stuff is important, too."

"And missing," Ellen reminded him. "How many more do you have to write?"

Pete leaned forward on the table and shoved his fingers through his dark hair. "Two confounded more," he said, the voice of utter woe. "Then I have to cut out the words and the pictures and put them in the book. I'll *never* get done."

The kid was smart, cute, and utterly charming. And Ellen still couldn't believe that he'd lifted her Harley up when it fell over in the soft dirt of the forest bed, much less mounted and started it exactly as she'd coached him. It wasn't that she didn't think he knew how, but that someone with Asperger's would do it that impressed her. From what she'd read, those kids were slow to change their ways. Pete definitely had gained confidence since the first time she'd offered him a ride. He rode behind her as if he'd done it all his life. Of course, still with earplugs.

"You'll finish." Ellen got up from her side of the table and joined Pete on the other. "We'd better practice some good motorcycle safety."

"Huh?"

"Concentrate on where you're going and maneuver within traffic, allowing yourself space. Focus on your goal through the middle of all this mess," she explained. "Gotta watch out for others on the highway."

"In *homework*?"

"In homework, on the road, in life . . . there's always the unexpected. A lot of what you learn about bike safety applies to life."

The boy pondered her point for a moment. "What else?"

"Point your gaze well ahead of you, keep your eyes up . . . not looking back . . . like at Alfredo for his interference."

"But he did interfere . . . big time!"

"Yes, but that's done, and you can't change it. So we are looking ahead, okay? The more time you spend looking back, the less time we have ahead of us to do this job."

"Oh." Pete nodded. "That makes perfect sense. What else?"

"Keep looking from side to side for any other unexpected intervention or threat. The more information you have, the safer you are and more likely you are to reach your goal." His undivided attention spurred her on. "Of course, the Bible is the ultimate guide. Know what B-I-B-L-E stands for?"

Pete shook his head.

"Basic Instructions Before Leaving Earth. It was on a bumper sticker the kids in my Sunday school class sold to raise money for a mission trip."

"How old do you have to be to be in your class?"

"I teach middle school ages, twelve to fifteen."

"I'll be twelve in December. Think I could get in early?"

"Two months?" Ellen pretended to think hard, but she'd love to have Pete with her group. Granted, he was socially behind those kids, but she'd run interference for him. And her kids were good kids. It would be a good lesson for them. . .

"If your dad approves. I could pick you up Sunday mornings and bring you home."

"On your bike?"

"Unless the weather's bad. Then it's my truck. But you have to clear it—"

A knock sounded on the door.

"Hello! Anyone home?" It was Adrian.

Recognizing his father's voice, Pete grimaced. "Uh-oh,

unexpected intervention," he said, referring to her lesson. The kid was a veritable sponge.

"I think we can handle it."

Although her heart might not, after the huge flip-flop it just did. Ellen opened the sliding door that separated the living quarters from the deck. Adrian stood there in a turtleneck sweater and slacks that made pictures of cuddling by a cozy fireside waltz through her mind.

"Looking for something?"

"I understand my wandering son is here. The one who didn't check in with Mrs. Duffy before coming over this afternoon."

"Sorry, dad. But Mrs. Brittingham called her later . . . and I'm doing homework and learning motorcycle safety." He brightened his expression as though that excused everything.

Adrian glanced at Ellen. "Motorcycle safety?"

"Focusing on our journey, so that we can reach our destination—finishing this project." Feeling as though she'd just added another count to her case as nut job, she motioned Adrian to take a seat at the table. "Want to help?"

Adrian scowled. "I don't believe in doing Pete's homework for him."

"I'm doing all the work, Dad. Ellen's just sticking it in the book for me."

She nodded. "It's true. He's looked up all the information and typed it up in his own words." She pointed to the printer that held the stack of finished pages. "I'm just cutting and pasting so that we don't have to pull an all-nighter."

"And you know how messy I can be with glue," Peter reminded him. "Ellen's neater."

"He should have had this finished by now . . . on his own."

Pete inhaled a deep breath of indignation and let it fly. "I *had* everything ready to be pasted in my scrapbook and Alfredo lost it. He and Mrs. Duffy packed half my room in boxes while I was in school."

"Him again." The two words said volumes. But Adrian didn't dwell in the negative feelings he clearly had for Alfredo. He switched on a smile. "What can I do to help?"

Pete scratched Marley's head under the table. "Dad, do you know what B-I-B-L-E stands for?"

"Bible?" Adrian ventured, clearly blindsided.

"*Basic Instructions Before Leaving Earth.* There's a lot of truth in that bumper sticker," Pete added, as if he'd suddenly become a sage. "I think I should be in Ellen's Sunday school class because she teaches a lot more than those stories about old people I learned when I went to Nana's church."

Ellen didn't know whether to hug or strangle the kid, but Marley stood between them. "With your permission," she told Adrian. "I think it would be good for Pete."

"Perhaps." Adrian didn't sound convinced.

Ellen wondered why he seemed suddenly put off, why he shunned church. His parents evidently attended. Something to do with his wife's death, maybe? Her heart constricted. It had to have been an unbearable pain. That kind of experience could cause one to emerge from it in one of two ways. With faith one could emerge better, stronger in one's belief. Without God, it resulted in bitterness and shattered what faith one had. *God, if there's anything I can do to help Adrian, show me. Use me—*

"I see no reason why he shouldn't go . . . if he wants to," Adrian conceded, drawing Ellen from her prayer.

Pete jerked his fisted hand down to his side with a loud "Yes!" that startled Marley into a bark.

Ellen made the T for *time out* with her hands, even as an answering peace soothed her troubled soul. "Okay, interference over." She didn't know how, but it was going to be okay. Maybe this was Adrian's first step. "That's Sunday," she said. "Too far ahead. What do we need to do tonight?"

"'Concentrate on where you're going and maneuver within traffic, allowing yourself space,'" Pete quoted. "In other words, let's just get this job done."

Adrian laughed for the first time since . . . since the last time he'd been with Ellen, he realized. It was impossible to be around her without feeling good. She had this inner glow that was infectious. Faith perhaps. That definitely was an integral part of who she was. As was her humor and an indomitable spirit. She was such a positive influence on Pete . . . and him. So different from Selena.

"First," Ellen murmured almost to herself, "we have to match the summer foliage pictures Pete found with his text descriptions and the leaves I've prepared. We'll use the sofa."

Adrian watched Ellen as she spread the papers from the printer tray. Despite his attempt not to do so, he kept comparing her to Selena.

"I labeled the leaves," Ellen said, handing him a stack of a dozen or so varieties pressed between layers of wax paper. "You put the leaf down, and I'll match the pictures and text to it. Then once everything is stacked together, we can cut and paste them onto the scrapbook pages."

"That's what I'd done before Alfredo lost them," Pete reminded them.

How could Adrian be upset with his son when he'd lost his temper at the meddlesome man, only that morning? Adrian had been so wrapped up in Bright Star, he'd blocked out the upheaval in his household until he came upon Alfredo taking pictures of his office.

Of course, the man was only doing his job. And Adrian did apologize, but not before Alfredo had placed a frenzied call to Selena in Bethesda. When she'd rung Adrian a few moments later, he was appropriately conciliatory, but nothing more. He wasn't even certain why he was allowing all this work to be planned, beyond the decorations for their party. Or why he'd called her, "Darling." The word left a bad taste in his mouth.

Selena was certainly innocent until proven guilty. Adrian couldn't imagine her being a part of this security breach. Granted, she'd been in the Bethesda system this morning when **someone** had tried to take over during his session, but she didn't have skill and knowledge to get as far as the intruder had. Thankfully, Adrian had foiled the attempt. The series of password-accessible doors he'd set up when he took over the project from Mitch had alerted him to a foreign presence in time to foil the attempt and collect information that would help locate the intruder. As much Adrian was tempted to go with it himself, he'd turned it over to the FBI hands, lest he compromise the investigation. They were the legal experts.

"Okay, we're ready for the glue. Here." Ellen displaced his preoccupation by handing him a brown leaf the size of a dinner plate. "We'll start with the *plantanus occidentalis.*"

"Planta-occi-what-is?"

"A sycamore," Peter answered him. "It's like a camouflage tree because of the colors of the trunk, and its species is one of the oldest on the planet. It's definitely going to be a two-page section," he said as Adrian filled most of the page with the leaf specimen. "We have one in our back yard—the huge one."

"Really?" Adrian's gaze sought and found Ellen's.

With a hasty nod, she snatched its brimming warmth away, focusing on cutting out the picture of its summer look.

In that bedraggled ponytail, jeans, and sweatshirt, she almost looked like a child, herself. Quite the contrast to the young woman who'd run the Rotary meeting in a smart slack suit, softened by a ruffled shirt. Or wearing leather boots and vest while riding Sheba. An enigma, that's what she was—a wild mix of personalities that caused Adrian to wait with bated breath to see which would emerge next.

And she smelled like fresh air.

"Are you going to glue that on the page or just hold it there till the teacher grades it?"

Ellen handed him the glue stick and pencil. From her saucy grin, Adrian couldn't tell if she'd caught him discreetly inhaling her scent or was simply getting on with business. Regardless, he was grateful that most of the light was concentrated over the table.

"I usually lightly outline the leaf with the pencil and fill the area in with glue. Then press the leaf on it. Pete, I'd leave waxed paper between the sheets tonight, to make sure the glue is good and dry. Then take them out before school."

"I'm gonna sleep with it under my pillow so Alfredo won't lose it again."

"You act as though you're used to doing this sort of thing," Adrian told Ellen as she cut out the text that Pete had written about sycamores.

"Well, this *is* my line of work. Plants, trees, flowers . . ."

"And now children . . . or so Josh Turner says." Adrian had run into Josh at the local gas station and heard that Ellen had accepted the job at the community center.

"Yeah, I can't believe it yet. I mean, whoever heard of changing careers in the middle of the road?" Joy practically bubbled in Ellen's voice. "I didn't think it would be possible to follow where my heart took me, instead of where my head was set to go. You know, my training."

Adrian did know. Somewhere along the way, his head had trumped his heart, taking Alphanet Security from a place he lived to work to a place he worked to live.

"It's a cut in salary, of course, but it's also a cut in tedium." She pressed a cutout of the text about sycamores on the page. "I get to do more of what I love to do—the creative stuff—instead of the detail that running a bigger business entails. This place was taking me down, but I kept it going for Pop's sake. And, come to find out, he was keeping it going for my sake."

Adrian nodded absently, distracted by the shine in her eyes and the animation of her features when she talked about the youth center.

"Just goes to show you, all things are possible."

All things are possible. Perhaps for some. Adrian envied her and her deep-rooted faith, even as he celebrated on her behalf.

It had made sense financially to go public, become international. And somewhere along the way, his enthusiasm for his work was beaten down by the operation of an incredibly successful corporation. And for whose sake? Not his. He was miserable. Certainly not for Pete's sake. His son made it clear he cherished time with Adrian—something Adrian could not afford now. Adrian could buy his son everything but his time.

"So I'll be doing freelance work for area nurseries," Ellen continued, "which I love to do, and get to spend time at the center." One of her adorable snickers escaped. "It's like getting paid to play. Know what I mean?"

"I know *exactly* what you mean." Adrian locked gazes with hers. He couldn't help himself. So much life—so much joy—bubbled in her bright eyes. Enough to intoxicate him. To set him free.

A smile teetered on her lips. They were not an applied-full rose-red like Selena's, but rouged, like her cheeks, by the nip in the fall air. They parted ever so slightly. . .

He wanted to kiss her. Really wanted to.

"Me, too," Pete put in, from the table. "I'd like to be paid to play video games instead of going to school and bothering with all that detail of stuff I don't like."

Ellen retreated abruptly to the table. "At your age, you have to get your education first. Then make life-changing decisions."

Adrian gave his son a grateful smile. He'd nearly forgotten anyone else was there. He'd nearly made a fool of himself. What must she be thinking of him, devouring her with his eyes, staring at her lips with such obvious intent? He was engaged, for heaven's sake!

"But I *have* finished my education," he began in an effort to dig himself out of his embarrassment. "And Ellen's example has given me a lot to think about. For that, I am most thankful."

"Like what?" Pete hit Ctrl+–P on the keyboard, setting the printer in motion.

Adrian squirmed at the other end of the eleven-year-old's stare. "Like changing some directions."

Pete reached up and picked the printout off the shelf behind him. "I hope Selena is one of them . . . and Alfredo."

Adrian's stomach sunk. Pete was his mother's child. Direct, and with an uncanny sense for awkward timing.

"Hey, are you keeping your eye on the road," Ellen piped up, "or are we going to be here all night?" She shot Adrian a sympathetic smile.

It helped a little. But what if Selena was right? That she'd never win Pete's approval?

"This is my last tree," Pete shot back, oblivious to Adrian's concern. Or he didn't care. It was so hard to tell the difference with him.

"Then you start cutting out the text and pictures of the summer foliage, while your Dad and I paste." She handed him her scissors and glanced from him to Adrian and back. "Everybody straight on their assignments?"

As Pete nodded, Adrian shook the subject from his mind. He'd deal with it later. "You don't by any chance possess a whip?" he teased.

Just when he thought his world had struck an even keel again, Ellen turned a look on him that made him feel as though braided leather had curled around his heart. . .

"No worries," she teased. "I only use a whip as a last resort."

. . . and yanked it into her hands.

CHAPTER EIGHTEEN

It was after ten when Adrian pulled into his garage. He could have stayed longer, soaking in Ellen's sunshine, but Pete had started nodding off as the two of them pasted up the last few pages.

"You'd best go straight to bed. Tomorrow will come early," Adrian advised his son.

"I will." Yawning, Pete unbuckled his seatbelt, his newly finished project still smelling of glue in his lap.

Once the boy stepped inside the house, he turned suddenly and gave Adrian a big hug.

"And thanks for the help, Dad. Ellen makes homework fun, don't you think?" Pete backed away, studying Adrian's face—probing, like his question.

"Yes, she does."

"Don't you think she's more fun than Selena?"

Ah, Adrian thought there might be an agenda in that question. He chose his reply carefully. "Selena has her good points."

"You mean like sex?"

Adrian cringed, glad that Pete had abandoned his scrutiny to hang up his coat. Eleven-year-olds were entirely too worldly for his liking. Still, Adrian's neck grew hot with embarrassment. Granted, he'd not done the deed, but it had crossed his mind.

"Clearly you've been watching too much television to—"

"Hey, buddy, it's about time you came home." Mitch Knittel appeared in the kitchen entrance with one of Duff's cinnamon breakfast scones in hand.

"Uncle Mitch!" Pete exclaimed, barreling into Adrian's partner with a half-hug. "When did you get here?"

"Too late for dinner. But one will never starve in Mrs. D's kitchen, right, A?"

Adrian wanted to hug Mitch, too, despite the wicked twinkle in his eye that suggested his partner had overheard the father-son exchange.

"So I see. But I take it Duff's scones are not the only reason you're here."

"Look at the project Ellen and Dad helped me with," Pete said, thrusting it at Mitch.

The man's eyebrows shot up. "Isn't *that* interesting!"

He wasn't speaking of the project, which he thumbed through with appropriate fascination.

"Very well, Pete. Off to bed now, like you promised."

Pete took the book from Mitch. "I'm sleeping with this tonight. Security around here stinks."

Taken back, Mitch glanced at Adrian as Pete took off down

the hallway. "Security stinks in a lot of places," Mitch said, making his way to the table where a cup of coffee steamed. "Want a cup? I just made some."

Adrian shook his head and pulled up a chair. "So why exactly are you here?"

Mitch dropped into the seat opposite Adrian with a mile-wide grin. "I am free, A. As in cleared of any wrongdoing."

Adrian exhaled in relief. When he first saw Mitch, he'd feared his friend to be the bearer of bad news. "What—"

"Wanted to be the first to tell you." Mitch raised his coffee mug in salute. "And to be with you when Statler calls"—he glanced at his watch—"any time now. Shall we hither to the office, my good friend?"

Uh-oh. Mitch was waxing Elizabethan, which meant something was afoot and he couldn't wait to unveil it.

"Just tell me if it's good or bad," Adrian said following him to the office.

Mitch shrugged, noncommittal. "I guess it depends on how you look at it."

Mitch did tell Adrian that the moneys found in his account had been traced to a small time gambling syndicate in France, removing financial motive and unraveling the FBI's case against him.

"And they *think* they know how my password was obtained," he said, "but—"

The phone next to Adrian rang. He picked up the receiver and punched on the speakerphone. "Agent Statler, I presume."

Statler's voice crackled over the line. "Mr. Sinclair. I take it Mitch Knittel is there."

"Ready and waiting," Mitch piped up from the corner of the desk.

"And I take it we have a break in the case," Adrian said, settling into his office chair.

"We at least have a person of interest," Statler affirmed, "although we are investigating further."

Adrian waited. *Not one of my people. Please, not one of mine.* Yet, who else could've had access to Mitch's station?

"While studying the video surveillance, the lab tech picked up Selena Lacy watching your partner type in his password."

Selena. The name settled like lead in the pit of Adrian's stomach.

"And she was on the system this morning when someone tried to take over your Bright Star session," Statler reminded Adrian.

"I mean, it's so obvious, A," Mitch chimed in. "I remember her getting a little close that day, but she was pumping me about the stats on one of the clients, so I went into the system."

"She doesn't have the skill to take over one of my sessions," Adrian hissed.

Besides, Selena had the same government security clearance as Adrian and all his employees. They had to have it before they were hired, given the sensitive nature of their work for government contractors.

Mitch continued, "My PW is twelve characters, and my fingers fly on the keyboard. She'd have to be a sharp cookie to've seen what I typed and memorize it."

"Could Miss Lacy have the capacity to watch and memorize keystrokes, Mr. Sinclair?" Statler asked.

"She has the memory for numbers and a keen eye. She spied me inverting a number on my speed dial and corrected me. But it was only two numbers, not twelve keystrokes."

"People with eidetic, or photographic, memories can recall up to twenty-five or more numbers in sequence," Statler remarked. "Great asset if they're on your side."

But what motive would Selena have to be against him?

"Mr. Sinclair, is the name Phillipe Durande familiar to you?"

"Phillipe Durande," Mitch repeated when Adrian didn't reply. "Durande Industries . . . high-tech electronics."

Adrian shook himself. "Yes, Durande Industries became one of our clients last winter. Selena—" There it went—that heavy, queasy feeling again. "Selena acquired the account."

"The family fortune was built on arms deals before Phillipe Durande entered the twenty-first century with his high-tech company," Statler explained. "But what makes him interesting are his dealings with a certain member of the Saudi royal family . . . and his recent affair with Selena Lacy."

Adrian was glad he was sitting down. His knees were water. Adrian struggled to keep his voice level, despite the emotional upheaval stemming from the news. "Are you certain of this?" he said into the speakerphone. "*All* of it?"

There was a pause on the other end of the phone that held Adrian between relief and dismay.

"The video is circumstantial. It provides opportunity to retrieve Mr. Knittel's password."

"The only opportunity," Mitch added.

"She was on the system when someone attempted to breach it this morning *and* her connection with Durande is well substantiated," Statler continued. "We have phone calls of a sensitive nature confirming that they were intimate . . ."

Why hadn't Adrian seen this coming? Selena was a sexual creature by nature. His reluctance to satisfy her needs—

"And that someone used Durande to get to Miss Lacy and Alphanet. Which is why we need you to maintain your relationship with Miss Lacy."

"What?" Adrian stared at the speakerphone as if he'd misheard.

Mitch frowned. "What do you mean *maintain*? Selena is a security risk."

"She's hired an interior decorator who looks like a thug stuffed into a pin-striped suit. He checked out, but so did Selena. I suppose you want me to keep him on, as well?" At this point, Adrian wondered if he could trust himself. "He's been taking pictures as though he owns stock in Kodak."

"Our preliminary check on Alfredo Bianco came up clean," the agent replied. "He is a decorator for the House of Scoglio. Interestingly enough, he transferred to DC from the Paris company three months ago."

"Isn't that quaint?" Mitch quipped dryly. "Paris sounds like a regular hotbed for evildoers."

Adrian cut his friend a reprimanding glance, although he couldn't argue. The funds used to frame Mitch, the hacking trail that led to the dead boy, Durande and Selena—it all linked to Paris. It was too much to be coincidental.

His thoughts skidded to a stop and backed up. Would Peter be at risk? Should he send him back to his grandparents to protect him?

Adrian inhaled between his teeth, the hiss just a hint of his building anger. Anger that she might have compromised his friend's future and the business they had struggled to build.

But not anger over any probable infidelity. Not a sense of personal betrayal.

Logic prevailed. His feelings could wait. Had to wait. "What about Selena's financials? Is there anything extraordinary there?"

"Nothing . . . yet," Statler replied. "She's clean on that account."

"So at most, she was videoed staring over Mitch's shoulder—she could have been staring at the monitor, for all we know—and she's been having an affair with one of our clients, who happens to have some suspicious ties." Adrian wrestled to keep his pricked pride suppressed.

"That's why she is a *person of interest*," Statler emphasized over the speakerphone. "Sooner or later, the puppetmaster of this scheme will make a mistake, which is why we want to maintain the status quo. The rest are petty players. And now that we are on to them, we can feed them what we want and see where the trail leads."

"I give up," Adrian said, his glum stare fixed on the silent speakerphone after Statler hung up. "I can't make out any possible motive for Selena to be a part of this."

Mitch plopped into a leather-upholstered side chair. "You know, for all that fancy education you've had, you're still pretty clueless when it comes to women."

Adrian's lips twisted in a smile. "This, from a man whose only lasting relationship has been with a computer?"

"How long have you been engaged?"

"Two years, more or less." Adrian couldn't recall the exact timing.

"You haven't set a date, A," Mitch told him with an air of authority. "She's tired of waiting."

"There's not been time enough for Peter to accept her. I've had to consider that."

Mitch laughed. "That ain't gonna happen, my man. Selena was behind the door when maternal instincts were passed out. She's a huntress, not a nurturer."

Mitch was right. Deep down, Adrian knew it.

"You two are like oil and water. You just don't mix. She's made you something you're not and, if you ask me—which you haven't—you are miserable with the end result."

Adrian knew it without a doubt. He hadn't realized it until he'd met Ellen.

Ellen, who was so like Carol, and yet so different. They had the same big, beautiful heart . . . and faith.

"And that's why Ellen's been tripping your trigger, my man."

Adrian glanced up, startled that Mitch seemed to read his thoughts. But then, when it was all boiled down, he and Mitch were two of a kind.

"You should don a turban and hang a shingle."

Mitch threw back his head, laughing. "Man, I knew it! But you better move fast, because your son might propose before you do. Heck, *I'd* beat you to the punch if she looked at me the way she looked at you."

"Really?"

"I'm starting to dig Harleys," he warned.

This from Mitch, who used his bicycle more than his beat-up SUV.

Adrian ran his fingers through his hair. Ellen . . . Selena . . . He couldn't toss two years of what he'd considered a relationship out the window just yet. If Mitch was right, that Adrian had been at fault, putting Selena on hold, he owed it to her to remain loyal, but cautious.

Even though she had not?

"God, I don't know," he whispered in defeat.

"What?" Mitch asked.

Adrian pulled himself together. God hadn't been much help in his matters of the heart. Then again, he hadn't asked. "Regardless of what my feelings are, you heard Statler. The status quo must be maintained."

"I'm with you, A. You know that."

And for that, Adrian was grateful. "And you realize that you can't go back to work yet. That would tip everyone off that you'd been cleared."

Folding his hands behind his head, Mitch grinned. "That's cool. I can sit back and enjoy the show."

Show. The word played over again in Adrian's mind. He hoped he was a good enough actor to pull it off.

CHAPTER NINETEEN

At the cedar-lined drive leading to the Sinclair home, Ellen stopped her Harley and switched seats with Pete. Three Sundays had passed since she'd been giving the boy a ride to church. Today, he'd asked if he could drive her bike—with her behind him.

He'd come such a long way, both with regard to the motorcycle and in church. At first, Pete had been ill at ease in her Sunday school class, but when he offered to prepare a computerized light show for the junior choir Christmas program, he became the man of the hour.

"I sing rather like a cracked bell," he'd told the group shyly after Ellen had encouraged him to volunteer his talent, "but I have a program that can make the lights dance to your music."

At the moment, lights danced in his eyes as he straddled the leather seat and balanced the bike with his gangly legs.

"Just remember, it's like riding a bicycle, only faster," she shouted above the engine.

Pete licked his lips and gradually released the clutch with his left hand and accelerated with the right. As the bike started forward, it wobbled and he anchored it with both legs, stopping in panic.

"It's going to wobble when you first start, especially if you're timid with the acceleration. Give it a little more gas," Ellen advised.

"What if it runs out from under us?"

She laughed. "Don't worry, I'm backing you up."

This time the takeoff was smoother and in a matter of seconds balance was attained. Pete took his time with Ellen coaching him on the throttle to keep the wobble out of the ride. "If Dad sees me on this, perhaps he'll buy me a dirt bike, eh?" the boy called back.

"You never know."

Between the Brittingham and Sinclair properties, there was plenty of land and back roads for Pete to ride on.

The stop in front of the house was a bit shaky, but Ellen clapped her companion on the back and climbed off. "Way to go, buddy!"

"Land sakes, will you look at this!" Mrs. Duffy shouted from the front door. "Riding a motorbike big as Billy-be-dashed!"

"Where's Dad?" Pete asked, beaming.

"Here," Adrian replied, appearing behind the housekeeper. "I saw you coming up the lane from the dining room table. Well done, son."

"Where's Uncle Mitch?"

"Sleeping in. You wore him out with video games last night."

Pete cut the idling engine and dismounted the bike. "Guess what? I'm in charge of lighting for the Christmas show."

"I'm impressed." Adrian glanced past Pete to Ellen. "How about joining us for coffee? Your mother sent us some mandelbrat."

Who could refuse eyes like that? Although weariness had paled their usual intense blue and engraved circles below them. "Jewish Biscotti? I'm in."

Mrs. Duffy clapped her hands together. "Marvelous!"

Pete tugged his dress shirt out of his slacks as he headed inside. "I'm going to change. I'll be back momentarily."

"You're good for Pete. I can't tell you how grateful I am," Adrian told Ellen, taking her leather jacket and hanging it on a brass coat tree by the door. His hand at her back, he ushered her through the central hall toward the dining room.

"Yeah, well . . ." *Okay, mind, get back here. It's just a polite hand on the back of your sweater.* "Pete's good for me. And Ma and Pop can't wait for school to let out. I haven't seen Pop this energized about tinkering in the garage for years."

"I'm almost jealous," Adrian admitted. "At least someone has time to spend with the boy. A male influence."

"Once this security snafu clears up, you'll have more time."

Something was different about Adrian. As he pulled out a chair at the long polished mahogany table, it dawned on her that he wore ratty sweats, kind of like the ones she slept in—worn out and comfortable. As she slung her bag over the back of the chair, she saw that he wore old deck shoes, no socks.

Sheesh, ratty and disheveled looks good on him, too.

"Here we go. Fresh coffee," Mrs. Duffy announced, bustling into the room with a steaming china coffee pot.

"I apologize for my attire. As delighted as I am to have your company, I'm afraid I didn't dress for it."

He was reading her mind.

"I worked most of the night," he explained. "Couldn't sleep."

"You do look a little fried." Ellen mouthed *Thank you* to Mrs. Duffy for the cup of coffee she poured for her.

"So I've tried to tell him," the housekeeper said with a chiding glance at her employer.

"You know, I'm not shoving the *keep the Sabbath holy* thing at you, but even God needed a day of rest. And science concurs. I read about this study in Japan." Ellen helped herself to a thick sliver of Ma's mandelbrat. "They found that laborers who worked six days a week and rested on the seventh produced as much as those who worked seven days a week. Think about it."

Adrian sighed heavily and dipped the hard cookie bar into his steaming cup of coffee. "I would rest, if my mind would allow it."

"I'll just leave the pot on the table," Mrs. Duffy said, making her exit.

"The security breach thing," Ellen guessed.

"It's more tangled than ever."

"Maybe you need to get away from it. You could take Pete bike-riding on the Boardwalk in OC and hit the arcades."

"Good morning!" Wrapped in a silk kimono, Selena Lacy walked into the room on heeled slippers, adorned with feathery pompoms that fluttered with every movement. Her greeting was intended for Adrian. Her brief, but undeniable glower for Ellen made that clear.

"Good morning, Selena," Ellen replied. "I was just telling Adrian that an outing on the Boardwalk might do him some good. You guys could get one of those bicycles built for two. You know, like in the old *Daisy, Daisy* song?"

Selena took a cup and saucer from the china closet. "Do you mean a *tandem* bike?"

"Yeah, but I kind of prefer 'bicycle built for two.' Gram used to sing that song to me. It's more romantic."

Crap. She sounded like the bumpkin Selena obviously thought she was. A babbling bumpkin, no less. Ellen picked up her coffee under Selena's sharp scrutiny and took a sip, burning her tongue in the process.

"Maybe Ellen's right," Adrian spoke up. "I could use a break. Get outdoors and unwind a bit."

"That *had* been my intention when I chose the area," Selena reminded him. She stopped to give him a hug before taking a seat opposite Ellen.

Ellen couldn't help but note how the woman looked disheveled, yet impeccably so. Like a movie actress who climbs out of bed with one lock of hair out of place and no wrinkles in her nightgown. *Oh, and wearing lipstick,* she thought, looking at its imprint on Selena's coffee cup.

When Ellen got out of bed in the morning, she looked as if rats had nested in her hair. And if she'd worn make-up for a special occasion, raccoon eyes stared back at her in the mirror. How did women like Selena pull this off?

"So would you like to join us?" Adrian asked.

"*Us?*" If Selena arched her brows any further, they'd join her hairline.

Ellen didn't want to be the one responsible for driving them there. She wolfed down a small bite of the hard-baked delicacy. The sooner she was out of here the better. All was not well on the home front.

"Pete and me," Adrian explained with a strained smile.

Selena's stiff shoulders relaxed. "Of course, darling. Although I'd hoped to go to Seacrets, sip a pina colada, listen to the music, and pretend we're in the islands."

"Pete would love Seacrets," Ellen agreed. "It's like a pirate's hideaway. Families go there through the dinner hour."

From the look Selena slanted Ellen's way, that was not what she'd had in mind. Ellen shoved the remainder of the cookie to the bottom of her cup.

"Seacrets?" Pete echoed as he entered the room, changed into jeans and a sweater. "I'd love to go there!"

"Then we'll do both," Adrian decided. "I'll tell Mrs. Duffy not to plan on dinner. Would you care to join us, Ellen? It is, after all, your idea."

Fingers halfway to her mouth and dripping with luke-warm coffee, Ellen shook her head. "No, thanks. I have to help Ma at the produce market."

"Ellen . . ." Selena flicked a manicured finger toward Ellen's shirt, drawing her attention to where she'd dribbled coffee down its front along with crumbs.

"Hey, I look good in anything I eat, don't you think?" *Meanwhile, I'll just crawl out of here and slink home.*

"Look what I found," Pete said, pulling up the sleeve of his sweater to reveal what looked like hightech watch. "It was in a box on my bed."

Selena smiled. "I bought it for you in London, darling. Since *someone* tends to wander off without telling anyone where he's going."

"It has a GPS locator," Adrian told the boy. "As well as some games," he added, seeing Pete's brow furrow.

"Oh," he said, still uncertain.

"Go get the manual, and we'll set it up," Adrian said.

Pete hesitated. "So if I put it in my bedroom, you'll think I'm there?"

"Actually there's a lock on it," Selena explained, "so, no tricks allowed."

"Hah," Ellen chuckled as she rose from the table, "Ma needs one of those for Pop. He has a cell phone, but can't remember to turn it on, much less call." She turned to Adrian. "Thanks for the coffee. I'll be seeing you all . . ." She paused to think. "At your party this weekend, if not before. Enjoy your day."

As Adrian started to rise, Ellen motioned him back down. "Stay put. I know my way out."

"Peter, aren't you forgetting something?" she heard Selena ask as she reached the front door.

"Oh, yes, thanks. I'll go get the manual."

Ellen heard Pete thundering up the stairs again as she stepped off the porch.

As she straddled her bike, her smile faded upon glancing down at the coffee stains Selena had pointed out. Women like Selena could fall into a vat of Ma's marinara sauce and come up clean. All Ellen had to do was walk into the kitchen, and she was spotted with the stuff. Things like that didn't used to bother Ellen. They were a source of self-deprecating humor that rolled off her back. The bleak fact was, that while God loved her, stains and all, a guy like Adrian preferred the spotless Barbie-type.

Engine started, Ellen shifted the bike into gear and eased up on the clutch for a smooth take off.

God, I know I'm supposed to love my neighbor, but do I have to like her?

CHAPTER TWENTY

"I keep asking God if it's okay not to like her," Ellen complained to her buddies the following week at Sue Ann's home.

Sue Ann and Alex had driven to Salisbury to rent costumes for Adrian's party.

"She looks like a snob," Jan said. "At least from what I saw of her at the Rotary meeting. When Sue Ann introduced Scott and me, she shook our hands, but acted like she wanted to wash hers the moment we let go." She glanced at the garments laid over the back of Sue Ann's burgundy brocade sectional sofa. "Okay, what did you get me? And please," she said, clasping her hands in prayerful pose, "tell me it's not a Tinkerbell costume."

Alex and Sue Ann struck the look of kids caught with hands in the cookie jar.

Jan groaned. "I can't help it if I'm small. Come on guys, please tell me I'm not Tinkerbell."

Alex broke first with a grin. "No, you are not a fairy this year. You are an elf."

Jan rolled her eyes. "Gee, thanks."

"An elfin princess or something," Sue Ann said, taking up one of the packages. "From *Lord of the Rings*. I forget her name."

"Galadriel," Ellen put in. "Lady of the Wood."

Jan's eyes widened as Sue Ann unveiled a white robe of shimmering material. "It's beautiful."

Jan slipped the garment on. "It's a little long," she admitted ruefully.

"Oh, sugar, we can staple it up just for one night."

Not one of them was a seamstress. Staples and duct tape had been used in many a pinch during their high school days.

"What about me?" Ellen asked. "What did you find for me? I could be Legolas . . . or a female version of him. I have the bow and quiver."

"Who?" Alex asked.

"The elf archer in the *Lord of the Rings* books. I'm tall and thin . . . even have the props."

Ignoring her, Sue Ann revealed the contents of another bag. "Alex is going medieval, with Josh as her gallant protector, and I am a Greek goddess."

Jan looked up from hanging up her robe. "So what's Martin? Zeus?"

Sue Ann smiled, fox-like. "The big rascal himself. Martin always did have good legs."

"What am I?" Ellen insisted.

"I hope Scott picks a costume that goes with mine," Jan said. "I think I'll call him and let him know what I'm wearing." She dug into her purse for her cell phone.

"And last but not least, *voilà*!" Alex pulled the plastic bag off the last garment.

It was pink. Ellen didn't do pink. And she certainly didn't do ballerina. "You're kidding, right?"

"Look, sugar, it was this or Bat Woman," Sue Ann told her. "That was all they had in your size and no woman needs to be stuffed into spandex."

"Aw, man," Ellen groaned. "I'll just wear my gi. I can be the Karate Kid."

"Ellen, do something different for a change," Alex pleaded. "Try something feminine."

"And karate pajamas are not feminine," Jan pointed out.

"I'll wear a pink belt." Ellen could remember the dance classes she hated. And those painful recitals. "Did you two take Ma with you to pick this out?"

"On my honor," Sue Ann pledged.

Alex brushed the gathered tulle, shaking loose glitter that had been glued to it. "At least it's a mid-length skirt. And you've got the height to carry it."

"Besides, you'll knock Adrian's eyes out in this. Trust me."

"I'll knock everyone's eyes out if I waltz in, wearing that getup." Besides, no way would Ellen trust that twinkle in Sue Ann's gaze. The costume was pretty; it just wasn't her. She pushed in the top of the bodice with her finger and watched as it popped back out. "Sheesh, bodice by Rubbermaid. No way can I fill that thing out."

"Sugar," Sue Ann chuckled, "my grammy always said, what the Lord's forgotten, you can pad with cotton."

"Just try it on," Alex insisted. "Have we ever steered you wrong?"

They had Ellen there. Her friends always had her best interest at heart. "Do I have a name or am I a generic ballerina?"

"Swan Princess." Alex showed her the label to confirm it.

"I guess I should be grateful I'm not wearing feathers," Ellen quipped. "The last time I wore something like this, I looked like a klutz in a tutu."

"Sugar, we all looked like flat-chested, skinny-legged little klutzes in Miss Patty's dance recital."

"And you're a woman now, Ellen. Tall and graceful on that bike of yours," Jan told her dreamily. "I think you'll be beautiful—more beautiful than you can imagine."

But then Jan saw beauty in everyone.

"You always dress plain," Jan reminded her. "You need to accentuate the positive."

Ellen shot the petite woman a skeptical look. "Someone's been listening to Ma's records." She loved the song. "But that oldie also warns not to mess with Mr. In-Between."

Still, if she could look as beautiful as her friends thought she might . . . "And what good will it do to get all dolled up? Adrian is all but hitched."

Her three friends shared a quick, knowing glance as she

bit her tongue to keep from spilling any more beans. What was the matter with her? The way she was acting, you'd think her only goal in life was to impress Adrian. . . .

"Well, you should have seen the way he and Selena were arguing in the Food Mart the other day," Jan said. "I think he was embarrassed when he recognized me behind the bakery counter."

And he looked horrible Sunday morning. At least as horrible as gorgeous *could* look. Ellen wondered how the day had gone. Had Selena gone with them or had she developed another convenient headache? The way she manipulated Adrian, it was no wonder he looked so haggard. In fact, he hadn't seemed really happy with her since Ellen had known the two. And Pete was no fan, for sure.

"How about the way he looked at Ellen at the Rotary meeting." Sue Ann heaved a big sigh. "If you ask me, someone has turned that man's head, and it isn't Miss Lacy."

Sheesh, to listen to her buddies, it was almost worth a shot. Trying to impress Adrian. Trying to—

"Okay, I'll try it on," she said, taking it from Sue Ann. She had to be nuts. "But I'm telling you now, I'm gonna float in that built-in bodice."

Saturday evening, Ellen arrived in her coach—the backseat of Ma's and Pop's sedan. The tulle of her knee-length skirt itched and the stays in the strapless bodice gave it a life of its own when she moved to scratch. A pair of her low cut sports socks helped her fill out the top, lest she inadvertently depress the hard foam cup and walk about with a concave bosom. The low heels of the jeweled satin slippers that her mother had picked up for her—no way was Ellen wearing ballet slippers again in this lifetime—clicked on the paved walk, lined with ghoulish luminaries.

"Doesn't she look just like a princess?" Ma gushed as they walked along a string of parked cars that affirmed what Ellen already knew. They were late.

It took Ma, usually a stickler for punctuality, three times to get hers, and Pop's Raggedy Ann and Andy make-up just right. More amazingly, Pop let her apply it three times.

"Even got the crown," he agreed.

Ellen's crown was Sue Ann's touch—a tiara she'd won as the Watermelon Queen too many years ago to count. Between the three of them, they looked like a toy box had come to life.

"That fancy decorator spared no effort, that's for sure," Ma observed, looking at the façade of the house.

Orange-flamed electric candles flickered in all the windows, which highlighted black silhouettes of cats, rats, and even grotesquely twisted or hunched human figures looking in anticipation down on the approaching guests. Giant, elaborately carved pumpkins purchased at the Brittingham produce stand stood lit and on guard at either side of the front door. Scarecrows hung on the porch columns and at the far ends, bathed in eerie light, human-bodied ghosts fluttered in the night breeze.

"Bet he's got mannequins under that wavin' silk," Pop observed. "Gave my neck a tickle."

Ellen's heart beat like the deer's that panted for water in one of the Psalms as she stood at the front door, and it had nothing to do with the elaborate decorations or the hideous electronic laugh of the doorbell. She'd let her friends—and Ma—talk her into making a fool of herself.

Pete, wearing a pirate costume and a mile-wide grin, met them at the door. "Welcome to the Sinclair House of Horrors." He rolled his *r*'s in Draculesque style, but added a piratical "me hearties."

"Look at the big man, will you!" Ma exclaimed, stepping inside. "Don't tell me that's a real sword."

"It's hollow aluminum." Pete cut a wide swash in front of them. "It makes a great noise when I hit something . . . which I'm not allowed to do inside."

Ma gave him a hug, causing his eye patch to shift. "Well, I hope you can protect helpless Raggedy Ann and Andy from the bad guys," she said, straightening it.

"Trust me," Pete replied, "as silly as you look in those costumes, nobody will bother you."

Ellen joined in the resulting laughter. The kid was a trip.

"Wow, you look like a girl," Pete said in wonder as she handed him her cape. "*You* might need my protection." He fixed his gaze on her tiara. "Are they diamonds?"

"Fake diamonds," she confessed, her heart growing a little lighter over his unadulterated admiration. "Nothing worth protecting, I'm afraid." Then again, she'd always been a hit with kids. It didn't mean—

"Welcome. I was beginning to think something had delayed you." Adrian stood in the wide entrance, looking as if he'd stepped out of a Disney movie in a princely cropped uniform jacket, sash, and dark pants. Stepping forward, he gave her mother a kiss on the cheek and shook hands with Pop. "There is food in the dining room . . . some of your recipes, I suspect," he told her mother.

Ellen caught a glance of herself in the hall mirror, the tiara crowning the thick mass of hair her mother had pulled back in a ponytail and curled into spirals. Ellen couldn't recall the last time she'd used a curling iron on her straight clip-and-go hair.

"And look at you."

"I am," she quipped, despite the sudden dryness in her throat, playfully primping in the mirror. She flipped a soft layer of curls off her shoulder. "Boy, that spray stuff really holds, huh?" She licked her lips. She couldn't help it. She felt like they were shriveling and cracking under Adrian's dark blue scrutiny.

"You are . . ." He searched for the word.

Not a good sign.

"Stunning," he said. "Positively stunning."

Ellen swayed in his enveloping gaze. Was this what it felt like to be beautiful? She cleared her throat of a giggle that bubbled up out of nowhere. She'd never understood giggly, airheaded types, and now, she was one.

"Yeah, well, no wishy-washy stunning for this girl, ya know. It's positively stunning, or not at all." At this foot-in-mouth rate, she was going to break her teeth on her slippers' fake jewels.

With a slight bow, Adrian took her hand and lifted it to his lips. Ellen fought to keep her feet from lifting off as he brushed her knuckles gently.

Had she washed her hands since petting Marley? If he smelled dog instead of magnolia body wash, she'd die.

"Well, look at you," Sue Ann exclaimed invading the fairy-tale moment. "Sugar, you look beautiful. I told you that dress was made for you. Don't you think so, Martin?"

Beautiful, stunning, or even positively stunning, Ellen knew she had no business being alone with Adrian in this fairytale. Much as she hated to leave it, she did, withdrawing her hand from his.

"You do look great, Ellen," Sue Ann's husband agreed. Martin slipped his arm about Ellen's waist and gave her a squeeze. "I don't think I've seen you in a dress since our senior prom."

Ellen had gone with Tony Richardson, friends only. "It's not been *that* long, Martin," she managed.

"I'm going to mark this day on my calendar," Josh Turner said, entering the foyer, clad in an Elizabethan match to Alex's exquisite brocade gown. "Now I know why you're late. It took your mom that long to wrestle you into that tutu."

"And I'm going to mark mine." Ellen pretended to write on the air. "Josh Turner wore pantyhose and lace."

"Adrian, darling, I've been looking everywhere for you." Selena Lacy emerged from the dining room, looking like Venus De Milo with all her limbs intact. "I have someone I'd like you to meet." Upswept golden hair glittering in the hall light, Selena beckoned him to her with a playful crook of her finger.

"Don't run off, Ellen. I want to introduce you to my parents. They flew into Salisbury this afternoon." Excusing himself, Adrian joined Selena.

Selena slipped a possessive arm through his and gave Ellen a cat-like smile. "Hello, Ellen. Love the ballerina look." Her demeanor said otherwise.

"Why that—*ow*!" Sue Ann exclaimed. She turned, glaring at Alex. "Do you know how much these shoes cost?"

Ellen's heart slammed back to earth with a jar. What *was* she thinking? Or was that the problem? She'd given into her feelings instead of heeding logic. Silky, sexy Venus or the Swan Fairy with an itchy skirt and stuffed bosom? Ellen gave herself a mental smack. That was a no-brainer.

"Hey, Ellen!" Pete and Kevin McIntyre, one of Ellen's Sunday school students stood at the top of the steps. "Want to come see my video games?"

Turning to her friends, she shrugged. "What can I say? My main man beckons. I'll be back in a jiff."

As she started up the stairs, tulle shaking sparkles in her wake, she heard Sue Ann's sawmill whisper. "Sugar, you're worth a thousand of her," Sue Ann insisted, as Josh and Alex ushered her toward the living room.

"You're biased," Ellen said, "but I love you anyway."

And Ellen did. She cherished each one of her buddies. Bolstered, she took the remaining steps two at a time. Give her friendship and loyalty over beauty any day of the week.

CHAPTER TWENTY-ONE

"Duff, have you seen Ellen?" His parents at his heel, Adrian stepped into the kitchen where Mrs. Duffy sat with Bea, sampling some of the catered appetizers. Margaret and Harrington Sinclair had arrived that morning with hugs for Adrian and Selena and a new X-Box 360 for Pete.

"Look for a group of guys talking cars or bikes," Bea suggested. "My princess will be right in the middle. Mrs. Sinclair, what do you think of these crab balls?"

Adrian's mother walked over to the table with a royal bearing that would show, even if she wore slacks instead of a silver gown. Then again, she entertained and had been entertained by heads of state in over a dozen countries during her husband's career.

"I told you to call me Maggie, Bea," she said, the brogue of her Scottish roots soft upon her tongue. "Are these your recipe?"

"Oy, no. My recipe calls for more crab and less filling."

"The Crab Dip is Bea's recipe," Mrs. Duffy said.

Harry Sinclair chuckled, the slight paunch he'd put on since retirement jiggling in the process. "It was so good, I nearly burnt the roof of my mouth when the staff put out a fresh dish."

"Backfin Maryland Blue Crab and old-fashioned sharp cheddar," Bea confided, "the kind you buy from a wheel at the farmers market, not those processed for the grocery stores."

"Then you must tell us where this market is. I love a good cheese."

Maggie rolled her eyes. "There goes his cholesterol. Mine, too," she confessed.

"Your husband was telling me about the hunting in these parts, Bea," Harry said. "He promised to take me next week. Why don't you join us, Adrian?"

Adrian shook his head. "Too busy, Father. Wish I could." Selena could learn a thing or two from his mother and father's ability to appreciate down to earth, as well as aristocratic sophistication.

"Ellen bagged her first deer when she was seven," Bea bragged. "A five-point buck, no less. With a bow and arrow."

"I can't wait to meet your Ellen. Adrian has told us so much about her," Maggie said.

The phone on the kitchen wall rang.

"I'll get it," Adrian said, as Mrs. Duffy started to rise to answer it. He picked up the receiver. "Hello, Sinclair residence. Adrian speaking."

"Maybe she's with Peter. He simply adores her," the housekeeper added for his parents' benefit. "I'll be they're playing that new game you brought."

"That's our princess."

Rick Statler's voice sounded in Adrian's ear over Bea's wry laugh. "Adrian, our techs just reported that someone has hung a sheet over our video camera on your office door and the camera inside focused on your computer and safe is picking up weird lights."

Adrian tensed. He'd moved some of Alfredo's decorations specifically to avoid obscuring the cameras. Of course, it could be an accident. Except for the lights.

"I'll check it out. Thank you."

"Our man has gone in, just in case," Statler advised him as he started to hang up.

"Trouble, dear?" Maggie Sinclair asked.

"No, no. Just something I forgot to take care of. You two stay on and chat. I'll be back shortly."

"I'll go with you," his father insisted.

"Fine." It was assuring to have his father in his corner.

By the time Adrian reached the door, the agent Statler had assigned to monitor the premises was waiting. With his red hair slicked back and Argyle sweater, he could have stepped off the cover of an old *Archie* comic.

"Nice costume, Jenkins."

"Not a costume, sir." He didn't have Archie's personality. "Maybe the little ghost slipped," he said, nodding to a lighted string of equidistant ghosts and witches. All but one, that is.

One had been moved out of order and covered the camera.

Selena? Adrian's stomach clutched. He hoped not. For all his disappointment in her of late, he hoped not.

"Ready?" he asked.

The agent nodded, patting a slight bulge in his sweater.

Trying to act nonchalant, Adrian punched in the key code, shielding his hand with his body. When the green light showed on the entry pad, he opened the latch.

The only illumination in the room came from the orange candle in the window and the large flat screen television mounted over a bookcase, an admitted indulgence on Adrian's part, since he spent so much time in his office. Electronic sounds echoed the flashes of light and color that bounced off the walls. Seated cross-legged on the leather sofa opposite the TV were a pint-sized soldier and a ballerina, each manning a console while a pirate looked on.

"Hi, Dad . . . Grandfather," Peter said as Adrian flicked on the light switch. "You don't mind if we use your TV for my new X-Box 360, do you? It's so much bigger than mine." The boy blinked with conjured innocence.

"Peter, how did you get in here?" Adrian demanded as the others entered the room, Agent Jenkins closing the door behind them.

Ellen turned off the X-Box 360, her long pink-clad legs appearing from under a mound of tulle as she rose to her feet. "Holy cow, are we in trouble?" she asked, glancing from Jenkins to Adrian's father and then to Adrian. "Pete assured me he'd asked you."

"Yeah," the McIntyre boy agreed.

"Funny," Adrian said to his son. "I don't recall having been asked if anyone could use my *secure* office for fun and games. Any more than I recall having shared the entrance code with anyone." An alarm should have sounded.

Unless the code was entered without flaw.

"I've watched you open it a kadzillion times, Dad."

The more he learned about Peter, the more amazed Adrian was at the boy's brilliance.

"Condescension under the circumstances does not help your situation, Peter," Harry Sinclair warned. Although Adrian could tell from the twitch at the corner of his father's lips that the former diplomat's poker face was worthless with his grandson.

"Pete." Ellen gave the boy a disappointed look.

Pete hung his head. "Sorry, Grandfather . . . Ellen . . . dad."

"And I suppose you moved the little ghost over the video monitor as well?"

The boy could easily reach it from the staircase. Strange as it was, Adrian didn't know whether to be angry or proud.

"I didn't think it was such a big deal," Pete replied defensively. "We didn't go near your computer. I know better than that."

Adrian chose relieved. Relieved that it wasn't Selena. Just two kids and one startled, remorseful ballerina.

Face fallen, Peter heaved a sigh. "I'll disconnect it. Come on, Kevin."

As the boys began unhooking cables, Harry offered his hand to Ellen. "And you must be Ellen. I'm Harry Sinclair, Adrian's father."

Her face a bolder shade of pink than her dress, Ellen shook his hand with a self-conscious glance at Adrian. "Please to meet you, sir. Although not under these circumstances. The kid set me up."

She was priceless, Adrian thought. Utterly priceless.

"I hear you're a skilled hunter."

"I usually bag my quota . . . when I have time to hunt, that is."

Who else could pull off ballerina and deer hunting in the same breath?

"Your father's taking me next week. Perhaps you'd join us?"

"I'd love to, but one of us has to hold down the fort at the business. But that'd be great for Pop."

"If I'm not needed here," Jenkins interrupted, "I'm going back to my post, sir." His *post* was actually a small room over the garage, a temporary setup to monitor the party.

"Fine, thank you for your diligence, Jenkins." While Adrian acknowledged the agent, his gaze was only for Ellen. "I'll have to think of some kind of penance suited to the deed. Breaking and entering. Contributing to the delinquency of a ballerina."

A grin lighted on Ellen's lips. "I figured when he knew the code, it was okay."

Reaching over, Adrian straightened her crown. He couldn't help himself. He had to touch her, to assure her in some way that all was well. "No harm done, priceless."

At Ellen's raised brow, he realized what he'd said. "I meant princess, of course." He hooked his arm in hers. "Although one might say that both apply in your case." Adrian felt his neck grow warmer beneath the collar of his shirt. "Have you gotten everything, boys?"

With a nod, Pete gathered up the gaming system, while Kevin carried the rest of its paraphernalia. "I think I'd like a big screen television in my room for Christmas. The action is so much better."

Harry steered the boys out of the room ahead of Adrian and Ellen. "I don't think now is the best time to be putting in a holiday request," he advised his grandson. "How about showing me how this thing works?"

Instead of following, Adrian lingered as the door drifted partially shut behind the three. "I'd like you to meet my mother as well. The last I saw her, she was in the kitchen with Duff and your mother."

Ellen smacked her forehead. "We'd better go to her rescue. In case you hadn't noticed, Ma thinks she's the incarnation of an old Jewish matchmaker. I can't get it through her head that we're just friends. That you are engaged."

"Neither can I, at times." He shouldn't have put his hands on Ellen's shoulders, but they'd developed a mind of their own. It seemed right. Her, here in his inner sanctum. Although the tulle crunching between them was a bit off.

Her lips parted, her so alive eyes widening in surprise. He was going to kiss her. Every voice in his head, every beat of his heart demanded it. He lowered his mouth to hers—

"Well, isn't this cozy?" Selena's voice drove a barbed wedge between them.

Ellen recoiled, leaving Adrian still caught in the spell. Except that he couldn't be. Shouldn't be. Had no right to be.

"I think I'll go rescue your mom from mine."

Selena blocked Ellen's way. "You've been after him from the first day you planted your little claws in him. Playing up to Peter." Sparks flashed in her dark gaze. "And you . . . I'd thought you better than this, Adrian Sinclair."

"Now, you hold on, Selena." Ellen fisted her hands at her side. "I don't play up to anyone. Pete is a great kid. I like him . . . and I've tried to get him to like you, but you haven't exactly made it easy, with your airs."

"Airs?" Selena stepped inside, closing the door behind her. "It's *sophistication* Daisy Mae. Not that you'd know it if it bit you in that ridiculous tutu."

A ballerina squared off in a fisted martial arts stance against Venus the Valkyrie might have been hilarious in any other circumstance. In this one, it had to be stopped.

"This is my fault," Adrian said, stepping between the two. "I apologize to both of you."

Ellen pushed him aside. "I know the difference between sophistication and delusions of grandeur," she said to Selena, "and you've got a bad case of the latter. It's driving a wedge between you and everything you want. You're surrounded by good people, and you set yourself apart from them. You gotta stop measuring people in carats and look at their hearts. That's who they are."

"And I suppose those are fists full of heart that you're holding there. What are you going to do, punch me out?"

"Selena!" Adrian pulled her to him. "Just let this go. We'll discuss it later."

"No, it's prayer," Ellen answered her. "*Hard* prayer." Her voice cracked. "Prayer that you'll see what you have and won't throw it all away. Prayer that you'll believe me when I say I'm truly sorry for any part I've had in all this. You won't see me here again."

Panic stabbed at Adrian's chest. "Ellen, this is none of your do—"

"Work it out, Adrian," she said, cutting him off. Turning back to Selena, she lifted a warning finger. "But I'm telling you now, Selena, Pete is a part of Adrian. If you want the man, his son is part of the package. A great part of the package. And Pete needs a mom who will love him and support him. Don't hurt him."

Selena crossed her arms, lifting her chin in defiance. "Or what?"

Adrian seized her arm, the roughness shaking what had been haughtiness into astonishment. "Or you'll deal with me. Peter comes first . . . always. Ahead of the business, ahead of you."

It hadn't been that way, but that was the way it had become. Adrian fought to bring the reckoning sweeping through him under control. He'd been within a breath of telling Selena to pack her bags. But he couldn't. Not yet. The blasted investigation—

"What is *that*?" Selena pointed to something lying on the carpet.

Adrian reached down and retrieved it. "One of the boys must have lost a sock."

"That's a woman's sport sock," Selena informed him, no less bewildered than he.

"Aw, give me that thing." Ellen snatched it from his hand. "It's mine. You two deal with this. Me, my sock, and I are headed home before I die of an overdose of humiliation."

"Ellen, I'm sorry," Adrian called after her.

"Yeah," she called over her shoulder as she slipped through the door. "Me, too."

Adrian stared at the closed door, torn between running after his wounded ballerina and not wanting to make a further scene. Between telling Ellen what was in his heart and letting Selena know exactly what was on his mind.

"My God," Selena whispered from outside his confusion. "You really *do* care for that Harley-riding, little redneck."

CHAPTER TWENTY-TWO

Ellen's phone rang as she stepped inside the sliding glass door to the salon of her houseboat. She read the caller ID. It was Alex. Great, now everyone at the party knew how she'd been humiliated. She didn't want to answer it. She didn't want to talk to anyone about what she was feeling now, not even her closest friends.

But she picked it up. "Hey, Ally, what's up?"

"Where are you? Suzie and I were looking for you, and your mother said you'd gone home."

"Headache." It was true. Her head was hurting, almost as much as her heart and ego. She kicked off her fancy slippers, now soiled from the walk across the evening damp field. "Beside, that kind of soiree isn't my thing. Too fancy to my taste."

Alex lowered her voice, as though other ears might be

listening. "Are you okay? I mean, *really* okay? Because you don't sound like it."

The emotion welling inside Ellen threatened to explode, either in anger or tears—or both. "No, I'm not," she blurted out around the blade wedged in her throat. "I should never have worn this stupid tutu rig with the artificial bosom. Adrian almost kissed me, Selena walked in on us, and I lost one of my socks . . . and I don't need to tell you from where. I have been—what goes beyond humiliation?"

"Oh, Brit." The sympathy in her friend's voice reached across the phone line, but it wasn't enough to stop the hurt. "Suzie and I will be right over."

"No, don't," Ellen shouted. "*Please, Ally,*" she added in a softer tone. "I just want to be alone. Lick my wounds . . . talk to God. If He's still listening."

"You know He is. He always is. And so would we . . ." Alex paused. "But I understand. As much as I loved the company of you all, when my heart hurt the most, God was the one to turn to. Only He could help me change my heart."

"I hear ya." Between the guilt, hurt, and disillusionment, hers had had a blowout and needed a major change. No emotions allowed this time. Only reason.

"Promise me that you'll call me—no matter what time— if you want to talk."

"You got it."

"And that I'll see you in church tomorrow."

"You got that, too. My group's serving the after-service

luncheon," Ellen reminded Alex. Otherwise, she might have had second thoughts, as tired as she was.

"You're in my prayers," Alex whispered softly. "Bye."

Prayers. A hint of a smile played upon Ellen's staggered heart to know that someone loved her and prayed for her, even when she didn't want to see or talk to them. But that was how her buddies were. All for one and one for all. Just picturing her friends was a comfort. Imagining what they'd say. But for now, she needed the shoulder of her best friend of all.

She plopped down on the dinette and buried her face in her arm. "Jesus, what'll I do now?"

Adrian sat in his office in the still of the night, too exhausted to sleep. The guests were gone, oblivious to the drama that had ensued. As far as he could tell. Fingers woven in his hair, he hunched over his desk, trying to make heads or tails out of his thoughts. All that was really clear was that he'd bungled the situation with Selena and Ellen. The investigation, as well.

As much as he'd wanted to follow Ellen, he'd remained behind with Selena. Selena, who'd crumbled into tears, eroding away his ire in the flood tide after the door shut on the last guests.

"You've never loved me, have you, Adrian?" she'd accused.

Adrian fetched her a handful of tissues, trying to muster an answer beyond the painfully obvious. "I loved you for all that you've done for me, for the business. I wouldn't be where I am today without you." Except that that hadn't been enough. He realized that now.

Maintain, Statler had said. Adrian was trying.

She laughed without humor and walked up to him. "Silly Adrian. Brilliant as you are, you don't know the difference between love and gratitude, do you?" She heaved a sigh. "I'd hoped to build on your gratitude. Maybe Ellen is right." Pain razed her voice. "*Delusions* of grandeur . . . or more so, of hope."

Adrian folded the tissues in her hand. "I'd like this to work, Selena." He might as well have said *I'd like an order of toast* for all the heart in it. But then, his had been carried out in Ellen's hands.

"Two years, I've hoped I could make you forget Carol. But you wouldn't let me. You and that blasted puritanical nobility of yours." She blew her nose. "I loved *and* hated you for it. In all my experience, I'd never met anyone quite like you."

If Selena were trying to make him feel guilty, she was succeeding.

"I give up," Selena told him. "I should have quit when you continually refused to set a date. I should have seen it was never going to happen."

Adrian caught her by the shoulders. "Selena—"

"I lost heart long ago, Adrian. Now I've lost the will, as well. You'll have my resignation Monday morning."

Maintain. "There's no need to act hastily, Selena," Adrian protested. Although who could blame her? "Besides, where will you go?"

"With Phillipe Durande. He has a better offer on the table than you."

Durande. What if she was being used? Conflict clawing at his chest, Adrian pulled her to him, brushed the top of her head with his lips. "At least stay on the job until you've had a chance to calm down. To think this through. I was a cad. . ." He stopped at that. He couldn't assure the woman in his arms that he cared as she wanted.

"I should have done this long ago, darling." Selena drew away and tugged at the large diamond on her ring finger. "I'll stay till everyone has retired for the evening," she said with forced brightness, "and then drive to Salisbury. I should have no problem getting a room near the airport."

She held out the expensive ring to him. When he refused to take it, she tossed it on the desk.

"Fine, then. I'll drive you."

"You will not." Her brave façade cracked with emotion. "Don't make it any harder on me than you already have."

Adrian shook the memory from his head and dropped the ring into his desk drawer. He *wanted* to talk to Ellen. He ought to call Statler, though. Adrian glanced at the clock. Three A.M. But Jenkins had already been told the short version of what happened. That Selena had broken their engagement and quit. The how and why that had not taken place in range of the video surveillance was none of his business. And Ellen would have been in bed for hours.

How was he going to explain himself to her, apologize, declare feelings he feared to trust? Oh, but they felt real.

A knock sounded softly on the office door. "Adrian? Are you in there?"

His mother.

Adrian got up and opened the door. "What are you doing up at this hour?"

He'd explained to the household after the guests left that he and Selena had had a tiff, that the engagement was off. He'd had to say something after the dramatic exit she'd made before the lot of them. The gravity of the situation hadn't been helped by the high-five that Mitch and Pete exchanged or the joyous clasp of Mrs. Duffy's hands. His parents had been diplomatically sympathetic.

"I was going to ask the same." His mother had a knack for turning his questions on him. It was a gift, given her husband's line of work. "Is national security at risk, or will you join me for a cup of tea?"

He was nearly forty years of age, and still, the love and warmth in his mother's eyes had the ability to lighten his burdens. Much like Ellen's. Was there love in those beautiful hazel-brown eyes, as well? The kind Adrian longed for?

"So how long have you been in love with Ellen Brittingham?" his mother asked after preparing two cups of tea in the kitchen.

Adrian sat back in his chair, blindsided. "Is it that obvious?"

"Every time you mentioned her name, which has been repeatedly since you met Harry and me at the airport . . . well, I've never seen you so animated. At least not since Carol."

"Carol." Thinking of his late wife didn't hurt as it had before. Instead of sharp pain, there was sweet melancholy.

He could almost see her smiling from some ethereal plane. As though encouraging him to move on.

"I wish I'd had the chance to meet her." At Adrian's puzzled look, his mother explained. "Ellen. She must be very special. Although I must warn you, Peter has intentions where she's concerned. He plans to marry her when he graduates from college and can support her."

Adrian laughed. The invisible vise that had bound his chest since Ellen had left gave way. "Then I'll have to move quickly." Like tonight? He dismissed the idea. At least one of them would get some sleep.

"Something tells me Peter will gladly accept the young woman as mother . . . not to mention her parents as grand-parents. Bea practically glowed when she spoke of our laddie. What a delightful character. Very real, down to earth."

Adrian stared at his untouched tea, but it was his ungrace-ful ballerina that consumed his thoughts. What could he say to her? How could he explain why he didn't go after her and kiss away the tears that glazed her eyes? How much could he tell her about Selena without breaching security?

"I always thought you'd settled when you asked Selena to marry you. Prayed to God you'd come to your senses."

So much for prayer. "Selena helped make me what I am."

"Ah, yes, the *big* business. The urbane socialite. Hasn't made you happy, has it?"

"It's grown into a monster. Like a tiger by the tail, I can't let it go."

"Don't be absurd, darling. Of course you can. With God and love, all things are possible."

Ellen's words that night on her houseboat echoed in his mind. *Just goes to show you. All things are possible.*

Adrian recalled his skeptical reaction. His envy of her change of career in midlife, her enthusiam to make that change. No reservations, no haunting fear of the unknown or failure. Nothing but confidence and joy . . . enabled by a deep abiding faith.

"Darling, God understood your anger at Him after Carol's loss. Still, He's been with you all along." His mother reached across and placed her hand upon his arm. "He's been clearing the way when you couldn't . . . or wouldn't."

Adrian took a sip of his tea. "So you think this is God's handiwork, eh?" A long-starved part of him wanted to believe it.

She pressed her hand to the smocked yoke of her robe. "It's the answer to a mother's prayer for her son . . . and grandson. The change in Peter is nothing short of miraculous." She rose from her chair and took her teacup to the sink. "Don't take my word for it." She returned and hugged his shoulders. "Ponder upon it," she said, bending over and pressing a kiss to his cheek. "True love is *God's* love. That's the measuring stick."

True love is God's love.

Adrian knew what Scripture said about God's love. His mother had seen to that. It was unconditional. No holds barred. He'd become flesh, submitted Himself to human torture and temptation, and died because He loved us so much. Adrian had heard the story time and again.

But this time, a tingle of awareness began to seep into Adrian's consciousness. It called every sense to attention, to an almost burning, totally undeniable knowledge. Its fire meshed Adrian's estranged spirit and mind as one for the first time since Carol died. With a new vision, Adrian realized he was not alone. Had never been. Someone had been with him who had felt the torture and frustration of such a love. A love where His words, like Adrian's prayers for Carol, were not enough. They'd been cut short, not by death of a loved one, but by disbelief and ridicule that led to His own death. Nothing He'd said had saved his love—those He'd died for. Death itself had been the key. Death and rebirth.

Adrian knew what he had to do. He had to let his past and present die, so that he might live again. Anew. No longer bitter and lost.

"God!" A thousand words in one, the prayer of repentance, the plea for God's forgiveness and peace for a troubled soul tore from Adrian's chest, leaving it to bleed. And bleed it did, until every heartache, past and present, every emotion he possessed had left him.

Time passed beyond him. Collapsed, head on folded arms at the kitchen table, Adrian became dead. Dead to feeling. Dead to his surroundings. Dead to all but this enveloping Spirit, Who slowly began to breathe life into him . . . new life.

At long last, hope, joy, and peace were his for the taking.

CHAPTER TWENTY-THREE

Her hand on the doorknob of the Brittingham kitchen, Ellen took a deep breath to fortify herself and let herself in. The kitchen smelled like fried sausage and something cinnamon-sweet. Ordinarily the scent would have triggered her stomach into a backflip of anticipation. Today, nothing.

"Come in, *schoene punim*," her mother called out from the sink. "How are you feeling?"

"Not like a 'beautiful face.'" Ellen walked up to Bea and gave her a hug. "But thanks, anyway."

"Any time you want to talk," her mother offered.

Ellen had called her parents from her cell phone as she walked home and told them to make excuses for her; that she'd spilled something on her dress and had walked home to change. But she'd not fooled her mother any more than she'd fooled Alex. But unlike Alex, less than an hour later, the boat dipped and Ma was knocking on her door.

Ellen wouldn't talk about it then . . . and she still couldn't. Not and make any sense. "Maybe later."

It was too confusing, so out of character for her. She'd been acting like Jan, wanting what she shouldn't have. For the first time in Ellen's life, she'd known what it was like to feel as if she was caught up in a blooming fairytale . . . and it had to be with an engaged man. Talk about a crash-landing when Selena walked in. Not even the discovery of one of her stuffer-socks on the floor had made her feel any lower. Ellen couldn't feel any lower. And she was angry. Angry at herself for dolling up, for hoping when she knew better. As much as she'd prayed for peace and resolution, it didn't feel as if her words went any higher than the flying bridge of her houseboat.

The last look in a mirror this morning as Ellen had dressed for church confirmed the fact that sleep had eluded her. Not when she could replay last night's high and low over and over in her mind, futilely editing the action and script. There wasn't enough ice in Antarctica to shrink the bags under the dull eyes staring back at her.

"Will you pick up Pete for church?" Ellen picked up a piece of sausage and took a bite. "I want to get to the hall and make sure everything is a go for the luncheon after the service. My kids are in charge of cleanup."

And Ellen wouldn't have to face Adrian or Selena.

"What, you're not eating breakfast?" her mother chided.

Ellen pressed another piece of the meat into a slice of bread. "This is good enough."

"But I've got *latkes* mixed and ready to fry, just for you."

Ma thought she could single-handedly solve the world's problems with food, especially Jewish comfort food. But not even her potato pancakes could fix the smarting hole in Ellen's chest.

"Save them for dinner. I just need enough in my stomach now to offset the ibuprofen I took for my headache." If only there was a pill for heartache. Who was she to threaten Selena over Pete's welfare?

"Alright, but if you ask me, you need to get your blood sugar up."

"This will do it." Ellen gave her mother a peck on the cheek. "Thanks, Ma. See you later."

Although what Ellen really needed was for God to take away this hurt so she could think clearly again. So that she could take a deep breath without further wounding her fickle heart. The one that insisted on falling for a guy that her head knew was beyond her reach. As she walked toward the barn where she parked her bike, she raised her eyes to the bright fall sky, searching for relief.

God, I know You do things in Your own time, but, for pete's sake, please hurry up. I feel like I'm dying here, and You're not looking.

Adrian walked into Faith Community Church behind his parents and shook hands with Josh Turner, who was handing out programs.

"Nice shindig last night. Although I may never live down wearing tights," he said.

"Thank you. Glad you enjoyed it."

Adrian had to hand it to Selena—she was a consummate actress, the perfect hostess till the end. He'd laid as low as a host possibly could. Small talk, introductions . . . Adrian couldn't recall half of what he'd said to his new neighbors and townspeople. It was as if he'd coasted until the last hurrah. Or good-bye.

"Oh, look, there's Bea and Edward," his mother said, pointing out the couple midway up the center section of the church. "There's a spot behind them."

"There's another right here," Adrian said, nodding to a red cushioned pew on the left. He couldn't very well say that the Brittinghams might not feel so warmly toward him. He'd left Ellen out of his terse explanation of his breakup with Selena.

Bea Brittingham glanced over her shoulder and, upon seeing his parents, waved them over. The soles of his Italian leather shoes feeling like lead, Adrian followed. Would Ellen sit with them? His heart skipped at the prospect, although he was at a loss to know if it was with anticipation or dread.

"How's Ellen's headache, darling?" his mother asked of Bea as she settled in behind her.

"Hanging on, I think. But she's got *chutzpah*," the woman replied. "She'll bounce back."

Adrian struggled not to squirm under Bea's unfathomable appraisal. Had Ellen told her what had happened?

"Going to be good bow-hunting weather tomorrow," Pop told Harry Sinclair. "Cold, light winds."

Obviously her father was clueless. Or being polite for Adrian's family's sake.

And where was Ellen? Adrian wanted to ask but held back.

His mother spared him the agony. "Where is Ellen? Did she stay home?"

He hoped not. He'd come today in hopes of seeing her. Although that was only part of the reason. He'd hoped to *see* God, as well. Plus, Peter was helping at the luncheon afterward.

"She's in the church hall with Peter and her Sunday school group," Bea replied.

His father chuckled. "I've never seen a boy so excited to wash dishes in my life."

"Ellen has coaxed him out of his shell." Adrian clamped his mouth shut. The last thing he wanted was to call attention to himself. Not until he made things right—if he *could* make things right.

The organist struck an attention-getting chord, sparing him once again.

Thank you, God. The gratitude sprang from the heart. After last night, Adrian didn't trust his reasoning.

Although he went through the motions of the service, in his mind, Adrian alternately practiced what he'd say to Ellen and prayed that he'd get it right. All his education and Selena's coaching were rendered useless by the desperation in his chest. He couldn't propose. Not when she hadn't forgiven him for putting her in such a horrible situation. Totally his fault. Totally unplanned, but nonetheless his fault.

"Robert Burns once wrote, 'The best laid plans of mice and men gang aft aglee.'" Reverend Ingerman raised his voice, breaking into Adrian's self-condemnation from behind the oak podium on the raised sanctuary. "Which is to say, no matter how well man plans, things go astray."

Had Adrian planned his behavior, this wouldn't have happened.

"I think that is because, quite often, God has a better plan."

If Adrian didn't know better, he'd swear the man was looking directly at him. Probably because he and his family were new faces in the congregation.

"A case in point is well illustrated by the Pilgrims who landed on Plymouth Rock in 1620," Reverend Ingerman continued. "Many of you may not know this, but they weren't heading for Massachusetts. Instead, a mighty storm changed their plans. *Three times.*

"Three times, the Pilgrims had changed their course for Virginia, and three times, they were deposited back on the shores of Massachusetts by stormy weather. Too late to plant and without plows and farm implements, they came to the one place in thousands of miles of coastline where the land had been cleared, shelters built, and crops had been planted—and then abandoned. One of the fiercest tribes in the area, who would have met them on the shores with death and destruction, had perished of a mysterious plague.

"Coincidence? I think not. But their good fortune doesn't

stop there," the minister said. "The one survivor of that tribe was Squanto, who spoke perfect English and showed them what to do with this foreign food crop called maize." After a pause, Ingerman leaned into the mic. "They'd been heading for a Jamestown disaster. God had a better plan."

Adrian couldn't help but think of how disastrous his plans had been. Not only with Selena, but with the business. Yes, he'd landed squarely on the coast of success, but it had gnawed at his spirit until he nearly had no spirit at all.

"As the season for Thanksgiving approaches," Reverend Ingerman said in closing after comparing how Jesus disrupted the plans of His people for the plan of salvation, "I want you to consider your lives today. What plans of yours have been foiled? What storms have blown you off your charted path? Step back. Ponder them prayerfully. Perhaps God has another plan. Or perhaps He's testing you, refining you in the storm so that when you reach your destination, you will be prepared, mentally, physically, and spiritually for the path you've chosen. If you have learned nothing else from what I've said today, let it be this. Regardless of where you are on your journey, God is with you always. Be you in the storm, adrift at sea, or safe on shore, He is with you and has Your best interest at heart." Clearing his throat, the minister opened his hymnal. "Our closing hymn is on . . ."

In the storm: last night. *Adrift at sea:* Adrian's life of late. *Safe on shore:* God, he wanted to be. And with God's help, he would be. He could start over. Would start over. Beginning today. With Ellen.

Ellen glanced at her watch as she did a last minute check in the community hall. The first of the parishioners should be coming over at any moment. The corn and gourd centerpieces on brown paper table covers, salt and pepper shakers, and chairs were all in place she noted with a beam of pride. The kids in her class had done well. The girls manned the buffet line to keep the vegetable soup dipped in bowls and sandwich trays filled, while the boys worked the coffee, tea, and cider bar.

One thing about working with young adults—it kept her mind off herself. At least it had, until Pete showed up and her heart staggered against her breastbone.

"Good news," he'd shouted as he burst into the back kitchen of the hall, cheeks ruddy and blue eyes bright.

Behind him came her mother and father, who brought in four trays of cinnamon pecan sticky buns that Bea had made for dessert. "What's that, sport?" Ellen had asked.

"Dad isn't marrying Selena!" The boy raised his hands to the ceiling. "There is a God!"

And Ellen had no doubt that He was mightily ashamed of her part in the breakup.

"I think they were arguing because we were in his office," Pete went on, unaware of the kick of his words. "But as soon as the last guests left, Selena took her suitcase, got in her car, and took off . . . and Dad told us it was over. No wedding." Spying Kevin McIntyre, Pete grabbed the boy's arm and swung him around with glee. "No evil stepmother for me.

I'm not even going to wear her dumb watch." Pete unfastened the bulky watch from his wrist.

"I don't know, Pete. That's a pretty cool gizmo." Not to mention that it cost an arm and a leg.

"Can I have it?" Kevin asked, wide-eyed with greed.

"Nope." Ellen took the watch from Pete and shoved it in the pocket of her dress jeans. "But I'll hold it for you till you're through doing dishes." She sighed heavily as the boys raced out into the dining part of the building to join the others setting up the tables.

"God's ways are not ours." That was all her mother had said before heading over to the church.

And they surely weren't Ellen's, whose emotions seesawed up and down so that she hardly heard Reverend Ingerman's message coming over the speaker system in the hour that followed. If Adrian had broken off the engagement because Selena was a haughty snob, that was one thing. If Selena had broken it off because she caught Adrian about to kiss Ellen. . .

Ellen had almost felt his lips on hers. They were so close. . .

If Selena had broken it off because of that, then Ellen shouldered at least half of the blame, because she'd wanted Adrian to kiss her. She couldn't believe he was going to, but the selfish side of her wanted it so badly.

"Dad!" Pete's greeting startled Ellen from her self-recrimination. "I didn't know you were coming."

Nor did Ellen. Adrian was the last person she expected to

walk through the door. Adrian, who approached her like a man with a mission. Adrian, who caught her by the arms as her feet finally obeyed the command to move.

"We have to talk."

Ellen broke his plaintive hold. "I can't. I have a church-load of people to feed." She nodded toward the door where others filed in behind him.

"After the meal, then," he conceded grimly. *And not a minute more* read like a ticker across his gaze. Pete tugged at his hand.

"Come on, Dad. Grandfather and Grandmother are sitting over here."

"But there's clean-up. There's a lot of clean-up," she called after him. And where's Alex? Sue Ann and Jan didn't attend church, at least regularly, but Ellen needed Alex to run interference.

As Adrian accompanied Pete to the table where the Sinclairs and Brittinghams were settling, Ellen beat a path for the kitchen, driven by the drum of her heart. After digging out her cellphone, Ellen punched in Alex's cell number.

"Alex, I need you now, in the community hall kitchen," she said the moment her friend answered. In a rush, Ellen explained the recent events in rapid succession. "Like, what'll I do? I just can't deal with this right now."

"Don't panic. Take a deep breath," Alex told her calmly, "and remember, God is in charge. *And you can't avoid Adrian forever.*"

Ellen exhaled on Alex's last words. Of course her friend was right. She *was* panicking and God *was* in charge.

"Trust God on this one," Alex said, "And I'll be there as soon as I drop Mom off. Dad has a cold and she wanted to skip the luncheon to go spoil him."

Trust God. Ellen closed her eyes. When she opened them, she spied one of the smaller members of her group struggling with a tray loaded with teetering glasses. "Look, I gotta go. Thanks, Ally."

Ellen intercepted the disaster about to happen and steadied the tray as the boy carried the tray over to the counter, but she felt as shaky as the glassware.

God, I am trusting that You know what You're doing, because I am so not ready for this.

CHAPTER TWENTY-FOUR

Casually clad in jeans and a sweatshirt, Ellen kept a watchful eye on the dishwashers and helped the driers put away the clean dishes. *Like a mother hen surrounded by precocious chicks,* Adrian mused, watching her from the door of the kitchen. *And sometimes,* one *of the chicks,* he amended as she flicked water back at two playful girls who'd inadvertently gotten her wet.

As for Pete, he was soaked to his shoulders from rinsing the dishes and thrilled to be a part of the group. Good thing Duff insisted he carry a spare shirt when she heard he was a dishwasher. Although Pete took his job very seriously and examined each plate or fork with such care that the driers huffed with impatience and dishwasher Kevin McIntyre groaned on getting do-overs. Adrian didn't know if this new level of tolerance was God or Ellen-enforced. Probably a bit of both.

"Everything is cleaned up on the hall side," Bea announced, stepping past Adrian into the kitchen. With a conspiratory wink, she waltzed past him and marched over to Ellen. "I'll take over in here. I think someone is waiting to speak to you."

Panic grazed Ellen's face for a moment as Bea took over her tea towel. "Ma, I'm—"

"A nickel holding up a five-dollar bill. Go!" She jerked a finger at Adrian. "You, too."

Looking somewhat as though she were off to an execution, Ellen removed the damp apron she wore about her waist and jerked her head toward a door at the other end of the counter. "Come on. I'll show you the craft room," she said to Adrian.

She led Adrian through a back hallway and into one of the rooms lining it. Once inside, she moved away from him with an exaggerated shrug. "So what is there to say that wasn't said last night?"

It was Adrian's turn to panic. He'd rehearsed precisely what he was going to say all night long, throughout the sermon—

"I love you."

No, no, that was the end.

"What?" Bemused, she crossed her arms over her chest and stepped back, bumping into a table lined with chairs. "Well, you can't." One brow hiked up, adding a question mark to the statement. Giving Adrian hope.

"Yes, I can." He closed the distance between them, his heart about to crash in overdrive. "And I do. I think I've loved you from the first time I saw you salute me on your motorbike."

"A Harley Davidson Soft Tail Springer Classic is not a *motorbike*," she mimicked his accent. "It's a Hog . . . the king of motorcycles."

"And the finest Hog I've ever seen," Adrian said. "I love it almost as much as I love you." He exhaled in frustration. This wasn't even close to what he'd had in mind. "Blast it, I love you." He ran his fingers through his hair. *God?*

It all came back to him. He blurted it out, laying it at her feet for mercy. How sorry he was for putting her in such a situation. How wrong he'd been to prolong an engagement that in his heart he knew was never to be.

"I'd been going through the motions of what I thought I should do," he explained. "I wanted to find a mother for Pete and show my gratitude to Selena for all she'd done for me—for my company. I thought I could make it work."

He caught her face between his hands, resisting the overwhelming urge to kiss her. But not yet. There was so much more on his heart that needed to be said.

"But when I met you, my heart felt alive again—for the first time in so long, I didn't recognize what it was." He swallowed, his mouth suddenly dry. "I thought it was gratitude for bringing Pete out of his shell."

"How do you know it isn't now?" Ellen asked, searching his face warily. "I mean, you just said how you mistook gratitude to Selena for love."

Adrian groaned. "I know, I'm an idiot. Give me logic. I can

deal with that. Introduce emotions, and I babble like . . ." Where had all his years of education gone? "Like an idiot," he finished lamely. "Can't you see what you've done? You've snatched me off the cover of *Forbes* and *GQ* and put me on that of *Mad Magazine*. And I am mad. Logic has flown out the window. I can't think straight anymore. I'm crazy for you."

Adrian searched her face for some clue that he'd made one iota of sense. But stunned was not the look he'd been going for. Shoulders sagging, he dropped his arms to his side and backed off.

"God, help me, I'm making it worse, aren't I?" He raised his eyes to the ceiling. "Where are You?" he cried out in frustration. "I could use a miracle right now, because, on my own, I've made a muddle of my life."

Ellen could not believe her eyes or her ears. First, Adrian declared his love for her and, God knew, she wanted to believe it. She'd almost felt sorry for the man and his obvious frustration. Certainly, she'd never seen Adrian like this before. So undone. So *not* together. Part of her wanted to gather him in her arms and assure him that it was going to be all right.

Except that she didn't know what to believe anymore.

He drew in a deep breath and exhaled. "Well, there it is. I've confessed to God and to you."

God again? But Ellen thought Adrian was a skeptic.

"And I'd do it again, in front of the church, if it would convince you." He raked his fingers through his hair. "I've no idea where the blasted storm is going to send me now."

Storm?

"I wouldn't have made a good Pilgrim. Probably would have remained in England and suffered persecution—"

The minister's sermon. Ellen had heard it over the intercom from the sanctuary. Adrian was talking about the sermon. And for some weird reason that quickened her heart as much as his declaration of love.

"Because that's what my life would have been if I'd continued with the status quo instead of listening to my heart. Except that God had another plan." Adrian drew himself from what had become introspection. "And I know with all my heart *and soul*," he declared, "that that plan includes you, Ellen Brittingham."

His heart *and* soul. Ellen's doubt began meltdown. If God changed the course for the Pilgrims, why not for Adrian? Selena had never been Adrian's match, not the real Adrian's. On the surface, they were a picture perfect couple, but it was what was inside that had to be compatible. Still, who'd have thought that polished, worldly Adrian could love a klutz with two left feet and grease behind the ears? Much less, that that same polished and worldly man would be standing before her raving like a lunatic about love and Pilgrims?

And looking as though his world depended on her response. Hers!

God *had* been listening to her prayers. But He'd changed *Adrian's* heart instead of hers.

Ellen examined his broken expression. Having felt that same brokenness all night long, she knew instinctively how to fix it. With the love that God lay before them for the taking. The love that filled her to overflowing.

She crooked her finger at him and mustered her best John Wayne voice, because her own was still frozen with shock and awe. "Come here, Pilgrim." And it covered up the nervousness that suddenly set in.

As Adrian came within reach, she gathered the knot of his silk tie in her fist and drew him closer.

"Are you gonna stand there lollygaggin' all day, or are you gonna kiss me like a man?"

The anxiety on his face gave way to a mix of relief . . . and a look that Ellen felt to the core.

He's gonna kiss me! Half-panic and all joy, the thought pinged from sense to sense, ringing full alert as he gathered her in his arms. Or was she melting in his? Regardless, it was getting hot in this kitchen . . . or wherever she was. Things were getting kind of delirious with those gorgeous blue eyes looking as though they were going to consume hers and his breath warming her lips.

God, is this what paradise feels like? All clamped together and breathless and—

Holy moly . . . *fireworks!*

In reverse. The lights went out overhead. Not that Ellen cared. She was wrapped up in Adrian's arms, her own wrapped around his neck. Wild horses couldn't drive them apart.

"Oh . . . excuse me."

But the minister could. Still holding her as though his

next breath depended on it, Adrian lifted his head, enabling Ellen to see Reverend Ingerman backing out the door.

"We, uh. . ." Was that her voice squeaking? ". . .were just closing up." It wasn't exactly a lie. She had intended to turn off the lights and close the door when they'd finished with their conversation.

As though he came upon embracing couples in his Sunday school rooms every day, the reverend replied. "No problem."

But she could imagine what was running through his mind. After all, Selena had talked to Reverend Ingerman about her upcoming marriage to the man Ellen was kissing.

Oy, what a mess. She had to—

Adrian squeezed her. "I hope the good reverend doesn't travel too far. Something tells me we may need his services in the near future."

Whoa! Did he . . . was he . . . ? Ellen's heart thudded against her breastbone so hard, she wasn't sure it would recover.

"Let's take this one step at a time, Pilgrim."

Admitting their love for each other was one thing. Marriage was another whole ballgame.

But her heart was too busy doing backflips to bother with reason. This was its moment.

"Dad? Ellen? Where *are* you two?" Pete's voice sounded from the hallway.

A moment interrupted.

"We'll continue this later," Adrian promised, letting her go.

"Sheesh, this is Grand Central," Ellen said as Pete zeroed in on their location.

"Can I ride home on the Hog?" the boy asked as he barreled through the open door.

"Sure. If it's okay with your dad," Ellen replied. Although she was likely to fly. She gave Adrian a sheepish glance.

"Blast," he said. "I was going to ask, but he beat me to the punch."

"You're old enough to get your own motorcycle," Pete dismissed him. "So when we get to the end of the lane, can I drive again?" he asked Ellen.

Ellen slipped her arm around the boy's shoulders. "I think that can be arranged. But you'd better slip into that dry shirt first, or you'll catch a cold."

"Right." Pivoting and nearly tripping over his own feet, Pete stumbled toward the door. "This has got to be one of the best days of my life."

Adrian slipped his arm around Ellen. "I'm inclined to agree."

Something welled inside of her until she thought she'd burst. Was this what love felt like? Now she knew why Marley raced off around the room, tail wagging and jumping up and down. High-octane love.

Instead, Ellen tucked her head under Adrian's chin, snuggling close with a sigh.

"Me, too."

CHAPTER TWENTY-FIVE

Although it was a sweater-crisp day, Ellen's leather jacket felt good as she gunned the twin cams of her bike and passed a car on Piper Cove Road. Behind her, Pete squeezed her waist and pressed his head against her back. She prayed the high from the surge of power would transcend his fear of it. Not to the point of recklessness, of course. She would teach him all the precautions. Her heart swelled at the thought. She loved Pete as much as she did his dad. It was as if God had opened up her heart and the boy had stumbled in with all his insecurities and anger. And Adrian had come tumbling after.

What a trio they were. What an awesome God that threw them together.

Ellen closed her eyes in thanksgiving, just for a second. First rule of the road. Keep the eyes on it.

"Can we go around one more time?" Pete hollered into her ear as they approached Three Creek Road.

"Around" meant passing their home, getting on Route 589, and looping back through Piper Cove, proper. But the sun was shining and so was Ellen, from the inside out. Besides, it was only an extra twenty or so minutes. Nothing to worry the folks at home over. Everyone knew Ellen would be the last to leave, although she'd had to insist that Adrian drive his parents home.

"Why not?"

A crafts bazaar filled the sidewalks and park as Ellen wove the Harley through the traffic of the seaside village. When she was Pete's age, the town would have seemed abandoned, now that the tourist season was over. Pop told her that in his day, even Ocean City was such a ghost town they turned off the stoplights. Now, many of the tourists have moved in to stay.

Spotting Josh and Alex walking hand in hand toward the park swings, Ellen beeped the horn. They didn't notice. That someday it could be her and Adrian, caught up in a world of their own in the midst of a crowd, struck Ellen with nothing less than wonder.

"Can we stop and look around?" Peter asked.

A squeal of brakes behind them brought everyone's attention to where the impatient driver of a big yellow Hummer waved a group of pedestrians across the street. Dismissing the jerk, Ellen considered pulling over and running Alex down to tell her about Adrian. It was so tempting. She could almost taste the banana split of an emergency *sundae* meeting. But not yet. He hadn't finished saying what she thought he was saying. Even though, deep down, she knew. She was just having a hard time believing it.

Sheesh, she was getting as ditzy as Jan, who was in a perpetual state of love struck. "Better not. Maybe you and the others can come back later. I think this lasts all afternoon."

With Piper Cove in their wake, the gold stubble of harvested cornfields and woodland spread before them. Overhead, a chevron of geese made their way toward the river, although Ellen couldn't hear their honking over the Harley. It was the kind of day she could ride forever. The kind she could imagine sharing with Adrian and Pete.

God, I could just stop this bike and hug Pete till his eyes bulged, but I'd probably scare him!

In the rearview mirror, Ellen spied the Hummer coming around a bend in the road practically on two wheels. If the driver were in that big of a hurry, he should have left yesterday. Keeping her speed steady, Ellen hugged the right side of the narrow farm road to give him plenty of room to pass.

Except he didn't. He closed the distance between them. Pete nearly squeezed the breath out of Ellen as the big turbodiesel roared in their ears. What kind of nut was this? Make that nuts. There were two men in the vehicle.

"Hang on, buddy," she shouted to Pete.

The best way to handle this was to get off the road, but with deep drainage ditches down both sides, she had to wait for the driveway that led through the woods to an old farmstead. The house had burned down years ago and the land was rented out to a local farmer.

Pulse racing with her engine, Ellen maneuvered a sharp bend in the road and accelerated out of the turn. Going too fast to make the turn into the driveway, the Harley shot over a portion of the ditch and landed, fishtailing on the dirt drive. Ellen fought to keep the bike under control, legs extended as she brought it to a stop a short distance into the wooded lane. The Hummer rounded the bend and passed them by. Then braked.

And backed up.

Fear stabbed at Ellen's chest. These weren't everyday jerks. They were following her. Except somehow she knew it wasn't her they were after. Turning, she pulled the ear plugs out of Pete's ears, making certain he could hear her.

"Pete," she shouted over the idle of the engine. "When we reach the field around the next bend, you'll see an old deer blind just on the right. Looks like a shack covered with straw and vines. I want you to slide off and run for it. Stay there, no matter what happens. I'll swing back for you once I lose these guys."

"I'm staying with you," Pete argued as she accelerated.

"I can't lose them with you on the bike. Trust me!" She felt Pete burrow his face into her back. "Trust me, buddy. I'll be back for you." She had to drop Pete off without them seeing it. "You know what to do, right?" she felt Pete's nod.

The last thing Ellen saw as she took the sharp bend was the yellow Hummer turning into the abandoned lane. They had to be after Pete. Something to do with Adrian and security. If she could lead them away—

She skidded the motorcycle to a halt and practically shoved the boy off. "Over there," she said, pointing to the camouflaged, dilapidated shack. If she hadn't known where it was, she'd have missed it. "Trust me. I'll be back. Understand?"

"Hide and don't come out . . . except for me or the police."

God bless him, his eyes were as large as the lenses of his glasses. "Go!" Ellen pulled away, spitting dirt and pine needles behind her. In the rear view mirror, she spied Pete stumbling toward the shelter. Familiar with the layout of the land, she sped toward the farmstead, nothing more than a collapsing barn and charred house foundation, all overgrown with trees and brush. As she reached it, she slowed to make certain that the Hummer following on the wooded lane spied her.

Her cell phone! She snatched it from her chest. Why hadn't she given it to Pete? *Come on, come on,* she groused as she turned it on. She hated that cartoon intro. She dialed 911 twice before it finally rang. At least the readout said it was calling. Who could hear over the Harley's engine? The moment it signaled a connect, Ellen began shouting into the mouthpiece.

"Send the police. Rayne's Farm. Kidnapping in progress. Send the police, Rayne's farm. Kidnapping in progress." With no time to identify herself, she kept repeating the same phrase again and again until she finally saw the yellow of the Hummer through the trees.

A cold lump settled in her chest. She could lose these guys. She knew the back roads. They didn't. She just prayed the men in the Hummer had not noticed Pete was no longer aboard. At least she and Pete had both worn black jackets.

Jaw clenched, Ellen tossed the phone aside as the Hummer shot past the deer blind without hesitation and headed toward her. Maybe the local authorities could trace its location. Regardless, there was no time to chat. Determined, she eased off the clutch and opened the throttle.

Hang on, God.

The first hour that Ellen and Pete had not shown up, Adrian wasn't overly worried. A delay in the cleanup. Or maybe his son had coaxed Ellen into a longer ride. Regardless, he couldn't get through on her cell phone. But as the second hour turned, Adrian climbed in Ed Brittingham's pickup truck as his parents, Mrs. Duffy, and Bea stood on the Sinclair porch.

"You know, there's a craft fair today in town. Could be they're just there," Mr. Brittingham said as Adrian fastened his seatbelt. But the older man's drawn expression conveyed more concern than his words.

"Wouldn't Ellen have called?" Adrian asked. "I kept getting a busy signal."

"I admit, it's not like her. She's not much of a talker, and she keeps her phone charged. I taught her about keeping everything she has in tiptop—"

Ed broke off as a state police car shot past the Sinclair driveway, sirens blazing. Adrian could almost see the blood drain from the man's face—could feel his own blanch as well.

"Don't mean nothing," the older man said, as if to persuade himself. "But it can't hurt to check it out."

He gunned the truck engine, jerking Adrian as he sped down the lane in the direction the police cruiser had taken.

Adrain latched onto the passenger side grab handle.

God, please let them be safe. If they've been in an accident, God, spare them. I promise, I'll never let either of them on one of those motorbikes again. Just spare them.

They barely rounded the bend when they spied the police car go around another in the winding farm road. Determined not to let it get away from him, Ed Brittingham sped up, slowing just enough to maneuver the curves, the drainage ditches waiting to catch anyone who misjudged.

"Well, I'll be dogged," Ed said, when the cruiser turned into a wooded road. "What're they doing, headed into the old Raynes' place?"

"Just go," Adrian told him. He didn't know why. Had no clue who the Raynes were. But the hair prickling at the back of his neck told him this was no coincidence.

As Ed pulled into the lane, another cruiser turned in behind him. "Haven't been back here in two years." He sped up with the police car on his bumper, maneuvering the twists and turns in the lane as fast as was safe. "Ellen and me used to hunt—"

"Look, look there!" Adrian pointed ahead to where a young boy ventured out into the lane from the woods, waving to head off the first police car. His stomach rolled over as he recognized Pete. His glasses were gone, but it was Pete.

It took him forever to unfasten his seatbelt. And another eternity for the truck to slow down enough for Adrian to bail out. Then Pete was in his arms.

"Dad! They went after Ellen."

"I'm Officer Benton, State Police. Are you the one who placed the 911 call, son?" the officer from the first car asked.

Pete pulled far enough away to shake his head. "N–no," he said, breathless. "But these guys in a b–big Hummer chased Ellen and me off the road."

The more Pete told them, the colder Adrian grew. If they'd struck the Harley, they could have killed both Ellen and his son. So murder wasn't their intention . . . yet. How had she seen the deer blind? Instantly, he knew the answer. She was a hunter. And with the same motherly instinct of the birds she hunted, she'd led her predators away from his son.

"She promised she'd come back, Dad."

And she would have, if she could. Adrian knew that. He also knew he needed to call Agent Statler. He fished out his cell phone from an inside coat pocket and speed-dialed the number.

"Which direction did she go in, son?" the police office asked, eyeing Adrian with mild curiosity.

"She disappeared behind that old barn," Pete said, pointing to a huge overgrowth of tree, shrub, and vine over what had been a home and what was left of a barn. "They went after her."

"Statler," came the answer from the other end.

"There's a back road that cuts through the woods there to 589," Ed Brittingham informed the officer.

Adrian turned away, shielding the mouthpiece. "Rick, I think there's been an attempt to kidnap my son. We have the boy, but the perpetrators may have Ellen."

The officer gave Adrian an annoyed look. "Excuse me, sir. If you have any idea why anyone would want to kidnap your son, or this Ellen, perhaps you'd best share it with us. And the sooner the better."

"Let me speak to the officer in charge, Adrian," Statler said flatly.

Adrian gladly handed over the phone to the state police-man. "I'm afraid it may have to do with a security breach in my company," he explained to Ellen's father. "I . . . I'm not certain."

If there was any animosity toward Adrian for involving his daughter, Brittingham masked it. Instead, he addressed Pete. "You remember how long ago it was that she led them off, son?"

Pete's face crumbled with the sob that tore from his throat. "I don't know. I gave Ellen my watch so I could wash dishes. It felt like forever. I stayed here like she told me."

"Can't be too long ago," another officer, the one from the second car spoke up. He extended his hand to Ed Brittingham. "Ed," he said, obviously familiar with Ellen's father.

"Brian, what's going on?" Ed asked.

"We got a 911 call to come here, kidnapping in progress."

He shook Adrian's hand. "I'm Lieutenant Stapleton. We responded from the Berlin barracks as soon as the call came in. Maybe twenty minutes ago."

"What took you so long?" Adrian snapped. The man hardly looked old enough to shave, much less be a lieutenant in the police force.

"This is a big county, sir. We do the best we can." Stapleton bent down to Pete's level. "What color was the Hummer, son? I need to put out an APB for it."

"Yellow. Big Bird yellow."

"Here you go, sir." Officer Benton returned Adrian's cell phone. "Agent Statler has agents meeting us at your home to coordinate a search. Looks like we'll be working in concert with the FBI," he continued to Stapleton.

I don't have my watch. The significance of Pete's words finally registered with Adrian. "Wait! Ellen has Pete's watch. It's a GPS locator watch. We can see where Ellen is on the computer in my office."

"Then what are we waiting for?" her father exclaimed. "Let's go." He herded Pete toward the truck with Adrian on their heels. "Let's go find our gal."

God bless Selena, even if she's behind all this. Or bless whatever prompted her to give Pete that watch.

Heading home instead of searching for Ellen went against Adrian's instinct. He was used to having control of the situation and it was totally out of his hands. But going home would give them her exact location.

Adrian climbed into the truck next to Pete. He hated this

sense of helplessness. God had given him a second chance at love and it was slipping through his fingers. Fear and frustration threatened to drown him, to pull him under in a sea of despair. There was one thing still within his grasp. The one Reverend Ingerman declared the most powerful option mankind possessed in the storm.

Adrian rose above the crashing waves of doom and doubt, his spiritual eyes fixed on the only One who could calm the storm.

I need you, Lord. Ellen needs you. Please bring her home to me. I don't think I can bear losing the woman I love again.

CHAPTER TWENTY-SIX

Ellen worked at the duct tape binding her wrists behind her back. Her fix-it-all product had come back to bite her in the tush, doing what it was designed to do—hold fast. Unfortunately, it was the only thing that worked so far. She'd been so close to losing the Hummer on a timber road when she'd done the unthinkable. She'd looked over her shoulder at where she'd been—at who was chasing her—instead of at the road.

It was a wonder she'd not broken her neck when her bike hit a dead tree that had fallen across the dirt pass. Suddenly she was airborne, the Harley cartwheeling after. By the grace of God, it missed her by an arm's length, and she missed a thick pine as they both crash-landed in underbrush. How long she lay there in shock, trying to make sure everything was still attached to her body and working, she had no idea. She'd almost forgotten why she was there, staring at the out-of-focus tree branches overhead, until the faces of two men appeared in her vision.

One was middle-aged, fit, a dark buzz cut graying at the temples. The other was a younger clone. Neither were in good humor that they'd lost Pete. And things didn't improve when Ellen disabled the older guy with a well-placed kick as he tried to help her up. She'd have done more too, if the other fellow hadn't pulled a gun. Gun trumped black belt, especially when this black belt wasn't hitting on all cylinders.

"Will you *please* be still? They're going to kill us anyway."

Bedraggled in a silk jogging suit that had likely never known human sweat, Selena Lacy sat tied to the opposite side of a creosote pole from Ellen. It supported the rusted tin roof of a dilapidated boat shed on some boonies property Ellen had never seen before. Maybe somewhere off one of the creek branches near Fenwick. They hadn't been on the road long once she'd been caught.

"Ah, come on, you've got more brass than that." Her shoulder still ached from the impact of her fall, but all in all, Ellen considered herself pretty lucky and totally confused. "Although I can't figure why you're in here with me, since you were working with them."

When they'd dragged Ellen inside the boatshed, Selena was waiting, trussed like a chicken. Once the men bungee-corded Ellen to the pole, as well, they'd left by boat to pick up what was to be Ellen's ransom—the files from one of Adrian's projects.

"It wasn't supposed to turn out like this." Selena heaved an exasperated sigh. "*You* were the final straw."

The accusation pricked at Ellen's already frayed nerves. "Uh, I believe Adrian's trouble started before we'd even met," Ellen reminded her. "You know, since those guys took the speedboat, the Hummer is right outside. If we could get loose—"

"But he never loved me. He wouldn't set a date for the wedding. *Two years*," she said through gritted teeth, ignoring Ellen's suggestion. "Two years, we were engaged and nothing. A few months in this godforsaken backwater, and he forgets I exist. All he can do is talk about you. 'Ellen did this with Pete. Ellen is great with kids. Ellen has Pete excited over a motorbike.'"

Ellen grimaced. "Motor*cycle*." What was it with these city types?

But as ridiculous as it seemed, Ellen was relieved to hear that she wasn't the first straw to break the relationship down. Not that that was doing her much good now. She pulled at the elastic cords securing them to the piling and tried once again to get her taped hands under her hips. If she could slip her hips and legs through, get her hands in front of her, she could pull the tape off with her teeth.

"You are cutting off my breath," Selena hissed.

"You won't have any to cut off, if I don't get loose. You're the one who said it. They're going to kill us whether Adrian gives them the file or not."

"I never should have slept with Phillipe Durande. But I wasn't like Adrian. I had needs."

Oh, brother. "Hold it. Too much info." Did Adrian know

this? Not that it would do Ellen any good at the moment. Or in the future. If there was a future.

Okay, God, let's work this out. I know You're here.

Selena ignored her. "Phillipe and I had had a past. And we revisited it just one night, six months ago, but Phillipe threatened to tell Adrian unless I helped him gain access to the Alphanet client system. They were just going to steal *one* bank's credit card information. He owed someone, he'd said, and . . ." She sighed in defeat, then flipped some internal switch to cryptic. "I'd thought it might get rid of Mitch. That red-headed, junk-food–stuffing nerd never liked me."

And just when Ellen had a twinge of sympathy toward the woman. "So then you decided to get rid of Pete? For God's sake, he's eleven."

Ellen stopped struggling. It was no use. She was too long-bodied or her arms were too short.

"Peter was a last resort. And no one was supposed to get hurt," Selena added defensively. "When the American and French authorities started tracing the credit card breach to Durande's hacker friends in Paris, he pushed me harder for access to Bright Star. But Adrian was the only one who had access to the codes by then, and I was in too deep to just back away."

The woman actually believed she was a victim. Heat rushed through Ellen.

"No, you had another choice. You could have confessed to the bank fraud and fingered the people who were *pushing*,"

Ellen said. "Instead, you put Pete at risk. You were going to be his stepmother, someone he should've been able to trust." It wasn't Ellen's place to judge, but it was hard not to.

"As if that was going to happen," she disdained. "The kid hated me, too. And that housekeeper—"

"Just who or what are these codes for?" Ellen asked. "Terrorists?"

"Of course not," Selena huffed as though Ellen had insulted her integrity. "*They* are arms competitors. They wanted to see what the American defense contractors have in the way of cyber-warfare. I knew Adrian would hand over the codes—even the Bright Star file—to save Pete . . . or you," she added grudgingly.

"Not if I can save myself first." Ellen started wriggling again. If she weren't bungeed to the blasted pole—

"We are loose ends. They are going to kill us, you *simpleton*," Selena said with a spiteful pull on the cords. "You see that device over there by the door?"

Lord, give me patience . . . and strength . . . and patience.

Ellen strained to look around the pole. All she could see was a battery-sized box. Unlike all the other debris in the abandoned boathouse, it was not corroded with age.

Her mouth went dry as she eyed the wires running from the box to the door. "What is it, a bomb?"

Selena's answering sob made Ellen's blood run hot and cold at the same time. "And I helped them. They have no right to kill me. It's not fair."

Cold. Slight accent. French maybe. That was the voice on the other end of the telephone that Adrian pressed to his ear.

"Since we couldn't secure the access codes surreptitiously, we want the entire Bright Star file now. If we see that any data is suspicious or missing, you'll never see your friend again. Are we clear? That means no FBI. No tipping off your client for twenty-four hours."

Everything was happening so fast, Adrian's head was spinning. Statler wanted him at home when the kidnapers called. He'd no more than walked into the house when the phone to his office rang. Selena must have given the number to the kidnappers. Aside from Mitch and their office manager, no one else had it.

Adrian read Statler's hastily scrawled question aloud. "How will I know Ellen will remain safe during those twenty-four hours?" His stomach clenched at the implication.

"You don't."

Adrian glanced at the sofa where Mitch sat with Peter. Despite Mitch's comforting arm about the boy's shoulder, Pete was wrapped in his own arms, bottom lip clenched in his teeth. Although Adrian and Mitch had tried to get the boy out of the thick of things, Pete had a stubborn streak that rivaled his mother's. And he loved Ellen as much as Adrian.

Statler shoved another question in front of Adrian.

"And what about Miss Lacy?" Adrian read again. "How is she involved in this?"

Selena had given the agent tailing her the slip at the hotel in

Salisbury. The man hadn't seen her leave her room, but when she missed checkout at noon, he'd had the hotel manager open her door. She was nowhere to be found, although her suitcase was there, still packed. The beds hadn't been slept in.

Wherever she'd gone, she'd left in a hurry, leaving Adrian to wonder yet how deeply she was involved in this. Perhaps she was in danger, as well. Not that she didn't deserve to be.

"Miss Lacy has been helpful, but that's hardly your concern now."

That settled that. Selena had indeed betrayed him, his son, and Ellen.

"You have one hour to hand the file over to me at the Ocean City Inlet parking lot. Do you know where that is?"

Rick Statler, who monitored the call nodded.

"Yes, I do," Adrian replied.

"Once we verify the information, I'll tell you where Miss Brittingham is."

Adrian glanced over to where one of Statler's men worked on finding Ellen via the Childfinder network. With luck, they'd locate and rescue Ellen before the exchange. She couldn't be far.

Stall, Statler wrote hastily.

"You do realize that our client will know his project has been compromised."

"Come now, Mr. Sinclair. We both know the technical advances on Bright Star won't be discarded, just because my client is privy to them. It won't make them any less effective."

The agent working on Adrian's computer leaned back in his chair. "Got her!" he mouthed. "A creek off Light House Road, just across the state line," he informed Statler in a low voice.

Adrian had been on that road before. When he'd taken Selena to dinner at the Links. It wasn't far. They might possibly rescue Ellen before he handed over the files.

"One hour. The Inlet Parking Lot, Thrasher's French Fries. Am I clear?"

"Fine," Adrian said to the caller. "I'll be there with the file in one hour. But how will I find you?"

"Buy yourself some fries at Thrashers. I'll find you."

The line at the french fry stand might have shocked Adrian, considering it was early November, but given the events of the past few hours, he merely took his place at its end. The boardwalk arcades were open for the number of tourists who obviously didn't mind a brisk breeze. A couple clad in sweatshirts, hoods raised, passed by on a tandem bike, basking in the sunshine and ocean air, reminding Adrian of Ellen.

He took a deep breath to break the bonds of anxiety constricting his chest and checked his watch as the line moved forward. It had taken him a half an hour to get wired and make the trip from his home. Another ten minutes to find a space in the busy parking lot. Adrian glanced about at the people making their way to and fro. Young people without care to the weather, some in tee shirts, others wearing coats they'd not bothered to fasten. Older couples bundled to the neck, rosy-cheeked and laughing. Some with grandchildren. And parents with cotton candy-smeared toddlers begging for coins to ride the arcade ponies and cars.

No one looked like a thug. Just people from all walks enjoying the good weather at the beach. And FBI agents dressed like them, blending in.

Statler's voice came over the receiver lodged in Adrian's ear. "Just remain cool."

Adrian had covered it with a Redskins toboggan. Not exactly his style, but it did the trick.

"Our chopper has spotted the Hummer outside an old boathouse. They're directing our team to the dirt road leading into the marsh."

Adrian closed his eyes momentarily. *Thank you, God. Just let them find Ellen safe.*

"We have to approach with caution."

Because Ellen might not be alone. His heart clutched. But the FBI had handled situations like this many times before. And God was with her.

God.

Adrian set his heart on that. The rest of his senses sought out the blackguard who'd taken her. Who sought to steal technology from his client. Perhaps catching him—or them—would lead to the mastermind behind it all. Adrian moved up in the line, now able to see the staff working in the steaming cubicle over vats upon vats of hot oil.

God. . .

"What size?" a young man in a white tee shirt and apron shouted at him, startling Adrian from his less than eloquent plea.

"Small, please," he managed.

Quite the operation. One taking the orders while another dumped steaming, golden fries into his bin. With a few shakes of salt, another tossed them and stuffed them into paper tubs. At the end, a cashier handled the transaction while customers sprinkled malt vinegar over their delicacies. What was he to do after he bought the blasted fries? Meander, Statler had told him. Stay in the area and wait until he was approached.

He handed over a five at his turn to pay. "Keep—"

"We found the women—"

"—the change."

"—but there's a snag. Explosives."

God in heaven! Sheer desperation fortified Adrian's knees as he followed the suit of the couple in front of him and sprinkled vinegar on his fries.

"We've got our experts on it."

God? Adrian turned away from the busy kiosk, stepping back suddenly as a boy on rollerblades narrowly missed him. The anguish of losing Carol stabbed at him. He couldn't lose Ellen, too.

No, he argued against the doubt. God would not have brought him this close to happiness, only to take it from him. Adrian had to believe that this was the door opened for him after his heart had been closed with Carol's death. He had to.

Dodging his way through the traffic to the south side of the boardwalk, he stopped in front of a souvenir shop and pretended to study the contents of its window. Cheap shell jewelry, shellacked cedar boxes, plaques, hermit crabs. A bizarre assortment of goods.

Absently he took a fry from the small tub and bit into it, barely registering the surprising burst of flavor. He caught a glimpse of himself in the glass. He was losing his mind. He shouldn't be here. He should be with Ellen, doing something—anything—to save her. Why didn't Statler say anything else?

"Trade you popcorn for those fries, man."

A young man in an Ocean City sweatshirt and jeans held out a box of Dolle's popcorn.

Adrian connected with the young man's gaze. Clear. Gray. Somber. There was no trace of the humor in his voice there. Pulse quickening, Adrian shook his head.

"No, thank you."

"Aw, come on, Pop, you gotta have something for me."

Like the memory stick of Bright Star in his pocket? But what if this was just some kind of whacked out—

Statler's voice crackled in Adrian's ear. "Not yet."

Focus, Adrian told himself when what he wanted to do was get his hands on the man—

No. He had to remain calm and see this through. Finish it. Get to Ellen and take her home to Peter. "I'd want more than a crummy box of popcorn for what I have to offer. Now move on, lad. These aren't ordinary fries."

"This isn't ordinary caramel corn, either."

He was so young. Looked like a college student, a cleancut one. And his accent was . . . well, he had none that Adrian could pinpoint. Definitely not the man who'd called and demanded the file.

"This could be like Cracker Jacks. A prize in every box." Smiling, the man glanced around casually, although there was nothing casual in his sharp gaze. He was looking for Adrian's accomplices. Expected them.

"There's no prize in these fries. Nor will there be a prize until I know Ellen is safe." There, the pussyfooting about was over. Adrian wasn't good at it. "Tell me where she is, and I'll give you the file."

"No can do, Pop. I have to verify it's the real deal first."

"How do I know she's safe?" *With a bloody bomb attached to her,* Adrian wanted to add. It was all he could think about.

"Stall him," Statler said. "We're close."

Adrian wanted to shove the tub of fries down the man's throat. "How long will it take for you to verify it?"

"I don't know, man. I'm just the pick-up guy. Once they're verified, the woman's all yours."

"Adrian, whatever you do, don't let him use a cell phone."

Adrian tried not to react to Statler's emotionless warning. Cell phone. Bomb. It didn't take a rocket scientist to realize the danger.

"I'll go with you then. As soon as you've gotten what you want—"

The man shuffled his feet, antsy. His wandering eyes

stopped on a jogger bent on tying his sneakers on the other side of the boardwalk. One of Statler's men.

"—I'll get Ellen," Adrian continued, heart stilled in his chest, "and we'll both be happy." Was the thug onto them?

"How about you give me the info now, or I'm out of here. And in case your boys watching us follow me, well—" He took a piece of caramel corn and popped it in his mouth. "We have insurance," he said through chewing it. "Not good for the lady."

Not good for the lady. Adrian felt physically sick.

"Not any more."

Statler's voice accelerated Adrian's alarm. What did he mean by—

"Ellen is safe," the agent said. "Give him the stick."

"So what'll it be, Pop?"

Adrian struggled to keep his knees from giving out with relief.

"Give it to him. He'll lead us to his accomplice."

Right. Get back with the plan. The man couldn't know that Ellen was safe . . . that his insurance policy just expired any more than he could know that Mitch had altered the information on the memory stick. Even if the crooks got away with it, it was flawed.

"Pop, we ain't got all day," the punk grumbled.

Adrian batted down the anger that now rose in relief's wake. Just for a moment, Adrian envisioned fulfilling his impulse to pummel the man. Instead he reached into his jacket pocket and handed over the flawed Bright Star data.

CHAPTER TWENTY-SEVEN

"You should go to the hospital, just in case," Bea Brittingham said as Ellen entered the Sinclair home ahead of Agent Jenkins.

"The paramedic said I'm fine, Ma. Just a little bruised and sore from the tumble on the bike."

"Your face is scratched," her mother fussed, pinching her cheeks.

"Ow, that really helps."

If Ellen were honest, she ached all over now that she was safe. A hot bath in mineral salts and a comfy bed called to her. But not as much as wanting to see Pete . . . safe. And Adrian. She had to see him too. So much was left unfinished between them.

"Ellen!" The boy materialized in the open door of his father's office and barreled toward her. His tackle of a hug would have bowled her over, had she not braced for it. Yet, as enthusiastic as his welcome was, he was somber when he pulled away. "You *said* you'd come back."

The fear that Pete had lived through mixed with pain in his gaze. It told her how terrified he'd been, not just for himself, but for her. And suddenly, it was swept away by relief and joy. Pete hugged her again, squeezing her ribs so tight, it gave new meaning to the phrase *love hurts*. And the way she felt about him, the love she felt, hurt just as much. More. If anything had happened to Pete—

"Well, here I am," she mumbled into his hair, refusing to entertain any notion beyond the fact that Pete was here and complaining in her arms. "I didn't say when, did I?"

"Good thing you had the watch in your pocket." As if afraid that she'd run away, Pete slowly released her.

The watch. Ellen had forgotten all about it. When the agents arrived at the boathouse, she'd about given up on trying to get loose. Exasperation had set in, both with the unyielding bonds and Selena's non-stop chatter.

Selena was convinced they were going to die and hadn't cooperated in the slightest. She ranted on and on about how this was all Adrian's fault. How she'd wanted to be a good wife and mother, but the man and his son had rejected her. How it wasn't easy being a woman in a man's world.

For all his intelligence, Adrian Sinclair was a dunce when it came to women.

Then Ellen had heard the men approaching the building. She shouted for all she was worth that the door was wired. At least she'd assumed it was. It was where the box of explosives had been placed. So the men ripped off a piece of rusted out siding and entered that way.

It still made her queasy that she'd been right.

"Adrian's on his way home," Harry Sinclair announced, stepping out of the office. "The FBI has both men in custody."

"Praise God," Bea said, her hand still resting on Ellen's shoulder. Ellen didn't mind her mother's possessiveness. But for God's grace, she might never have known that touch again. Or seen Pop's quiet smile that said, "All's well, pumpkin."

Just as the grim realizations threatened to knock out her knees, Adrian's father gave Ellen a gentle hug. "Thank you, young lady, for saving our grandson. Brilliant, quick thinking."

"For heaven's sake, Harry," Adrian's mother exclaimed. "We're mobbing the poor girl. Why don't we go into the living room where Ellen can sit down and have a cup of tea while she's debriefed."

The way Maggie calmly took charge, one would think she'd had experience in this type of thing before. Regardless, Ellen gave her a grateful smile. The sooner her aspirin kicked in, the better.

Adrian jumped out of Rick Statler's car before it came to a stop in front of the porch. The worst was behind him now. Stiller and Jones, if that were indeed their names, were in custody, along with Selena. Perhaps if he'd been honest with the woman—honest with himself—this would never have happened. His son would never have been in danger.

But then, he'd never have met Ellen. Never known this

going-out-of-one's-mind madness just to see her, to touch her, to know that she was safe—and his.

Adrian burst through the front door. Mrs. Duffy, who carried a tea tray down the hall, stopped dead in her tracks.

"Ellen?" he asked, throat suddenly constricted.

"In the living room with the family," the housekeeper told him. "Slow down now and act civil."

Good old Duff. Always the nanny in charge, even with him. And heaven knew he didn't want to rush in like a madman and frighten—

"Adrian!"

Adrian turned in time to see Ellen coming toward him at a run. It was only natural to open his arms and catch her as she jumped into them, wrapping her long legs about his waist. Momentum sending him into a spin, he held on to her as though she were the most precious thing in existence. Which, his son aside, she was.

His lips found hers as she looped her arms around his neck. Or hers found his. They were both mad, but it didn't matter. All he cared about was that she was here, where she belonged—in his embrace. And planting explosive little kisses all over his face.

"Aw, this is sickening," Pete said, a world away, where Mrs. Duffy's civility still reigned.

Adrian could well imagine what it looked like. What he and Ellen looked like. Two desperate souls who'd nearly lost each other. A man and a woman in love. A man who was never going to let her go.

Until she began to slip out of his grip. Slowly she regained her footing, but that was as far away as Adrian would allow her to move. He looked into her eyes—those beautiful hazel eyes—where the same emotions catapulting through his mind and body looked back at him.

Her lips moved, a bit swollen from his fervor. "Okay, let's get this over and out."

Over and out? "I beg your pardon."

"Look," she said, "I nearly died back there, and all I heard was how slow you are to commit. So prove Selena wrong and propose. Now. Time is wasting."

Adrian heard a gasp, perhaps more than one. His mother? Her mother? Duff? All three?

"Sounds like someone has met their match," Mitch noted from inside the office. He had probably never left the computer console. Until now. He peeped around the door jamb. "Well, A?"

"Come on, Dad. Ask!"

Ellen cocked her head, frazzled ponytail tilting in concert. "For Pete's sake, Adrian, has the cat got your tongue?"

No, it was panic. A ring! "I . . . I don't have a ring. I can't properly ask without an engagement ring." And he couldn't give her Selena's. It was ill-fated, pretentious. Simply not Ellen.

"Like I care about a ring." He loved that little noise Ellen made when she laughed.

"I have one." Adrian's mother took off one of her many rings. He recognized it instantly as his Scottish grandmother's, a gold band of Celtic design. "All these circles and knots symbolize the everlasting."

He recalled his grandmother telling him that. And everlasting was what he wanted. Adrian took it and held it up for Ellen to see. "It's old, my grandmother's . . . if you'll accept it. Or you can pick your own—"

"What's not to love about that one? Take it, bubeleh," Ma advised.

Ellen wriggled her bare left ring finger and smiled, full of mischief. "So now what's your excuse, Sinclair?"

"I have none. Despite the spontaneity of the moment, it seems God and our mothers have taken care of everything." He cleared his throat. "Ellen Brittingham . . ." Some of that mischief entered his voice. "For *Pete's* sake . . ." He glanced aside at his son. Rosy-cheeked, bright-eyed, and anxious as he gave Adrian an encouraging nod. Thus fortified, Adrian plunged into Ellen's expectant gaze. "And mine—most definitely mine—will you marry me?"

Hardly the most romantic proposal, standing in a hallway with an audience, the bride-to-be looking as though she'd been dragged through the dirt.

But beautiful and brimming with life and love. He'd never tire of that face, smudged or not. Never.

"Yes."

As Adrian slipped the ring on her finger, Ellen reached out with her right hand and ruffled Pete's hair, drawing him into their intimate little world. "For *Pete's* sake . . . and for ours."

"Definitely for ours," Adrian agreed.

L eave it to Ma and Maggie Sinclair to throw this party together in one month. Seeing stars from the camera flashes as she walked into the Piper Cove Country Club on the arm of her new husband, Ellen bunched up the skirt of her white brocade sheath so she wouldn't trip over it and embarrass herself in front of the room full of guests. She and Adrian had been married in her church beneath a royal blue canopy, a staple of a Jewish wedding, held up by Alex and Sue Ann on one side and Mitch and Pete on the other. Instead of a traditional wedding procession, their parents had brought the bride and groom to the canopy, and Jan had stood in as maid of honor and Harry Sinclair as Adrian's best man.

Only Ma would have the chutzpah to put a *chupah* in a church, but Ellen never complained. This was the wedding her mother never had, since she and Pop had eloped. And it had been beautiful. The ceremony, a blending of the Jewish and

Christian traditions that captured Ellen's heritage, ended with the breaking of the glass and good luck shouts of "*Mazel tof!*" from both sides of the church.

"And now, ladies and gentlemen," the DJ announced, "I give you Mr. and Mrs. Adrian Sinclair."

Ellen snorted. "Kind of got a nice ring to it, huh?"

"Absolutely." Adrian leaned over and kissed her on the cheek as they entered the crowded room and took a seat at the head table.

The scents of the food reminded Ellen's stomach that she'd not eaten since grabbing half a bagel that morning, while her cousin Marsha from Brooklyn styled her hair. One side of the room was the Kosher table, with roasted and potted meats and noodles, no dairy, chopped liver, Challah bread and chicken soup with matzah balls. The other boasted Eastern Shore cuisine—crab imperial, fried chicken, prime rib. The Brittinghams had spared no expense.

"I'll never remember your relatives' names," Adrian whispered, smiling amidst the camera flashes as he held Ellen's chair for her. With Adrian's parents being only children, a few Boston family friends and an aunt and uncle from Scotland took up four of the twenty-plus tables that had been set up for the affair. Everyone else was associated with the bride—family and friends.

"Don't feel bad, I won't either," Ellen confided, sitting down between their respective parents. She barely recognized half the guests her mother had invited. Ma was definitely going to have to help her with the New York relatives, although Ellen would know the personalities instantly from the many family stories Ma and her sisters told when they got together.

Ma was in seventh heaven as the buffet to end all buffets was opened and served. She hardly ate a bite, but Bea made sure her new grandson visited both tables. Pete was as impressed with the resiliency of the matzah balls as the soup itself after one he'd tried cutting with a spoon flew out of his bowl and rolled halfway across the open dance floor in front of the head table.

"Whoa," he exclaimed, sounding more like Ellen by the day.

"The trick is to get the ball from bowl to belly," Ellen said as Pop discreetly rose and retrieved the errant morsel before someone slipped on it.

"Ellen Brittingham Sinclair," Sue Ann exclaimed from a nearby table where the buddies and their escorts sat. She pointed playfully at Ellen's heaped plate. "If you can eat all that, you'll never hold up for the dancing."

"All these people make me hungry," Ellen shot back. "And Pete and I are going to have a double slice of Jan's wedding cake creation."

"You'd better toss me the bouquet tonight, Brit, or I'm taking it back," Jan warned her. "You promised: a bouquet for a wedding cake." Of course, it was said tongue in cheek, but Ellen couldn't help but feel a little guilty at being so happy, when Jan had yet to find love. Tink was the only one of the three of them who hadn't—and the one who craved it the most.

"Hey, I'll do my best," Ellen promised. She just hoped Scott Phillips wouldn't be Jan's intended. The guy still gave Ellen the creeps.

Lord, Ellen prayed later as she stood with her back to the single ladies who'd assembled in the center of the room. *You made my dream come true. And I didn't even know Adrian existed. Do it again . . . for Jan.*

Ellen gave the bouquet a sling, up and to the far right, exactly where Jan had said she was going to be. *Okay, God, I know I'm fixing the game, but—*

Jan squealed in delight. "I got it! I got it!"

Yes! Ellen turned to see the petite blonde clutching the bouquet to her chest and staring at Scott Phillips as though it were a done deal.

Well, it was just a dumb tradition anyway. With a forced smile, Ellen stepped aside and watched as the eligible bachelors gathered behind Adrian, who looked to die for in a tuxedo. Front and center of the group was Scott.

The DJ started the count. "One, two, three . . ."

The garter, handmade by Ellen's mother, went sailing over the reaches of the men, none of whom were as enthusiastic to make the catch as the women had been, Ellen noted. The circle of ribbon and white lace struck Joe Phillips, who'd predictably chosen a place in the back, square in the chest—and hung on the mechanical pen he always carried in his shirt pocket.

Startled, the shy and unassuming Joe took it up on one finger, as though it might be contaminated, and with a somber face that turned scarlet enough to rival that of the roses adorning each table, carried it over to where his older brother stood. "I believe this is for you."

"Oh, no, sugar!" Sue Ann bolted from the crowd and separated the two men before Joe could hand over the prize. "Fate is fate. Joe caught it fair and square." She turned the disconcerted bachelor to where an embarrassed Jan stood, her former enthusiasm frozen. "She's yours," Sue Ann drawled, adding with a wicked glance Joe's way, "at least for the next dance."

"Well, then," Adrian said, sidling up to Ellen as the DJ directed Jan and Joe to the center stage for the garter-on-the-lady's-leg bit. "That's done."

"And you done good," she said, planting a kiss on his lips.

Wow, who'd have thought it? This time last year, it was her in the garter seat, wishing she were anywhere else. If she'd known Adrian was in store, she'd have never taken the blooming thing off.

"Now all we have to do is serve a little cake around, shake a few hands, and we're outta here," she promised, as much to herself as to her husband.

Tonight, they'd spend in the grand suite of the Baylander Hotel, just the two of them. Then, since Adrian was in the midst of selling his business and needed to be close by, they'd decided to take a short ski trip to the Poconos . . . with Mrs. Duffy, Pete, and his buddy Kevin.

"I can hardly wait."

"Me, either."

Okay, it wasn't exactly a storybook honeymoon, but then again, Ellen was no Cinderella. Just a woman head over white cowboy boot heels in love.

Dear Reader,

FOR PETE'S SAKE is dear to my heart for many reasons. First, I had fun writing it. This was a healing milestone for me. Since I'd lost my husband, writing had become more of a chore, even painful at times to celebrate love when mine was gone. I feared I might never write romance again. God knew better.

Then there was Ellen. Who couldn't fall in love and have fun with her? I know Ellen personally. She is an amalgam of me, and a few other independent spirits I know. (I grew up with grease working in my family motor repair shop and was a 4H leader and camp counselor, just a few of my experiences working as a kid magnet.) Although, I admit, Ellen is far more outspoken and I never mustered the nerve to ride a motorcycle. Seeing what a '66 Mustang could do on the highway to Ocean City was thrilling enough for me.☺

Thirdly, there was Pete, whom I fashioned after my own son. Diagnosed with a mild case of Asperger's Syndrome, he has been both a gift and a mother's heartbreak on his behalf. These usually gifted, loving children are hobbled by anger/frustration levels and social handicaps that often make them seem like insensitive jerks when they are anything but. For those of you who would like to learn more about Aspergers Syndrome, go to http://www.aspergers.com. The good news is that therapy and education can make these people wonderful, loving, and productive professionals such as teachers, scientists, mathematicians, and more.

Lastly, there was Adrian, who really threw me a curve. I didn't know when I created this suave *prince* for my Harley-riding *Cinderella* that he was unhappy with his big career and worldly image! I love it when a character takes over and shows who he really is, even if it required a little tweaking of the pages written before he took charge.

Practically set in my back yard, this series brings back wonderful memories of people and places, especially on the waterfront. And the seafood? It's a way of life in these parts. So take a deep breath of salt air and savor the flavor of the good old Eastern Shore.

And don't forget to drop in at www.LindaWindsor.com and visit a spell, sign up for my occasional newsletter, and maybe drop me a line at the address below.

Bless you, as always, for your encouragement and support,

Linda Windsor

Email: Linda@LindaWindsor.com
or write to:
Linda Windsor
c/o Harper One
353 Sacramento Street, Suite 500
San Francisco, CA 64111-3653

Discussion Questions

1. How is Ellen different from her friends? What about her is most endearing to you? Have you ever known an "Ellen" in real life?

2. What concerns do Adrian and Ellen have in common? From what or where does each draw their strength?

3. To paraphrase the Apostle Paul, our afflictions can also be counted as blessings. How does this apply in this book in regard to Pete and Adrian?

4. What draws Ellen to Pete? What about Ellen draws Pete to her? Do you think it unbelievable that the dog Marley can sense Pete's insecurities and accommodate them?

5. Is Adrian totally blind to Selena's manipulation? At what point does he begin to see that he is "making do" for a lifemate?

6. Life is filled with change. What changes to Adrian and Ellen make in the course of this book? What kind of changes would you like to make in your life?

7. Ellen talks about *God things*—things that happen or come together in which she feels God had a divine hand. Have you had any *God things* in your life? Are they easier to spot with hindsight?

8. How is Ellen's mom different from Adrian's mother? Are their motives and support any different?

9. Do we see unconditional love reflected in Ellen's friends and their support of her and each other? How? Do you have friends like these?

10. Can you empathize with Selena at all by the book's end? What personal conflicts do you see in her? Are she and Ellen alike at all? How?

11. How do you think Adrian and Ellen are good for each other as lifemates? Soul/Spirit-mates?

12. What would you call this story? Cinderella? Pygmalion (or My Fair Lady)? The Prince and the Biker . . . er . . . Pauper? What elements do you associate with your choice/choices?

LINDA WINDSOR, a native of Maryland's Eastern Shore, is the author of eighteen historical novels and nine contemporary romances for both the secular and Christian market. A Christy Award finalist, Linda has received numerous awards in both the ABA and CBA, including the Romantic Writers of America's Beacon Award. She lives in Salisbury, Maryland.

Linda Windsor

Introducing

AVON

INSPIRE

Celebrate the grace and power of Love

Discover Avon Inspire, a new imprint from Avon Books. Avon Inspire is Avon's line of uplifting women's fiction that focuses on what matters most: family, community, faith, and love. These are entertaining novels Christian readers can trust, with storylines that will be welcome to readers of any faith background. Rest assured, each book will have enough excitement and intrigue to keep readers riveted to the end and breathlessly awaiting the next installment.

Look for more riveting historical and contemporary fiction to come from beloved authors Lori Copeland, Kristin Billerbeck, Tracey Bateman, Linda Windsor, Lyn Cote, DiAnn Mills, and more!

AVON  INSPIRE

An Imprint of HarperCollinsPublishers
www.avoninspire.com

E-mail us at AvonInspire@HarperCollins.com

AVI 1107